Black Snow

Black Snow

Liu Heng

Translated from the Chinese by
Howard Goldblatt

THE ATLANTIC MONTHLY PRESS
NEW YORK

Published simultaneously in Canada
Printed in the United States of America

Library of Congress Cataloging-in-Publication Data

Liu, Heng, 1954–
[Hei ti hsüeh. English]
Black snow: a novel of the Beijing demimonde / by Liu Heng;
translated from the Chinese by Howard Goldblatt.
ISBN 0-87113-530-2
I. Goldblatt, Howard, 1939– . II. Title.
PL2879.H38H4513 1993
895.1'352—dc20   92-32130

DESIGN BY LAURA HOUGH

The Atlantic Monthly Press
19 Union Square West
New York, NY 10003

First printing

Black Snow

1

A fat white guy was squatting in the yard. Li Huiquan, his knapsack slung over his shoulder, noticed the frosty grin as soon as he walked through the gate, so he went over and wiped it off. Chunks of coal for eyes, a chili-pepper nose, a wastebasket hat—the same stuff he'd used as a kid. The new generation hadn't come very far. He stuck the cucumber mouth back on upside down, turning the frosty grin into an icy frown. As a kid he'd used steel taps from his father's shoes, giving all his snowmen the same tiny mouths and identical bashful expressions.

The door of the west wing opened just enough to allow a woman's head to pop out. Her tight perm made her look like a pug-dog. Before he could even say hi the pug-dog head snapped back inside. He didn't recognize her—probably a new tenant. He couldn't see anyone in the north wing, since the curtains were drawn, and the south door of the south wing was secured with the same black padlock Auntie Luo had been using for the past ten years or so. She could be anywhere right now, running around as an emissary for planned parenthood or distributing rat poison—a woman of many causes, concerned with both this world and the next.

"Looking for someone?"

The woman from the west wing had slipped up behind him. Her red nylon parka was like a little fireball. Thirtyish, pudgy— he was sure he'd never seen her before. Her haughty vigilance made him squirm.

"Yeah."

"Name?"

"Li."

"The Lis from the rear compound?"

In no mood to talk, he ripped off the chili-pepper nose and buried it in the snowman's forehead. Then he skirted the water faucet and took the path that ran east of the north wing. The outhouse door was ajar, revealing a dung pit that gaped like the mouth of Mount Fuji, yellowing snow piled around its edges. The path was blanketed with virgin snow. When he saw the little add-on kitchen—his handiwork—with its plastic awning in shreds and draped over the sill like dirty fingers, he stopped, feeling a sudden, urgent need for a smoke. For years he'd dreamed of standing in his own backyard again, but now that he was actually here, he felt awful. His legs nearly buckled.

"Nobody lives there now."

The vigilant woman was right behind him.

"I know."

"That fellow Li was sent to a labor-reform camp."

"I know."

"You related? The old lady dropped dead because of her son's stupid high jinks, or so I've heard. We just moved here last year. Chairwoman Luo will be back soon. She knows everything. Ask her. They were longtime neighbors . . ."

Li Huiquan turned slowly, and the murderous glint in his

teary eyes nearly caused the woman to jump. "Spiteful bitch!" the look said.

"Are you finished . . ."

His voice sounded gentle enough, at least to him, but she shot out of there like a spooked jackrabbit. Everyone on Spirit Run Street surely knew about his troubled past and had probably vied to see who could appear more concerned about him over the past few years. He could just see his old neighbors as they sighed and shook their heads. He doubted that any of them would greet his return with much enthusiasm, however, and some probably wished the government had shot him and been done with it.

The man's back and happy to be here. The man's still in one piece. The man . . . His mind was hopelessly confused. He fished in his pocket for the key, and just touching it nearly unhinged him. I've got to think about something else, or I'll go nuts! After several failed attempts he managed to unlock the door, and as it swung open, mildew and other stale odors hit him full in the face. There wasn't much to see in the outer room, so he went straight to the bedroom. But he was back in no time, rubbing his hand over the washstand and sniffing the inside of the wardrobe. After flinging his knapsack onto the bedstead, he sat down and lit a cigarette since he didn't know what else to do. It was one of those aromatic Everlast filters.

The first thing he'd done after getting off the highway bus at Yongding Gate was to buy a pack of decent smokes at a corner market. Now what should he do? The place was like an ice locker; the chill was causing his feet to grow numb and his eyes to blur. He held back as long as possible, but when he finally glanced up at the wall, the tears broke loose and slid down his cheeks, wetting his fingers. These are damned good cigarettes! He wiped his face with his sleeve between furious, deep puffs.

Mother's face was blurred in the window set within the

tiny frame. She was gazing at him through a thick layer of dust. She must have known he was back.

"Huiquan."

Mother's voice. Wordlessly he began sweeping out the room, listening to the echoes of her voice in the dusty corners. After wiping the wardrobe mirror, he stood there with the broom in his hand and looked at himself: the posture, the scowl on his face—he looked like a beaten-down peasant. How could he cut such a pathetic figure? Full, dark lips, high cheekbones, and large, lifeless eyes—certainly not handsome. But then he'd never been handsome. Some said he looked like a wild man from the south, and in high school his nickname had been the Cantonese. At one time he'd even thought he looked Vietnamese.

His origins were a mystery that no one, certainly not he, would ever solve. A friend of the man he would later call Father had found him one day near Beijing Station, and he knew neither the identity of his biological parents nor the date of his birth. As a teenager he had been obsessed with solving these mysteries, but no longer. All he found out was that on a rainy autumn day in 1959 someone, probably his mother, had wrapped him in grimy swaddling clothes and dumped him in an underground-cable ditch east of Beijing Station, probably hoping he would have the good sense to drown when it rained or be buried by an inattentive worker. She'd had the right idea, and everything would have been fine if his father's friend hadn't happened by. Now that he was grown, he often regretted not having been buried there, near the station, where there was always so much activity.

Lighting a fire in the stove cheered him a little. The stove was so rusty he couldn't see the bare metal, but the bricks around it were still in good shape. The fire crackled. In place of briquettes he cut up one of the dozen or so pieces of lumber that lay under the bed. A friend they called Hobo had entrusted the lumber to him after stealing it from a construction site near Chaoyang Gate. Hobo had planned to use it for furniture but didn't dare take it home and had asked Huiquan to hold on to it for the time being. Even on the day of his arrest he hadn't revealed Hobo's secret. But then a motorcycle accident on Loop Two Road had claimed Hobo, and since death invalidates loyalty, he planned to burn every last piece. That would remove his feelings of complicity and tie up all the loose ends.

Hobo had been a goofy-looking guy whose flat face and head looked like they'd been pared with a knife. Auntie Luo, as representative of the Neighborhood Committee, had made a visit over New Year's to tell him about Hobo's accident, and his friend's flat face was the first image that popped into his head. She told him the motorcycle was stolen. He was depressed for days as he thought about the gory mess his friend had become when he wrapped his motorcycle around a telephone pole. Just about everything had fascinated Hobo, but the motorcycle had been his undoing. He was probably better off dead, since now he wouldn't have to live for the latest fad.

Auntie Luo dropped in at noon, while Li Huiquan was sitting at the table over a bowl of instant noodles. Steam spewed from the kettle on the stove. Her smile showed how pleased she was to see him.

"You weren't supposed to be home till March, were you? I was going to visit you at New Year's."

"They sprung me a couple of months early."

"For good behavior?"

"You know how it is . . ."

"Just look how you've straightened the place up. I guess there's hope for you yet."

Although she'd gone completely gray, Auntie Luo still had

rosy cheeks and a quick mind, even at the age of, what, over sixty? Mother would have been sixty-four now. He wondered what she'd look like. She was pretty feeble toward the end and so wrinkled it nearly broke your heart. Auntie Luo was lucky she didn't have any delinquent kids to worry about. He was a piece of work, all right.

"Did Xiaofen graduate?" he asked.

"She's in grad school. But I couldn't tell you why. She practically exists just to get my goat . . ."

"How's Uncle Luo?"

"Goes fishing every day—summer, winter, anytime. One of these days he'll fall through the ice and never come up! If there were a law against fishing, he'd be in jail—" She stopped in midsentence to feel his lined jacket. "Nice . . . Oh, I almost forgot. I have your residence card, your grain card, and your ration book. I'll get you a card for bottled gas in a few days. The precinct station said you wouldn't be back till March—"

"I just came from there."

"What did they say?"

"Not much. I have to report to the beat cop once a month. They told me to go to the Street Committee. What do you—"

"Slow down. Let Auntie take care of things. The beat cop's name is Liu. About your age, no more than twenty-five. Not a bad sort, a little on the snippy side. A few days ago he asked me to help him find a wife."

Huiquan smiled. Auntie Luo was wasting her breath if she thought she could get him to like a cop—he'd never had any use for them. They all had bad attitudes, and he felt like thumbing his nose at every one of them. Except for Political Instructor Xue, of course. But he didn't consider him a cop, just a nice old guy with smiling eyes and a crinkly nose. The world could use a few more people like him. That very morning, when they returned his personal effects to him, the political instructor had handed him some bankbooks.

"Hang on to these; they'll come in handy someday . . . like when you get married. Don't spend it unless you have to."

"I know . . . See you later."

"I don't want to see you again—ever."

He picked up Huiquan's knapsack and walked him to the bus stop, like a father seeing off his son. Huiquan had been there not quite three years, but the old man had spent half his life there—a tough life, however you looked at it. Among all those cocky young cops out on the street you'd be lucky to find two or three decent ones. He had no use for them at all.

As soon as he found work, he'd write to the old guy. Such a nice old fellow—he didn't want him to worry. These thoughts reminded Huiquan of a pocket dictionary he'd owned as a kid. In all his years he'd never written a real letter to anyone—never wanted to, never knew how to. Writing meant one mistake after another, and who needed that? Just thinking about it usually pissed him off. But now, to his surprise, he was considering writing to someone, anyone. He wondered whether the dictionary were still around and whether the literacy classes in camp had done much good. He wouldn't know until he tried.

That afternoon, after helping him install a chimney and a wind scoop, Auntie Luo brought over half a basket of briquettes. By then he had retrieved his bicycle and was removing the protective grease. Once he had it gleaming, he pumped up the tires and rode off without even stopping to wash his hands. With the bankbooks in his pocket and a warm stove at home, he felt it was time to take a long-anticipated turn around the neighborhood. With no one to watch him and no one to tell him what to do or what not to do, he'd go anywhere he wanted. He knew this freedom would take some getting used to, but for now he felt like riding until he dropped.

The sky was clear. There was still plenty of snow on the walks, but the streets were turning wet and shiny black. Smiling pedestrians walked gingerly. He circled Temple of the Sun Park twice and then sped into the Legation Quarter, hands in the air as he glanced right and left. Not even the scowls of foreign women, with their prominent noses, lessened his sense of joyful liberation. Stopping at the Japanese embassy, he scooped up some clean snow from around the flower bed and cleaned off his hands as he studied the photos in a glass-enclosed display case. Some neatly dressed Japanese officials were shaking hands, while beside them some enormous bare-assed men were hugging each other. The handshakes looked normal enough, but the grimaces on the faces of those intertwined man-mountains were a sight to behold. How could grown men like that not be ashamed of the disgraceful figure they cut? Yet even that picture didn't darken Huiquan's mood, although he experienced a tinge of disappointment. Three years earlier the spot given over to the sumo wrestlers had been occupied by a lovely Japanese girl in a gold crown and a skimpy loincloth—not quite naked, but pretty damned close. After taking a good look, Hobo had claimed she was Japan's empress, naked. Huiquan had scoffed at the idea at the time, but as he lay in bed that night he couldn't rid his mind of that loincloth, and he promised himself he'd go back for another look. Unfortunately they arrested him before he had the chance. No telling where she was now, and he was disappointed to see in her spot a bunch of fat slobs hugging each other.

He passed through Yongan District and went to a bank on Spirit Run Street to withdraw fifty yuan. But now that he had the cash in hand, he couldn't think of anything to spend it on. Ah, a good meal, of course. Now, where to go . . . The names of renowned Beijing restaurants glided through his mind, and his intestines quickly got into the act. He didn't like the idea of eating alone, but where was he going to find a companion? Hobo was dead, and Spike Fang was serving a life sentence, which was nearly the same thing. No sense feeling sorry for himself, since his friends were much worse off than he. They had spun the wheel of life and lost.

Thoughts of Spike Fang ruined his appetite. As he looked across the street, someone took a pratfall on the ice. Normally he would have laughed, but not this time, as the poor soul sat there staring red-facedly at his bent knees. Huiquan actually considered going over to help. But in the end he just mounted his bike and rode off, feeling a little sheepish.

Spike had only himself to blame for what happened to him. After popping off like that at the station house, he was lucky they hadn't shot him. Spike was the handsomest man Huiquan had ever known: tall, with large eyes and rosy, slightly effeminate lips. He was reliable, and he was clever. But he had his secrets, and Huiquan had never pried. Someone had once told him that Spike had a hot girlfriend, but Huiquan never broached the subject.

Huiquan didn't like women. Every time he tried to talk to them, he blushed, a reaction he viewed as a sign of weakness, so he avoided them. Fighting was what he liked. It was the only thing he liked. Once a fight began, he had no peers, friends included, no matter how they swaggered. He had never lost a fight. The sight of blood didn't bother him. He'd carried a rolling pin up his sleeve, and as soon as fists started flying, out it would come. He was so well known for the bloody numbers he did on the heads of his knife- or switchblade-wielding opponents that the mere mention of the name Basher Li threw the fear of God into every punk son of a bitch in Chaoyang District.

He earned his friends' respect by never refusing to help them out of a jam. Their respect was all he wanted—he couldn't be bought. But he never turned down a meal, and there wasn't a restaurant in Beijing he hadn't graced with his presence. He was also known as a big drinker. That night three years ago he would have enjoyed a wonderful meal if he hadn't been hauled in. Spike was treating him to a bottle of real Maotai—his way of showing off—but they were both behind bars before the bottle was empty. Spike, who was useless in a fight, carried a straight razor for courage, a nicked weapon that he used only once. But once was enough to send him up for life. Not something you want to tell your grandchildren.

No, they really screwed up that time.

Huiquan headed east until he spotted the yellow apartment building. He was in Eastbridge. He parked his bike across the street, in front of a photo studio whose door was covered with portraits, each one bigger than the next, each subject better looking than the one before. Who were all these people? And what had made them happy enough to smile like that? He lit a cigarette and puffed it furiously as he walked hesitantly up to the sidewalk in front of the yellow building. He cocked his head to see into the stairwell. The cold air gusting from the building made it impossible for him to stand still. It swept the concrete clean. There were some stains but no blood. No trace remained of what had occurred there three years earlier.

He had a cold, and when he heard that the dispute was over some slut, he saw no reason to get involved. But Spike did everything but get down on his knees and beg. Then the hotshot in the leather jacket had dragged the little slut along instead of coming to settle things alone, and when Huiquan told her to get lost, she just scrunched her head down into her fur collar.

"This doesn't involve you!"

The words were no sooner out of his mouth than a fist caught him on the jaw and sent him reeling; his head nearly cracked like a melon when it banged against the cement wall. He never saw Spike stab the guy—just a momentary commotion. By the time things quieted down, he was alone with the guy lying on the sidewalk bleeding from a gut wound. He looked up and down the street, but Spike was nowhere in sight. The girl in the fur coat was flying down the street screaming bloody murder. You wouldn't catch Huiquan running away; it might look bad. If not for the girl, he'd have made short work of his opponent. Instead, he wound up being disgraced. He got to his feet and, without even stopping to give the guy one last kick, picked up his rolling pin and sashayed off. The crowd that had formed kept its distance, and he walked all the way to Spirit Run Street unhindered. They arrested him beneath the memorial arch, a short way from his home.

"I've got a cold . . ."

He put up no resistance and didn't say another word. The cops sent for a doctor. His temperature was over 103, and his lower teeth had been knocked loose. As it turned out, the other guy wasn't seriously injured, and Spike would have gotten off lightly if not for his big mouth. Huiquan still found it hard to believe that Spike would confess to a rape, which he'd committed that summer at Northern Kiln, his victim a peanut vendor from the countryside. She was over thirty, nearly a decade older than Spike. The idea sickened Huiquan.

An announcement of the verdict was posted in camp. Beneath Spike's name came the entry *Li X X* followed in parentheses by the comment "sentenced separately." He brooded over this for the longest time, finding it insulting to have received a lighter sentence than Spike. After all the fights he'd been in, only the final one had sullied his reputation. Three years in a labor-reform camp for getting popped on the jaw! He wished he'd killed the guy with his rolling pin, even if they shot him for it. His own incompetence disgusted him more than Spike's cheap tricks with women.

But those feelings were gone now, and as he stared at the icy cement sidewalk, he was reminded of how catching a cold had saved his skin. Spike, on the other hand, had been the architect of his own tragedy. No one had told him to lose his cool over a woman, and it served him right. It served Huiquan right, too, for that matter, since he shouldn't have got involved in something that didn't concern him. From now on anyone asking for his help in a fight would learn what it felt like to be on the receiving end of one of his punches. Three fucking years! For what? What was he thinking?

As he crossed the sidewalk, he had the uneasy feeling he was being watched. Someone tapped him on the shoulder as he was about to climb onto his bike, giving him a fright.

"Two cents!"

An old lady with her hand out, a blank look on her face. He sighed in relief and smiled foolishly as he paid the parking fee. At a sidewalk stall he bought a skewer of lamb and a couple of bowls of wontons. The food tasted great and made him even hungrier. He rode around some more, but by now the feeling of novelty was gone. The streets were lined with newly constructed, nearly identical matchbox apartments. The street-level shop windows were fancier than they'd been before; lots of girls were wearing high boots, and nylon parkas were everywhere;

fancy cars weaved in and out of traffic; the children looked well fed and happy.

Yet none of this had anything to do with him, just as whether or not he was happy had nothing to do with anybody else. He had served nearly three years in a labor-reform camp, his mother was dead, and he was all alone. Did anyone out there give a damn? Up and down the street they strolled, men and women, not one of them so much as glancing at him. It was as though he didn't exist—no parents, no friends, just a pair of eyes and a beat-up old bicycle. He flitted around aimlessly, talking to no one. No one knew him, anyway. If they had known him, they'd probably have avoided him. Looking around and feeling good about himself—big fucking deal!

What was there to feel good about?

As night was falling, Huiquan rode up to a small tavern at the entrance to Spirit Run Street, ordered a shot of strong liquor and a plate of sliced pork, found a corner table, and sat down. He'd promised Political Instructor Xue that he would behave himself when he got out, that although he would keep smoking, he would quit drinking. But this drink really hit the spot. There'd be plenty of time to behave himself once he found a job. He ordered another shot. The blackened sky outside was lit up brilliantly. Streetcars clanged past, motorbikes moved through the cold air—*putt putt putt*—loud and crisp. But none of this had anything to do with him. He looked at the clock. Eight o'clock. Television time back at camp. He didn't own a TV, so that was out. He didn't feel like going over to Auntie Luo's, since Xiaofen might be home, and he didn't want her to see him looking like this. He decided to stay put. There was nowhere else to go.

The drinks were just what he needed. He closed his eyes and tried to think of the name of the TV series, but it wouldn't come. He'd watched it just the other night, a drama, and now he couldn't even recall the name. Amazing! At some point he began to hum, to the chagrin of the other customers, who eyed him suspiciously. It was the TV-program theme song. Everyone knew it, but the other customers were too busy trying to figure out where this young fellow had come from to give it much thought. He opened his eyes. They were bloodshot.

What about tomorrow? He was still humming, off key by now, as he pondered the question. He needed an answer. Otherwise even a simple question like Is life worth living? would stump him. All day long he had been happy and carefree, and now he was suddenly blue. Why was that? Of course, life's worth living. What a stupid question!

Ah, fuck! He blacked out.

2

Someone was moving around in the room. He assumed it was Auntie Luo until he opened his eyes and spotted a pair of black boots pacing the floor. The red stripe down the trouser leg made it a cop. He closed his eyes again. Steel tongs scraped the sides of the iron stove: stoking the fire, stirring up ashes, adding coal. The bed creaked. He must have sat down. The wind whistled outside. Was it light out?

He couldn't move. After sprawling on the bed fully dressed the night before, he'd been out like a light. He dimly recalled throwing up once but couldn't remember where. His bed was as hard as nails, his feet were nearly frozen, and he ached all over. He'd drunk too much, but it was just what he'd needed. The little tavern was a nifty place. He liked it. That and his frigid bed had quickly become his two favorite places. By cruising the neighborhood most of the day, he'd managed to find a place to hang out, a spot he could head for anytime he pleased, as long as he had money. He didn't need lots of people around him.

Cops pissed him off.

"Up and at 'em! It's almost noon . . . Get up!"

His patience exhausted, whoever it was laid his hand on the comforter and shook Huiquan. The tone of voice and the actions were those of lawmen everywhere: strength in the hand but no respect for others. He sat up and glared at the man through sleepy eyes. Young with fair skin, bushy eyebrows, a slightly under-slung jaw, and gentle eyes—probably the beat cop Auntie Luo had mentioned. What was his name?

"Too much to drink?" the cop asked him.

"Nope."

"Then why'd you smash the glass and dishes like that? They lodged a complaint with the Neighborhood Committee. If you can't hold your liquor, why drink? They demanded restitu-tion."

He couldn't remember; he really couldn't. The cop didn't seem to be picking a fight, and he obviously wasn't the joking type. Huiquan fished out a pack of cigarettes and then stuck his hand back in his pocket.

"How much . . ."

"One-sixty. If Auntie Luo hadn't spoken up for you, you'd have been fined as well. She probably saved you a good five yuan. Not a very good start, becoming a public nuisance on the very day you get out."

"I don't remember; I honestly don't—"

"Forget it. You've got real talent at hanging on to telephone poles and singing . . ." The cop chuckled.

Huiquan had a sinking feeling as he suddenly recalled where he'd thrown up. The outhouse. Squatting down had been easy enough, but when he'd tried to stand, he'd promptly emp-tied his stomach and must have squatted in the freezing crapper for at least a half hour.

He handed two yuan to the policeman, who took all the

coins out of his pocket and laid them on the bed—not enough to make the right change.

"That's okay—tell them to keep the change."

"I already paid for you. But if I'd known you were going to be this extravagant, I'd have said I gave them a month's wages. Here's thirty-eight cents. I'm still short two frigging cents."

He looked everywhere for those two cents, but all he came up with was a nearly empty pack of cheap cigarettes. He stuck one in his mouth and tossed the pack over.

"Fifty-three cents a pack. You win this time."

This was no run-of-the-mill cop. Huiquan was slightly mystified but not upset, not yet. The cop's boots were scuffed, there were grease stains on his trousers, and his fingernails were dirty. Certainly not finicky about his appearance. Huiquan climbed out of bed and poured his visitor a cup of water.

"What's your name?"

"Liu, Liu Baotie. Everybody calls me Little Liu. But you . . . you can call me Old Liu. Spirit Run Street is my beat, East and West lanes. We'll be seeing a lot of each other, so keep your nose clean. I don't play favorites, so there's no need to be afraid of me. The devil himself is my friend as long as he stays out of trouble. I know you just got out. What do you plan to do? We need to talk. This uniform says I'm a cop, but underneath I'm like your older brother. You've got no one else at home, so you might as well take me into your confidence."

"I . . . I don't have any plans at the moment."

"No harm in that, but guzzling booze won't do you any good. The bad thing about people like you is you don't bother to think things through. You don't know shit. Little Nine in West Lane, you know him? His mom sells ices at the corner—"

"Yeah, I know who you mean. A jerk. I ignore him!"

"No sooner out of reform school than he steals three color TVs. And he loses his ID card. His mom pleaded for him, but what good does that do? If it'd been up to me, I'd have had him shot. And she's pleading with me! People like that have no idea what's going on, so sooner or later life passes them by. They'd be better off finding a shit hole someplace and jumping in. Right?"

Huiquan nodded. Not that he liked what he was hearing, but he could handle it. This guy Liu was no pushover. No telling what lay behind that benign appearance.

"I've read your file. Fighting, right? No big deal. Stay out of fights, and you'll be okay. If you feel a need to fight, come see me. Try me out. Got the guts?"

Liu Baotie wasn't joking, and that made Huiquan fidget.

"I didn't think so. But get into a fight with somebody else, and it's the same thing as fighting me. And that means you and I have problems. Yech! Why's your water so brackish? Take a couple of minutes to scrub out your vacuum bottle . . . Time to go. No more booze, now. If you've got time on your hands, read a book."

"Such as?"

"Hm . . . Can't think of any right off the bat . . . There's Qiong Yao . . . I've never actually read any—"

"Who's that?"

"Overseas Chinese, I think. A woman. She's all my kid sister and her friends ever talk about . . . Her stuff's supposed to be pretty good. Look around—you can find her books everywhere."

"I don't like books written by women."

Liu Baotie looked at him uncomprehendingly.

"I'm not much of a reader."

"Okay by me. But you have to do something. Well, time to go. I'm out on the beat every day, so if you need me for anything, leave word at the Neighborhood Committee. You'd better shake a leg. It's lunchtime.''

The cop walked off with a bounce in his step, as if he had springs on his heels. One of the camp inmates, a basketball player from an athletic school in West City who always lined up in the front row for calisthenics, walked the same way. You didn't notice it at first, but when he ran, his head bounced up and down like a racehorse. He'd fought the guy once in the kitchen, and the little wimp had started bawling as soon as the first punch landed.

But this guy, the cop, was not one to be taken lightly. Assuming a patronizing stance, he had tried to scare Huiquan with the fist-in-a-velvet-glove tactic. Huiquan would not only have to toe the line, but he'd also have to make sure the cop knew he was doing it. It would be stupid to lock horns with him. Besides, what the cop said made sense, and as long as his intentions were good, there was nothing wrong with throwing a scare into somebody. Huiquan knew his own mind. The last thing in the world he wanted to do was beat up on someone, unless that someone was himself. That you can get away with. But how to go about it? And what good does it do? Back in camp he thought that people who swallowed nails and things like that were a bunch of malingerers, but now he saw they had the right idea. Everybody runs into hard times once in a while, and since you can't take your frustrations out on others, a little masochism can't hurt. What are your options, after all?

Huiquan didn't know what to do with himself. After taking a turn around the bedroom, he went outside and looked around the courtyard. It wasn't any colder outside than it was in the house. After preparing and eating a bowl of instant noodles, he sat down and began chain-smoking. But even after the floor was littered with butts and the room was blue with smoke, the painful sense of emptiness lingered.

He knew he couldn't return to the transformer factory, since it had nearly gone belly-up shortly after he was fired. Then, a year or so before he was released, Political Instructor Xue had talked them into taking him back as a replacement for his mother—in other words, if not for his sake, then for hers. But the deal had barely been struck when the factory declared bankruptcy, and the workers were required to defer receipt of thirty percent of their salary. They couldn't have hired him on even if they'd wanted to, which was fine with him, since he hated the place. He had no use for collective enterprises, especially if they required him to wind copper wire alongside a bunch of old fogies. He'd done enough of that for one lifetime. But what else was he qualified to do? Eat. But so were other people, and they either earned their money for food or were supported by their parents. He had a mouth, and that was all.

Auntie Luo arranged for an orphan's stipend. But being on the public dole at his age was mortifying. Besides, even if the Street Committee gave him twenty-some yuan a month, what good would that little bit of money do? Half would go for smokes, and the rest wouldn't be enough to keep him in gruel. The bankbooks would tide him over for a while, but he hated the idea of using up his mother's life savings, which came to less than a thousand yuan anyway. Besides, Political Instructor Xue had urged him to keep it for when he got married. Did the old guy know something he didn't know? Sure, the world was filled with marriageable girls, and maybe he ought to consider marrying. But other people's lives had nothing to do with him. Absolutely nothing. Why waste time thinking about it? He wondered whether there was a job out there somewhere with his name on it.

He picked the butts up off the floor, dumped the bits of tobacco into the empty pack, and rolled one last smoke. He had never minded doing cleanup work, for which he'd been praised on a number of occasions. Back in camp, after sweeping out the guards' office, he would pick the butts and scraps of stationery out of the dustpan without letting on—no one ever found out. Smoking had been prohibited in camp, but he had sampled every brand imaginable—even though the guards smoked their cigarettes down to the nub. He felt sorrier for those poor slobs than he did for himself. People will do anything if you push them hard enough, so smoking someone else's butts was nothing to be ashamed of.

Refusing to believe that he would have to join the ranks of the unemployed, he rode over to a local store and stocked up on rice and noodles, oil, salt, soy sauce, and some vinegar. Then he tossed his ration book down on the counter and told the clerk to "fill it up." In went noodles, eggs—just about everything but sesame paste—plus some carrots and a head of cabbage. He walked home, pushing his loaded-down bike along unsteadily. He was comforted by the knowledge that he had all he'd need to get by. If he had to make it on his own, that's precisely what he would do: he'd manage like everyone else, since he was as good as they were. He'd cook his own rice, make his own dough-drop soup, fry his own vegetables, and scramble his own eggs—no reason why he shouldn't eat well. Mother had always cooked for him before, but now it was his turn. If he didn't know how to do something, he'd learn. He would eat to please himself, and to please Mother. He'd live right or know the reason why!

The kitchen was dusty, but his mother's smell lingered. The spatula, brush, cleaver, and aluminum steamer all hung from hooks on the wall, the pots were stacked on a three-legged rack, and bottles and cans rested on the windowsill alongside packets of spices. A bomblike gas cylinder stood darkly in the corner. He cleaned the kitchen, putting everything in its proper place. Spotless, shabby, and cramped, it felt as though Mother were still alive and hunched over the stove, cooking dinner for him. Back then he had never stuck to mealtimes: if he came home late, she went into the kitchen without a murmur and cooked something for him under a naked eight-watt bulb. At the time he didn't realize how much he loved her, and now that she was dead, he understood what a shit he'd been, a selfish little bastard. But it was too late now to become a devoted son.

The gas bottle still had heft, and the stove lit with the first match. Three years, and there was still plenty of gas. Amazing! The sight of the blue flames dancing around the burner was reassuring. After mixing some baking soda and water, Huiquan cleaned the stove and the gas bottle, and when everything was spick-and-span, he went into the bedroom to sit until dinnertime. It was still early, but he couldn't think of anything else to do. Go window shopping? No, the thought of seeing all those people and all that merchandise made him fidget. Take in a movie? He couldn't possibly sit through a movie in his agitated state, so that was out. If only a friend would drop by. There must be lots of people without parents, but surely there are few who have no friends. Life is agony for friendless people. With no one to talk to, all the words turn to shit inside. It's murder.

Did he have what it takes to cook a decent dinner? He wasn't sure. He could use a drink, but he quickly put that thought out of his mind and decided to write to the PI instead. He dug out a pen and some paper but couldn't find his dictionary. He may have forgotten how to write a lot of words but not how to look them up; a dictionary would endow him with the ability to string sentences together. As long as he had his dictionary beside him, he wasn't illiterate. He knew he'd have to find it.

Even after turning the room upside down, he still couldn't

find the dictionary. Maybe a cat had walked off with it, or rats had chewed it up. When he emptied the wooden chest in the bedroom, he found plenty of books inside it but no dictionary. The yellowed pages looked as though they had dried out after having got soaked. He couldn't read them, but that was okay, since they didn't interest him in the first place; all he wanted to do was flip through them and look at the name on each title page: Li Ruoshan. The ink had faded, but the characters were neat and well written. The books had belonged to his father, a graduate of a civil engineering university. He didn't know what his father had done before 1949, but after liberation he had been an accountant at a flour mill in the western suburbs.

Accountants don't leave much of an impression, and few people, including his mother to some degree, had ever mentioned his father. About all anyone ever said about him was that he'd been a heavy drinker and that he had died of pancreatic cancer. Huiquan had already forgotten what he looked like, except that he had large eyes and a long face—and that he lay on his bed in the hospital without saying a word. That was Huiquan's last image of his father—from 1965—and the only one he had left. After finishing off an ice in the ward that day, he had tossed the paper wrapping into a filthy cuspidor, which he could still see in his mind's eye, since the clots of blood inside it had scared the wits out of him—he was six at the time—and even now the thought of it made him queasy, as though he had something dirty in his mouth.

He had no idea where in the western suburbs the flour mill was, but a twelve-yuan subsidy had arrived from there every month until his eighteenth birthday, at which time his link to the mill and to his father disappeared, and he and his mother had begun their life as widow and fatherless child. It wasn't easy, but they managed. Maybe he ought to try to get a job as a loader at the mill. Would they know who he was? Would they still recall the heavy-drinking accountant Li Ruoshan?

No one knew him. He was just an old accountant's bastard foundling.

As he was packing the books back into the chest, he spotted some of his schoolwork, which Mother had sewn together into a book. His grades weren't bad. In fact, at one time he had been a pretty good student, even though he hadn't realized it—but Mother had, and she had wanted him to be a good student always. He looked at one of his essays. Some of the words were so unfamiliar he could scarcely believe he had written them. It was an essay extolling the joys of joining the Junior Red Guards and crowing about his ideal of carrying out "the continuing revolution under the dictatorship of the proletariat." The solemnity of that pledge made him swell with pride for his youth. Squatting down beside the mildewed chest, he read his childhood essays with pride and pleasure until nightfall, captivated by his forgotten past. Yet if he had been offered a chance to relive those days, he doubted he'd have the courage to do so. He would probably wind up the same anyway. Many of his classmates had pretty much designed their own futures, but only one road had ever been open to him. Fate had decreed that he would be sighing over his past and fretting over his future when he was twenty-five years old and that he would experience deadening anxiety over his inability to find work. He had left that underground-cable ditch only to suffer a raft of miseries. He should have taken leave of the sorrows of this world back then and slept there for eternity.

Absorbed in reading the essays, Huiquan completely lost interest in his search for the dictionary and forgot about the letter to the PI. When it was time for dinner, he supplemented a package of instant noodles with a couple of hard-boiled eggs and then went out for a walk. He headed for the distant lights to the accompaniment of sizzling woks, taped music, TV announcers, the conversations and laughter of men, women, and children— sounds emerging from the rows of apartment buildings. The sounds were gentle, as though afraid of disturbing or saddening him.

He had to pee. The light in the empty public toilet was on. Someone had drawn a pair of spread-eagled legs above the urinal, with female genitalia crudely sketched in. Like a living object the drawing mocked him; it made faces at him. Disgusting. His life was a mess, and it was his own fault. He felt bored, purposeless.

The streets were aswarm with people now that the sun had set. They didn't know him, and they didn't know each other. No one spoke to anyone else, at least not that Huiquan could see. A few people stood beneath a streetcar sign, each one an island; but when the streetcar pulled up, they merged into a single dark mass, looking both intimate and hostile at the same time. No common courtesies, no sense of humanity—a microcosm of life itself. The streetcar left without him. The lucky passengers shouted, argued, and laughed as they left the stop, taking no heed of the person left behind. He was fated always to miss the bus.

Huiquan walked past brightly illuminated cafés and bars and then past darkened apothecaries and newsstands. He paused briefly, then crossed the street and entered a grocery store, where he bought a small box of pastries and a basket of apples, the basket woven from willow strips wrapped in red and green paper. The apples were slightly wrinkled, and their color was a little off. But the heft of the basket was reassuring.

At the pedestrian overhead at Chaoyang Gate he turned

south into Golden Rooster Lane. Counting as he went, he passed six lampposts. There it was, the one with the red curtains. An old woman was squatting at the base of the wall, making briquettes by the light of the streetlamp. Spike Fang's mother.

"Auntie Fang . . ."

She straightened up and looked him over curiously.

"It's me, Huiquan. I'm out . . ."

"I was wondering . . ." To Spike's younger brother she said, "Little Five, open the door!"

Huiquan followed her in and sat down, while Little Five poured him a cup of boiled water. Someone was watching TV inside but didn't make an appearance. After washing up, the old woman sat there without saying a word, and Huiquan knew he'd have to stick it out no matter how awkward it got. The idea that he might not be welcome here had never occurred to him, and he fidgeted with the pastries and fruit to make sure they were noticed.

"I wanted . . . wanted to come see you. How's your husband?" It was probably Spike's father who was watching TV inside, but his question went unanswered. Little Five, red-faced by now, looked up. He'd grown at least a head taller since the last time Huiquan had seen him and was every bit as good looking as his brother.

"What is it you want?" Auntie Fang asked him.

"Your son won't be coming back for a long time, and it's partly my fault. I'm really sorry. If you ever need anything, just send Little Five over to East Lane to get me, just as if I were your son . . . I haven't found work yet, so I've got the time."

Auntie Fang sighed. Someone turned the TV down.

"I'm glad you're out, and you'll be okay as long as you use your head. But we don't need help from outsiders. My third son is no longer a member of this family. We don't care whether he lives or dies. There's no need for you to worry . . ."

"Has he written? I'd like his address."

Little Five fetched an envelope and handed it to him. Huiquan had to strain to read the return address: "PO Box 356-11, Qinghai." He committed it to memory and then handed the envelope back. The numbers *356* and *11* didn't give anything away, and he wondered what sort of place they represented. Since there was nothing more to say, it was time to think about leaving.

"Sorry to bother you. I'd better go now."

"Take that stuff with you!"

As he reached the doorway, Huiquan finally heard the voice of Spike's father. It was angry and uncompromising.

Poor Auntie Fang looked pathetic even as she smiled.

Once he had fled into the welcome darkness of the lane, he didn't stop until he reached Outer Chaoyang Gate Boulevard. He felt like running headfirst into a lamppost. Spending good money just to make himself miserable! What had he done to provoke them like that? Just because their son was in trouble, why take it out on him? What about him—whom was he supposed to take it out on? He wouldn't be in this predicament if not for their son. He had expected a few questions and maybe a little advice, yet they had done everything but curse him to his face. That was the last thing in the world he had expected. Was he really so despicable? As he plodded along confused, someone ran up behind him.

Little Five, gasping for breath, was carrying the pastries and fruit. Huiquan felt like burying his fist in that innocent little face. Let his parents get good and worried, good and mad. That's what was called for.

"My dad told me to return these, since you're out of work. Here, take them."

"Little Five, you keep them—a gift from your big brother. You must be in middle school. What year?"

"I'm a freshman in high school!"

"High school? Don't bullshit me! If you don't want that stuff, toss it in the crapper! And stop following me, or else . . ."

Little Five recoiled fearfully.

"I'll be damned! A freshman in high school . . . Planning to go to college?"

"If I can."

"Then forget about me, and don't take after your brother. Go tell your dad Huiquan told you to study hard. See if he finds anything wrong with that. Do what you want with that shit. Now get lost!"

Little Five looked so pathetic, knowing he had to stop following him, so Huiquan patted him on the shoulder and took a shortcut toward Spirit Run Street without a backward glance. The movies had just let out, and the street was filled with disappointed, anxious crowds. He struggled against the rough tide, his chin stuck out defiantly, an attitude that helped him pass without incident. He made the people uncomfortable. The way they steered clear both discouraged and embarrassed him. He had no idea what he was up to.

Later that night, just before bedtime, he decided to write to Political Instructor Xue, dictionary or no. After laying out the paper, he wrote, "I'm fine," and stopped, not knowing what to write next. Not because he couldn't find the words but because his feelings were at war with the paper they were supposed to be written on. So he decided to write to Spike instead. Spike was in a worse predicament than he, but he didn't spend all *his* time whining. Huiquan felt he ought to be more magnanimous in dealing with friends who were worse off and in greater need of sympathy than he. But dejection set in, since the only thought that popped into his head was that Spike's real name was Guangde—Broad Virtues—a name that seemed now to belong to someone else. Why try to reestablish a link, necessary or un-necessary, with that name after the passage of three years? Still, that's what popped up, and finally Huiquan managed a short letter:

> I'm out now, but there's no work. How's it going? Do
> they work you hard? It's not cold in Beijing. How
> about you guys? My mom died, livver canser. Hobo's
> dead, moutercycle crash. He stole it. I've thought
> about things for three years and it wasn't worth it.
> That girl was the problem. Now you can't ever come
> home. It wasn't worth it. Do a good job there. Insides
> the same as outside, ones as bad as the other. Nobody
> runs your life, its still the same. Listen to me and do
> as your told. Don't think too much, and try to make
> some friends. Everything's OK if you got friends.

He managed to fill half a sheet of paper, and even though the characters were a mess, he felt good, as though Spike were sitting across the table from him, patiently listening to him chatter on and on about what was on his mind. He thought he'd written a pretty good letter and felt like writing more but was too tired. The words were getting jumbled up in his head, and he knew he'd have to pull them out one at a time to keep them from fighting all the time. In all the years he'd known Spike, he'd never said this much to him at one time. Now, with no dictionary, he'd filled half a sheet of paper, and that was gratifying. The heaviness in his chest had lessened considerably. He could change Fang Guangde into anyone he pleased, if he felt like it, and pour out his heart to whoever it was—Political Instructor Xue, Luo Xiaofen, his dead friend Hobo, even his mother and father. This simple secret came as a genuine but pleasant shock. For the first time in his life he had developed a personal relationship with a pen and some words. They were his friends now. He wouldn't mind writing some more.

That night he slept like a baby.

3

New Year's Eve was approaching. Li Huiquan had his picture taken at the Red Palace Photo Studio, something he disliked greatly, since he felt the camera made him appear uglier than he really was. Auntie Luo told him four prints were enough, but he ordered fifteen. The clerk reacted with a look of incredulity.

"Fifteen?"

"That's right, fifteen."

"We can't guarantee the quality of that many."

"I said I want fifteen!"

There was a nasty edge to his voice, and it was all he could do to keep from driving his fist straight into that jaw. He had ordered fifteen so he wouldn't have to come back for more later, and having his scheme viewed as just plain dumb devastated him.

When he came back to pick up his snapshots, he was more nervous than when he'd fetched his mother's ashes from the crematorium. He turned and walked out with the paper packet without first checking them, but as soon as he was alone, he dumped the contents into his hand. Fifteen identical faces lay in his hand at all angles, every one staring at him with the very same expression. All in all, they turned out better than he had expected. His lips seemed thinner than usual, since he'd squeezed them shut, and the look in his eyes was firm and focused. Certainly not what you'd call ugly. In fact, he was better looking than lots of people. He had no complaints.

Auntie Luo took him to the Street Committee, where they were shunted from door to door. They talked to a series of people until a middle-aged functionary finally gave him a pushcart license. His application for a fruit-peddler's license was denied because the quota had already been filled. Auntie Luo's contacts were either unable or unwilling to help, and the only license available was for a clothing stall, hats and shoes included. Huiquan didn't much care what he was permitted to sell, as long as he had something to do. He heard that fruit peddling was more flexible, with a quicker turnover, and that clothing sales were slower and the profit margin lower. He also heard that you needed a storefront or a black-market connection to make a real go of it. But he was willing to give it a try and was not overly concerned about the prospect of operating in the red, since he had only himself to worry about. He had to show confidence in himself; besides, if he kept his eyes open and his wits about him and wasn't afraid to work hard, he might do all right. No matter how little he made, it couldn't be less than his orphan's stipend, could it? He'd let the future take care of itself.

On their way out of the government compound they bumped into a fat man Auntie Luo called Section Chief Li. Auntie Luo told Huiquan to call him Uncle Li. Chief of which section and whose uncle he was Huiquan had no idea, but the man reminded him of the grotesquely fat Japanese sumo wrestlers.

"Aren't you going to thank Uncle Li for all he's done?"

Huiquan bowed respectfully, something he'd learned in camp. Inmates were required to bow to all guards, inspectors, and observers who spoke to them or even looked their way—that was the drill. Now he did it out of habit. But the man, too self-absorbed to notice, barely glanced at him—he was like a man looking over some merchandise. Huiquan, feeling like a roadside garbage can or a piece of cast-off clothing, wanted to crawl into a hole.

"That's him?" the fat section chief asked Auntie Luo.

"He's a good boy, like I said. See how he blushes."

That tickled the fat section chief, who sort of giggled as his patronizing gaze settled on Huiquan's face.

"You know why you got a license when plenty of retired and unemployed people can't get one?"

"I . . . because I need a job?"

"That's it?" Fatty sneered contemptuously.

"Because I'm an orphan?"

"The government cares about you; I'm sure you know that. Now don't pull any shenanigans, and don't get greedy . . . You've made one mistake. Now put that behind you, because if you revert to your old ways, no one will be able to help you—"

"I'll do whatever the government tells me to do."

Another one of those stock slogans from camp. His thoughts and feelings remained imprisoned even after he had been released from camp. Disgusted by his own servility, he understood that other people lapped it up. Even Auntie Luo nodded appreciatively. No matter where he went, there was always someone to tell him what to do and what not to do; by demeaning him they reaffirmed their own superiority. He had spent time in a penal camp, they hadn't, and he couldn't help feeling that warnings, rebukes, and notices concerned him alone: USE THE URINAL, NO SPITTING, NO TRESPASSING, FIVE-YUAN FINE—it all came down on him and only on him. Something was forever making life difficult for him, forever pointing out differences between him and other people, forever trying to deflate him spiritually. He wanted to resist, but he lacked the strength. So he would keep playing the fool, avoiding watchful eyes and suspicious looks. Might as well—he'd been doing it for years.

Auntie Luo strode triumphantly, oblivious to the crestfallen look on Huiquan's face as he followed her home like a prisoner.

"It's almost New Year's. You can spend the holiday with us."

"Thanks, but I'll be okay . . ."

"Well, I think I've done all right by your mother. If she were alive, she'd be chattering away—her son's in business; his prospects look pretty good; not the same boy he used to be. I want you to bring credit to your mom this time."

"Uh huh."

"Spend the holiday alone if you want to, but that doesn't mean you can go drinking."

"Don't worry."

"It's not too early to shop for New Year's. Fish, chicken— stuff like that. They'll keep. If you don't know how to cook something, come over, and I'll show you. You deserve a decent holiday. Then it'll be time to get down to business. Do a good job, and I'll find you a girlfriend. What do you say, silly boy?"

"You're the boss." He smiled, but wanly. A wooden frame and canvas awning would cost a hundred or so; a three-wheeler, another three hundred at least. That wouldn't leave much with which to lay in some merchandise. He had barely taken his first step on the new road, and already he was forced to dip into Mother's savings. That made him nervous, since there was no turning back.

A day or two before New Year's he spotted a rickety old three-wheeler at the East China Gate Consignment Store for 230 yuan. The price was right, but it was in such bad condition that riding it was out of the question. The frame looked okay—at least it had kept its shape; no tires, but the spokes and rims were passable; no bell, no chain, and no bed flooring, but it had brakes and pedals. Unable to make up his mind, he examined it from every angle. He had already been all over town. New three-wheelers started at four hundred, and there were no operable secondhand ones for sale. At a grocery store he'd seen a bamboo pedal pram that seemed sturdy enough, but something about it didn't seem right. If he wanted to sell clothes, he needed a three-wheeler—for the sake of appearance if nothing else.

"Interested in this one? What do you plan to use it for?"

A clerk materialized behind him.

"A clothing pushcart."

"Perfect. Can't go wrong! Now if you were planning to haul telephone poles or concrete or stuff like that, I'd advise against it. But all you're talking about is a few bundles of clothes. You can fix it up for less than a hundred, and it'll last you a good five, six years."

"Why won't it move?"

"Brakes are frozen. I can fix that."

Huiquan handed over the money, and the tire-less vehicle clanked its way from East China Gate to Dongsi and from there to Chaoyang Gate. His one-of-kind three-wheeler made him the center of attention, although the looks he got seemed benign enough. After picking up some parts at a bicycle-repair shop on Outer Chaoyang Gate Boulevard, he pushed his three-wheeler down East Lane of Spirit Run Street and through the gate of number 18. A green string basket hanging from the rusty, pitted handlebars was packed to overflowing with seasoned beef, a couple of braised chickens, a frozen carp, four pig's feet, and a bottle of wine—New Year's dinner. He bought whatever was available since he hated waiting on line and wasn't particular about his holiday meal. He was preoccupied with his three-wheeler, his new friend, his silent partner.

On New Year's Eve Auntie Luo invited him to dinner. She came by while he was sawing a piece of wood, a slice of braised chicken dangling from his mouth. He begged off. As she sniffed the air, she went over and lifted the lid of the pot. The pig's feet were simmering in a watery broth. Nothing green in sight—not a balanced meal. The sleeves of his sweater were worn; his shoes and pant cuffs were covered with sawdust; his hair was dirty and long. Auntie Luo felt sorry for him, but still he begged off. Like a man possessed, he kept using the wood Hobo had left behind, determined to make a first-class bed for his three-wheeler.

Auntie Luo returned later to invite him over to watch TV— some comic repartee and other interesting programs. A shame to miss it. But he shook his head without pausing in his sawing.

"I still have lots to do—"

"It can wait till after the holiday."

"I'd rather you let me finish—"

"There's plenty of time. Don't try to do everything at once. You don't want to tire yourself out on a holiday."

At first the sound of firecrackers outside was spotty, but the noise picked up until by midnight it sounded as though the world were exploding. Huiquan laid down his saw and poured some wine. The pig's feet had stewed so long the meat nearly fell off the bones. It was okay, a little bland, maybe, so he poured some soy sauce onto a plate and dipped the meat in it, and then he ate and drank until his taste buds grew numb. The fireworks sent up a shocking din; there was even something that sounded like the shriek of a bird. Red and green lights flashed outside his rear window from time to time. Extravagance wherever you looked, from people who were content with their lives. What were all those millions of people up to? What were they so happy about?

He sure wasn't one of them. If Mother were alive, it would be time to wrap dumplings, those tiny little things he had popped into his mouth like candy. He loved them. On his first New Year's in camp he had eaten seventy-six at one sitting, until he was so stuffed he couldn't sit, and had spent the afternoon walking around the athletic field. Yet even this memory failed to cheer him up. His hands were sticky from the stewed pig's feet and a layer of pork goo, and the wine was making him edgy.

He went out and stood in the yard for a while. No chill, no wind. The sky blazed with color; there were explosions all over the place. The yard, no more than seven or eight feet wide, was like a well under a sparkling azure sky. A stereo set was blaring a song, the kind whose lyrics are unintelligible. He imagined the singer to be fat and ugly. He'd seen those types on TV—nice voices and pretty smiles but betrayed by their looks. They writhed and cavorted on the screen, making movements that only accentuated their ugliness and transformed their songs into screeches and moans. Only attractive girls should be permitted on TV, but they were probably in short supply. Although Huiquan kept his distance from women, images of pretty girls still cruised through his mind. None of them seemed distinctly familiar, since they were all jumbled together—blurred objects whose intents were clear and explicit. There were times, special times, when he wished he could make those objects dancing around in his head do his bidding. But neither in the real world nor in the world of illusion were those appalling objects willing to fall under his spell. Helpless and inferior, he was forced to acknowledge his impotence.

Huiquan's thoughts turned to lewd walls—toilet walls

whose scars could not be whitewashed out of existence, battered walls about to topple under lustful assaults. Weird, obscene thoughts and excrement were in strange harmony there, forcing him to confront the filthy body he was trying to conceal. Huiquan knew there was no place he could hide. All alone on New Year's Eve, he added his own fantasies to those sordid walls. Rather than girls, maybe what had disgusted him all along was himself.

His self-disgust—if that's what it was—had begun at the age of fourteen.

Following the summer cleanup at Middle School 68, he had gone up to the boys' bathroom on the third floor and, without any prior instruction, done the deed. Standing behind the partition, drenched with sweat, his face flushed, strange things happened to his body, and a total loss of control had him palpitating with anxiety. A single female face kept reappearing: sometimes it belonged to his classmate Luo Xiaofen, sometimes to his language teacher. He tumbled into an abyss. He never revealed this incident to anyone, nor did he have the strength to keep it from occurring again. Sometimes he treated his body like a temple; at other times he tried to destroy it. He punished himself by keeping all girls at arm's length, but even that didn't lessen his sense of self-contempt. Among his friends he had the reputation of being a misogynist and a prude, someone who knew what lay behind the casual lewd comments they passed around. A thief, he stole feminine warmth and passion in his fantasies. Deep down he respected girls, was even a little afraid of them. Spike and Hobo needled him over the way he acted around them, but he couldn't have turned lustful if he'd wanted to. Better to use his rolling pin on the overweening head of one of his own than to lay a finger on a girl. Naturally he found Spike's admission that he had raped a peasant woman impossible to accept.

He took care of himself in his own way. It was a bit trouble-some, to be sure, but his way not only satisfied him but was secret, safe, and uncomplicated. The camp had more hiding places than he could count—groves, corn patches, irrigation ditches, virgin farmland—where his only observers were the sky above and the ground below. By the time he was there, he no longer had a crush on Xiaofen, so his infatuation was direction-less. He assumed a fatalistic approach to his inertia, knowing that he would keep sliding forward without the foggiest idea where that movement would take him. Aware that demons were toying with him, he was still powerless to resist.

He was tired. The popping of firecrackers had peaked and was now dying out. The infrequent explosion only accentuated the stillness of the black night. People had had their fill of fun, food, and games, and it was time for the city to sleep, before dawn broke. He had no peers, yet he still felt lost. Outside of his fantasies he could find no girl worthy of his affections.

Luo Xiaofen, no longer on his mind, was certainly not that girl. He hadn't seen her since getting out. She was vacationing in Harbin with her boyfriend, an assistant at the normal college, where she was a graduate student in math—a match made in heaven. Auntie Luo, bursting with pride and joy, told him they were getting married on May Day. Luo Xiaofen—Huiquan had grown up with her, had gone to elementary and middle school with her, but now they had nothing in common. She was in Harbin taking in the ice sculptures while he was on Spirit Run Street, in a dark corner, doing something so sordid it made him sick at heart. But that's how fate had arranged it. Fate was always mocking him.

He spent the first day of the new year fixing up his three-wheeler, and on the second day he took it out for a spin. The drawers he'd built into the bed brought him an enormous sense of accomplishment. He rode his bike over to check out some wholesale outlets, to familiarize himself with their location. They were all scheduled to reopen for business on the fifth, as though conspiring against him. Nothing to do until then.

After writing to Political Instructor Xue and mailing the letter, Huiquan stopped at a book stall and bought copies of *Ghosts in an Ancient Cemetery* and *Serpent Women*. Back home he sprawled out on the bed and read while eating one banana after another. Over the holidays he finished off an entire bunch, until his intestines were so slippery he felt like going to the can all day long. The books were okay; he just couldn't retain a memory of the plots. So he read them again, and they were as fresh and entertaining the second time around. He particularly liked the parts that were patent nonsense, like the description of a woman's private parts as a mushroom. There were lots of interesting places like that, and the books could have been written expressly for him. After he had reread them and tossed them aside, the walls seemed to him too blank, too pale. More bananas. By now he was referring to the authors as a couple of bastards. Time dragged. Tomorrow wouldn't be any different, and would it matter if it were? What difference is there between a big rat and a little one? Both are ugly; both are sneaky.

Li Huiquan was assigned a spot on the sidewalk south of Eastbridge, where numbers had been painted in white on the bricks in a long row of two-square-yard sites; some were occupied, some not. After setting up his stall, he covered it with the awning and rolled up his three-wheeler to serve as the counter. It was like a little tent, with a metal railing and a traffic light behind him. Off to the left was an east-west sidewalk, to the right its north-south counterpart. The parking lot for the Eastbridge Department Store was directly in front. He was on the edge of a whirlpool, with eddies of people swirling past, seemingly unable to stop.

Not a single pair of eyes cast an appreciative glance at his merchandise. Having barely extricated themselves from the tiring business of getting through the holidays, the passersby were either aloof or cantankerous. His designation was South 025. Not a particularly energizing number. He was the twenty-fifth clothing vendor within a hundred-yard area. Food stalls were on the north side of the street, with at least six selling roasted yams and several old men and old women peddling frosty oranges and half-rotten bananas. Their noses ran in the glacial air. They looked as though they were trying to milk the northwest wind for something, but try as he might to feel sorry for them, he couldn't manage to.

A shock of green appeared on his stall—a bundle of eight olive-drab padded army overcoats. He hung some from the frame, spread others out over the counter, and wore one. The old guy at the wholesale outlet had tricked him. Army overcoats, angora sweaters, and canvas deck shoes didn't sell. The only business he did that day was in old-men's ski caps, all twenty of which were quickly snapped up. Obviously, they were the bait for the other stuff. The wholesale cost was three-ten. He sold the first one for four yuan, the last for six-twenty. No one had to teach him. He learned a valuable lesson when the first customer handed over the money: don't lose your nerve in front of money, and forget about being polite. Giving a sales pitch gave him a rush, for some reason: his eyes lit up, yet inside he was cool as a cucumber. Here finally was something over which he had control.

He wished he'd kept one of the ski caps for himself. They were like Ku Klux Klan hoods—only the eyes showed—and that was just what a vendor needed. Huiquan felt endowed with the same mysterious power possessed by the old peddler of candied hawthorns who had been standing in front of the Eastbridge Department Store, right in the path of the wind, for hours without a murmur, without moving. He had some customers—not many, but a few—but Huiquan couldn't bear to watch him any longer, knowing he might scream if he did.

"Perfection-brand deck shoes from the Shenzhen free economic zone. Deck shoes, Perfection brand, made in Shenzhen . . ."

His shouts caught the strollers by surprise. He had heard that sort of hawking at East China Gate and at Front Gate before, but he never figured he was up to it. Too great a strain, he thought; more than he could handle. Now he knew that he had underestimated himself.

"Batwing blouses! Over here! Lookee see!"

This time it sounded horrible, but no one seemed surprised. Within seconds the shoppers had adapted to his strange shouts. They could have been made by a howling dog or a screeching cat, and still the shoppers would have reacted with nonchalance. He was home free.

"Batwing blouses! Sexy, sexy, sexy, girls!"

Oh, if he could only shout something really dirty to grab their attention. All day long he manned his stall, from early morning till dinnertime, but he didn't sell even one angora sweater or a single pair of deck shoes—nothing but those twenty ski caps. Even at that, the middle-aged woman in the stall to his right was envious, since she'd been there longer than he, and all she'd managed to sell were a measly pair of stockings and a couple of hankies. The stall on his left was manned by a fellow in his early twenties who nearly got into a fight with a customer over a leather jacket. The customer said it was imitation; the vendor insisted it was genuine kidskin. The customer rubbed it and insisted it was a foreign imitation. The vendor's patience was running out. Huiquan could tell by looking at it that it was genuine kidskin, but he kept his nose out of the dispute. No reason to get involved. When the fellow later offered him a smoke, he refused it. And when he lit up, he ignored the other guy. He had no intention of getting çlose to anyone. Better to be careful where strangers were concerned.

He was the last one in the row to pack up for the day. It was nine o'clock, a half hour after the department store closed. The parking lot was dark, the streetlights too dim to make much difference; there would be no more customers that night. A stall across the way, run by two men, was also packing up, but even at that late hour the vendors were reluctant to see the day end; there was a note of desperation in their voices.

"Nylon stockings, closeout! Eighty cents a pair . . . Eighty cents a pair! Closeout on nylon stockings. Last chance! Nylon stockings . . ."

Their three-wheeler came up the side street and onto the road, heading toward Hu Family Tower. One of the vendors pedaled as the other knelt in the bed and waved a pair of nylon stockings in the air. Their desperation was short-lived, quickly overtaken by a perverse joy. Their voices—one high, one low— roamed excitedly, carried on the night winds.

"Condoms! Two for eighty cents . . . Nylon condoms, red or green, take your pick! You say you're not interested? Take a whiff, take a look! Who wants condoms? Large or small, loose or tight, perfect for boys and girls . . . Come over here, you little pussy, I'll kick your ass. What am I doing? Getting ready to stick it to your old grandpa, that's what!"

They turned into a housing project and disappeared. Hui-quan stood there with a blank look on his face. He could have said stuff a lot worse than what those guys did, but he hadn't. A gust of cold air brushed past his heart, yet the back of his head was burning up. It was a sensation he knew all too well, from a lifetime of fights. He thought about his rolling pin. He wouldn't mind using it on the heads of the two "condom" peddlers, a couple of wild men who, incidentally, were having a hell of a lot more fun than he was; and even recalling his earnings from the ski caps didn't improve his mood.

The next day he sold a muffler.

On the third day he didn't sell a thing.

On the fourth day, less than half an hour after setting up shop, he sold army overcoats to four carpenters who had just arrived in Beijing from the south. After leaving Beijing Station, they had headed to the carpentry market at Hu Family Tower, and by the time they reached Eastbridge, their lips had turned purple in the arctic air. Huiquan's lined overcoats saved their skins, and their money slipped easily and quickly into his wallet. Before the sale he had attended to business in a halfhearted manner at best, but his dealings with the carpenters inspired him. The key ingredient to ensure a life of stability was patience. Even during the worst of times getting antsy or discouraged is counterproductive. Better to play possum than to run away, since no one can predict when opportunity will knock. A guy can't be down on his luck all the time, can he? Li Huiquan was thinking.

4

Business was booming during the first part of March. Huiquan had bought two hundred pairs of faddish shorts from a Willow Hamlet clothing factory in Shunyi County, and sales were brisk, to say the least. The factory manager was a distant cousin of Political Instructor Xue, who had referred to Huiquan in his letter of introduction as "a friend of mine," either to put his cousin at ease or to preserve Huiquan's self-respect.

After Huiquan had handed him the letter, the manager showed him the courtesy due a friend of his cousin by selling him the two hundred pairs of shorts. At first Huiquan didn't think much of them, but it didn't take him long to realize the bonanza he had in the form-fitting, multipocketed unisex cotton shorts. Available in two shades—dark and light gray—they were quickly snapped up by teenage girls, to his surprise and delight. Handing the satiny hip huggers to all those girls brought him a real sense of joy; maybe it was his mission in life to deck out the girls of the city—and at a tidy profit, no less. His asking price—twelve-sixty—brought frowns to the girls' faces, and maybe that was the source of his joy. One girl agonized for the longest time before

47

handing over the money, and when she left, Huiquan gave her one yuan too much in change. He couldn't explain this action, since she wasn't sexy or pretty or anything—quite nondescript, if the truth were known. But when she noticed the mistake, she quickly disappeared into the crowd before he demanded the money back. Her behavior turned his joy to ashes.

"Come back here!"

He wasn't even looking in her direction when he shouted. All he wanted was to frighten the panicky girl, for whom a one-yuan bill had produced a mixture of happiness and trepidation. The incident taught him a valuable lesson: they're all like that girl. He sold; they bought. They powdered their faces and added touches of mascara to cover up the grime. Their filthy asses, encased in Dacron slacks or leotards, were just waiting to be hugged by a pair of skimpy shorts. Their hands invariably trembled as they counted out the money (where it came from was no business of his), their fingernails transformed into demonic purple claws. There was nothing they wouldn't do as long as they had someone to lead the way, even if it meant going outside dressed only in a pair of panties—anything, so long as it was the newest fad. Huiquan knew he could depend on people like that for his livelihood and that he would have to serve them if he was to feast on them. He would cheat them outright if necessary. There was no law that said you had to treat people civilly.

His second visit to Willow Hamlet wasn't as successful as the first. This time Political Instructor Xue's cousin gave him a cool reception. Maybe the man had learned of his background. Whatever the reason, he would sell him only a single bundle of shorts, fifteen pairs, from which he might earn enough to buy a carton of cigarettes. But that was better than nothing. As he left, he said courteously, "I won't bother you anymore . . ."

"Drop by for tea anytime . . ."

A polite, tactful remark that clearly meant that the greater the distance between them the better. If not for the sake of his cousin, most likely he wouldn't have given Huiquan the time of day. Those two hundred pairs of shorts on the first visit had been a favor, a very big favor, and Huiquan would have had to be dense indeed not to realize that they had constituted a one-time transaction.

Surprised by how quickly his bonanza had petered out, he was nonetheless determined not to be discouraged, for by then he had begun to adapt to the atmosphere around Eastbridge. No one held a gun to his head to make him stand in the cold in the path of a stream of strangers; fate had arranged it. There was plenty there to keep him occupied, as long as he maintained the right attitude. Watching people and guessing their moods by their expressions was one of his favorite pastimes. On cold days there were a lot more gloomy faces than happy ones, and the sound of laughter was rare. When the weather warmed up, the number of happy faces increased, but the laughter and conversations sounded forced and unnatural.

The overwhelming majority of faces betrayed no expression whatsoever, in cold weather or warm. From east to west and north to south the passersby strolled past Huiquan's stall without a second glance. Those few who stopped to look at his goods or to ask a price usually had kind faces or innocent ones or slightly foolish ones. Once in a while a character would stop, pick something up, and examine it as if he were Sherlock Holmes looking for clues. Huiquan got a real kick out of watching these performances.

He had begun to form a set of guidelines for appraisal that pertained to his prospective customers. Those with juvenile, slightly dull expressions never bought anything. The ones who fancied themselves as shrewd took up as much time as possible before handing over the money, even if they could have bought the same thing in the department store behind them for less. So much for shrewdness. It was all part of a pattern. People are never their own masters. A mysterious force is always in control. Some people make out fine, some don't; some grow up looking like a squash, others blossom like flowers; some people nap comfortably in their cars, whereas others pick through trash behind department stores. Everyone is different, so it is impossible to compare people, impossible and fruitless. To himself Huiquan repeated his observation—people are never their own masters.

Huiquan was fated to wait patiently at pushcart stall South 025, like it or not, since he had to eat, since he had to live. Cars drove up and down the street behind him; silvery airplanes soared slowly in the sky above; a young couple argued on the sidewalk; a three-wheeler loaded with fruit flipped over; an out-of-towner, his back to the pedestrians, was pissing against the railing around a lawn, evidently unable to hold it any longer . . . None of this had anything to do with Li Huiquan. No power in the world could have stopped any of it from occurring right in front of his eyes. A prospective customer or a bomb going off next to him was about the only thing that could have disturbed his apathy. As he calmly took in the sights at Eastbridge, a simple world was revealed to him; the world was profound only if one clung to it stubbornly.

A little tortoise crawled out of the gutter and aimlessly threaded its way around and between the wheels and then, surprisingly, crossed the road and moved onto the side street. Huiquan was engrossed in its movements. If it had looked in both directions at first, it would never have made it. Ubiquitous fate kept it from being squashed. Now if fate could protect a tortoise, why couldn't it do the same for a human being? Huiquan wished that business would pick up, but if that were too much to wish for, then how about the gift of being able to spot his next customer in the crowd? That would please him as much as not having the gift would depress him.

More than anything he hated seeing a customer take out his money only to drop the merchandise and run off at the moment of truth. He wondered where the sudden impulse not to buy came from, since it always caught him unprepared. He sometimes suspected the person of playing games with him, and although he coped with these situations with as much equanimity as he could manage, he knew that the next time it happened, it would bother him just as much. All vendors were victimized in similar ways, but Huiquan wasn't like other people, who could release their anger by cursing like sailors or by perversely demanding that the customer make the purchase. He just crossed his arms in front of his chest and, like a street thug, glared contemptuously at the customer.

That glare of his made husky young men lower their heads and pretend not to notice. With others it was worse—girls were afraid to look back until they were ten or twenty yards away. Such a reaction usually brought Huiquan sufficient satisfaction; he would relax his menacing pose, his face taking on a barely detectable I-can't-help-it expression that gave him the pathetic appearance of a common hired hand. He had the look of one of those visiting carpenters or seamstresses or one of those visitors from the south who fluffed cotton or sold sleeping mats. With his high cheekbones and dark, thick lips he could easily have been mistaken for a southern peasant. Only a few of his fellow vendors knew that he was the famous (or infamous) Basher Li and that Chaoyang District was filled with people whose skulls he'd cracked. Those who knew were careful not to anger him or try to butter him up, wisely keeping him at arm's length and minding their own business.

One Saturday afternoon Huiquan spotted a familiar face in the crowd. As he watched the man approach, he tried unsuccessfully to recall his name or how he knew him. The man stopped in front of his three-wheeler and picked up a pair of white-soled blue canvas deck shoes that were dirty from all the handling.

"Made in Shenzhen?"

"There's the label. See for yourself."

But instead of looking at the trademark, the man stared at Huiquan and froze. A mole the size of a coffee bean decorated the spot above his right eyebrow; an errant tooth protruded through tightly closed lips. Finally it came to Li Huiquan—his rolling pin had danced on this guy's head.

"You're . . . Basher Li?"

"And you . . ."

"Brushes!" he said, giving his nickname first. Then, "Ma Yifu, from Gold Tower's West Lane. That time you and I . . . I thought it was you! How's it going, man?"

Now he recalled. When he and some friends from his high school bonehead class had cut school one day to go ice-skating at Red Scarf Park, they got into an altercation with some students from Red Monastery High who were lined up to rent skates. The challenge was given and accepted, and the two groups headed to a construction site at Six-Mile Villa. Ma Yifu was the leader of the Red Monastery students. The cost of that fight, which involved a couple of dozen combatants, was several busted heads and two broken bones. The details of the battle escaped Huiquan now, but he recalled that Ma Yifu sent a peace delegation to invite him and his friends to a meal at a famous restaurant. Some

time later Ma Yifu asked him to come along to a fight with some
guys from Wine Immortals Bridge. He went, but the fight never
materialized, for his reputation had preceded him.

Ma Yifu had put on weight. Huiquan didn't know what to
say to him, but he found the man's cordial pose distasteful. He
wondered whether this meeting, their first in five years, was as
accidental as it seemed, yet his expression betrayed none of his
questions.

"How're you doing?" he asked.

"Not bad! I work for the Jeep company. It's a joint Sino-
U.S. venture. One of those big-nosed foreigners is my boss."

"Better than me. I haven't been out long . . . I was inside
for three years; did you know that?"

"Yeah. I knew the guy Fang Guangde stabbed. From Hu
Family Tower High School. His kid sister and mine were classmates. They live at Hundred Clans Village. He was okay in a
couple of months. Oh, right—he went to Iraq last year. His old
man's a section chief for China Construction. Well connected,
they say. Shit, you and Fang Guangde got a raw deal."

Ma Yifu hadn't changed—still a fast talker, and a long-
winded one. Huiquan had hated that mouth of his from the very
first day, but now he wanted to hear the news that flowed from
it, since he had a lot of catching up to do.

"Been staying out of trouble these past few years?"

"Busted twice, but was in detention for less than a month
altogether. I wised up. I avoid anything that might get me into
trouble. Doing time ain't worth it, right?"

"Don't ask me."

"Can you make a go of it here? Clothes were a hot item a
couple of years ago, but they don't do so good anymore."

"It's the only license I could get."

"Yeah, but . . . this stuff's pretty old-fashioned. Does it sell? These shoes aren't bad. Are they really made in Shenzhen?" Ma Yifu was still holding the pair of deck shoes.

"Are you kidding? They're from Baoding. The label's a phony. But you need a foreign label to get 'em to sell."

"You're right there."

"You like 'em? I'll give you a pair."

"You don't have to do that."

Huiquan asked him his shoe size, fished a clean pair out of the box, and wrapped them up. Ma Yifu made a show of waving him off with one hand and digging in his pocket with the other, but in the end he took the shoes.

"I'll pay you later."

"Brushes, don't try to bullshit me!"

"What the fuck do you take me for? You busy tonight?"

"Who wants to know?"

"Meet me at ten o'clock at the Little Village intersection."

"Will I need my rolling pin?"

"No joking, man. A new club opened on Mill Road last month. It's open until two in the morning. Want to check it out?"

"Only if they sell booze."

"Come see for yourself. Satisfaction guaranteed. Ten sharp. I'll be waiting for you by the traffic-control tower. Bike or bus?"

"Bike."

"Good. That way you won't have to worry about missing the last bus. Okay, we're on, then."

"You haven't changed. You're still a goddamn chatterbox!"

"You think so? My girlfriend complains I don't talk enough."

"You've got a girlfriend?"

"Nothing serious. You'll see her tonight. I'm not sure about her."

Ma Yifu was putting on a bit of a show and was obviously pleased with himself. Showing off his girlfriend was probably the main reason he wanted to take Huiquan to the place, eager to bask in the glory of his conquest. Huiquan already envied him, no matter what his girlfriend looked like. Anyone who fell for Ma Yifu had to be scraping the bottom of the barrel.

Ma Yifu—Huiquan knew him then only by the nickname Brushes and never did find out what it meant—had come to the fight at the Six-Mile Villa construction site armed with a hoe. He charged like a wild man, swinging the implement—*whoosh, whoosh*—as Huiquan slipped the rolling pin out of his sleeve to meet the charge. Huiquan knew instinctively that the hoe was all for show. The look in those eyes was not that of a man prepared to fight to the death. He had guessed right.

"Take one more step, and I'll knock your fucking block off!"

Huiquan charged, Brushes' hand froze, and rolling pin met skull. Only his lined cap saved Brushes from at least eight stitches. Huiquan lit into him, raining blows on his back.

"I give up, man. I give up!"

Seeing the futility in trying to get away, Brushes quit the fight without a trace of embarrassment. Later, at the restaurant, he nearly groveled at Huiquan's feet.

"I've been around, but I've never seen anybody like you. As soon as I saw the look on your face, I knew you were somebody who didn't give a shit . . . Weren't you scared I'd take your head off with that hoe?"

"I'd have easily warded off the blow with my arm. I was ready. But you were too scared."

"You're a fucking piece of work! Out of my league. You ever run into trouble and need help, just give the word."

Huiquan had no reason to "give the word," but he was asked on several occasions to join one of Brushes' fights. He went one time, and though the fight never materialized, Brushes was openly appreciative. After that they bumped into one another every now and then when they were out of work. Eventually, though, they went their separate ways and fell out of touch. Huiquan's only friends were Spike and Hobo.

Now Huiquan was touched by Ma Yifu's sense of loyalty. After all these years he hadn't forgotten him. Not a bad friend when all was said and done.

Before going out that night he cleaned his bicycle and would have changed clothes if he'd had any worth changing into. He should have taken Auntie Luo's advice about buying a New Year's wardrobe. But he was used to making do and had never cared much for new clothes. This was the first time in his life he felt like taking better care of himself.

Ma Yifu was standing on the sidewalk by the traffic-control island at Little Village, dressed in a suit, his hair slicked down. More and more people were shedding their padded clothes and wearing suits these days, now that it was warming up. The sight of Ma Yifu standing there cheered Li Huiquan. He had a friend, someone who treated him pretty well. He knew other people, of course, but was too lazy to look them up. People don't easily forget someone like Basher Li. But Ma Yifu treated him with the deference of the old days, and that was immensely satisfying.

"How come you're dressed like that?"

"What do you mean?"

"I mean you look like a peasant! What do you do with all your money?"

"All my money? I'm lucky to break even. I've been at it two months now, and I've barely made back what I spent on my three-wheeler."

"That's what being on the up-and-up will get you."

"How does someone get by without being on the up-and-up?"

"Wait'll you meet this bunch of wheelers and dealers, and you'll know what I mean . . . That's it there, the one with the delivery van in front. It's a great joint. You'll like it so much you'll probably become a regular."

The front window of the building was flush against the sidewalk, under bright streetlights, but the club itself was dimly lit. Up close Huiquan saw that the plate-glass window was curtained to keep passersby from seeing what was going on inside. Orange lettering over the aluminum door frame spelled out KA-RAOKE. The name meant nothing to him. The take-out section in front occupied only a few square feet of space. There were no customers, just a haggard-looking girl behind the counter. Apparently recognizing Ma Yifu, she nodded, and he beamed as he opened a narrow, leather-covered door to the right, revealing the lounge. Soft background music and the gentle sound of singing greeted them.

"Close the door!"

"Hurry up, close it!"

Some of the more excitable patrons. Huiquan closed the door behind him and with barely disguised hostility took in the luxurious setting. The place was laid out like a railroad car, with booths on both sides separated by a narrow aisle down the middle. The low tables made the booths look like individual compartments. The aisle was barely wide enough for one person. At the far end a girl sat in a swivel chair, her back to the wall, a microphone stand before her, her eyes closed as she sang and swayed from side to side. She seemed right at home up there, singing one of those songs whose lyrics one can never figure out. Not blessed with much of a voice—obviously an amateur—she had more stage presence than most professional singers.

Ma Yifu led him over to one of the booths, where a chubby girl was drinking a Coke. By the look of Brushes' sudden diffidence, Huiquan imagined this must be the girlfriend. She was saving seats for them and didn't look very happy.

Ma Yifu pointed to her. "This is my friend . . ."

Huiquan, blushing slightly, nodded and sat down.

"This is my friend," Ma Yifu repeated, this time pointing to Huiquan. No doubt who the boss was here.

The chubby girl giggled. She was not pretty. Her nose was too flat, her eyes were barely visible, and she had an underdeveloped chin. Nothing worth getting envious about, but just about right for Ma Yifu, it seemed to Huiquan. Ma Yifu sat down and whispered something to his little princess, who nodded regally.

Ma Yifu stood up, walked over to an opening in the eastern wall that resembled the serving window in the camp canteen, and returned with three cups of coffee and three pastries on a small plate.

"Real Maxwell House!"

"Shh, not so loud!" the chubby girl groused at Brushes. Huiquan sipped his coffee. It was bitter, strangely bitter.

The girl on the stage stopped singing and stood up.

"Your turn!" she said.

A strapping young fellow walked up and took the mike from her as she planted a kiss on his cheek. Lovers, probably, but even then! Huiquan took another sip of coffee. It was beginning to taste a little better.

"What'll I sing?"

"Anything . . . Something with a beat."

Following a brief exchange between the young man and someone behind the window in the eastern wall, some raucous music blared, and the young man started grinding and shaking. Hardly what you'd call a musical performance. All he did was open his mouth a crack, as though he'd forgotten the lyrics, and at certain spots in the song he grunted or let out a shrill, falsetto shout.

The window in the wall supplied food, drink, and music. The patrons spent cash and emotions they couldn't unleash anywhere else. The young fellow up on stage reminded Huiquan of a cat in heat, with all those screeches, but inexplicably the more he listened, the more he felt like screeching right along with him.

He was beginning to like the place.

"Feel like singing?"

"Not me."

"Coffee sells for two yuan a cup, so you might as well get your money's worth. How about it, Huiquan? Want to give it a try?"

"I . . . can't sing."

"Then I'll do it if you won't!"

At eleven-thirty on the dot Ma Yifu gave his rendition of "Moonlit Night on the Fifteenth." The audience took his singing in stride, even if he couldn't make the notes fit the general mood no matter how hard he tried. He probably knew only the one song. Either that or his chubby girlfriend had told him to sing it. After he finished, he walked his girlfriend home, and while he was gone, they played back a tape of his performance. This time it sounded funny as hell, and the other patrons had a good laugh over Ma Yifu's scratchy voice, which sounded like leaky bellows. Huiquan wondered what he might sound like on tape. He'd never heard his voice before. It would probably be nothing like what he heard while he was singing. The temptation to go up and give it a try was very strong.

The microphone owned the empty stage as a haunting melody began to play. It was the theme song from *Shaolin Temple*, and Huiquan began to hum the tune. Unfortunately he could remember only the first half of the lyrics, and his courage vanished as he imagined how foolish he'd look up there all alone; there was nothing he hated more than making a fool of himself. As he sat indecisively, a young fellow weaved his way up the aisle and sat in the inviting swivel chair. After signaling the person at the window to turn off the music, he launched into a song, accompanying himself on a guitar.

People didn't patronize this club for the music or the menu. The booths around Huiquan were occupied by modish boys and girls engaged in hushed conversations. One couple across from him was kissing, one hell of a kiss, like a pair of exhibitionists. They sure were young, high school students by the look of them, and didn't seem to have a care in the world. Huiquan found that puzzling.

After finishing his coffee, he scanned the menu. Brandy went for two-fifty a glass. How big a glass? he wondered. Other items included spaghetti, tossed salad, ham sandwiches, and roast beef. And all of it pretty pricey. He went up to the window, ordered two bottles of Tsingtao beer and a salad, and then carried them back carefully, so as not to spill anything on the carpet.

"Your first time here? Why not go on up and sing a song?"

"I can't sing. I just want to enjoy my beer."

He found the waitress's friendliness troubling.

"Maybe later, after you've been here a few times. Be sure to tell us what you think of the place. We're open till two, you know. Is there anything else you'd like?"

"No . . . thank you!"

Ma Yifu's chubby girlfriend must have lived nearby, for he was back in no time, wearing a scowl. He obviously didn't feel like talking.

"What's wrong?" Huiquan asked him.

"She insisted on knowing what the fuck you do! Instead of trusting me, she tries to run my life. One of these days I'll dump her!"

"Why'd she ask about me?"

"Says you look mean, . . . but don't sweat it. She's afraid I'll get mixed up with a bad crowd and get into trouble. Afraid I'll pick up bad ways! What the fuck does a girl know? If I want to pick up bad ways, I don't need anybody's help!"

"She looks okay to me."

"Yeah, she's okay. What can you expect when you look like me? I was busted last year for scalping tickets at the Masses Cinema and did two weeks. She damn near broke it off over that. She's really got me on a short leash."

"It's probably for your own good."

"I know. I got the message. The benefits at the factory are good, and there are plenty of bonuses. That's why I keep my nose clean. There might be better jobs, but there are worse ones, too. If I've got money in my pocket, I have a good time. If not, well, that's the way it goes."

"When you gonna tie the knot?"

Brushes' answer was slow in coming.

"I'll tell you: she's willing, but her mom ain't. Still won't give her blessings, even now . . . Tell me, do I look like a lowlife? Back then I could get any goddamn girl I wanted!"

"Get off it! What do you have to offer anybody?"

"Of course, I'm not much compared with Spike Fang or with you. But enough of that. How about you—when can I meet your girlfriend?"

Huiquan forced a smile. "She'd scare you off!"

"Who is she?"

"Didn't you say you're buying? How about a brandy?"

"I'm a little short—"

"I've got money."

Doubts were creeping into Huiquan's mind about the wisdom of rekindling a friendship with Ma Yifu. He was sort of slippery and too concerned about himself. He still hadn't asked about life in the camp. An oversight? No, other people's problems simply didn't concern him. Worst of all, he hadn't even asked about Huiquan's mother. Too busy rambling on about his love life.

It was getting late. Trucks sped up and down the street, since speed limits weren't enforced at this late hour. A new batch of patrons gradually replaced the early crowd, breathing new life into the joint. Even the employees were energized.

At about one o'clock a bearded man walked in, and was greeted by waitresses and patrons alike. He acknowledged their greetings and sat in the booth opposite Huiquan's.

Apparently Ma Yifu knew him.

"How's it going?"

"Okay."

"Long time no see."

"Just got back from Guangzhou. Have they a hired the singer yet? Is it a he or a she?"

"They ought to stop wasting their time! The pros won't come, and they can't find a decent amateur. Hell, anyone can screech like a cat."

"Smoke? Your buddy here . . ."

"Friend of mine. Don't you know Basher Li?"

"I think I've heard the name."

"He just got out. He's selling clothes at Eastbridge."

"That so? Smoke?"

Their eyes met briefly when the man handed Huiquan the pack. As Huiquan lit up, his gaze settled on the stranger. Lots of white showing around pupils that bulged more than most people's. The lower half of his face was all whiskers, giving him a mean look. His suit was a little grimy, his fingers were long and pale. Hard to tell what he did for a living. No more than thirty. He was wearing three rings on his fingers.

Ma Yifu was sickeningly ingratiating.

Whiskers applauded a girl who had just finished singing and then went up to the window to visit with the person inside for a while. To Huiquan he seemed pretty shrewd, a man who had seen and done most everything. A middle-aged inmate at camp, nicknamed the Wire, had spoken and acted with the same self-assurance. The other inmates were amazed to learn that he had been arrested for selling funerary urns in a village where cremation had just been instituted. His so-called funerary urns were nothing but common, everyday pickle vats available at any store in town. You sure can't judge a book by its cover. Brushes looked like a completely different person in his natty suit and shiny shoes, while in fact he was the same stupid jerk he'd always been.

"Who's he?" Huiquan asked.

"Name's Cui; that's all I know. People don't ask questions like that here. If he wants you to know something, he'll tell you.

If he doesn't, you're better off not asking. You want to stay away from the big spenders here."

"You seem to know him pretty well."

"I used to run into him at dances at the Cultural Palace, and I've seen him here a couple of times. We're just nodding acquaintances. I have no idea what he does."

"Where does he live?"

"Over near Ten-Mile Fortress, I think. He doesn't come here much. You'd think everybody's his friend, but there aren't more than three or four people who really know him. The bastard's always got a wad of bills on him, though, so he must have connections."

Whiskers stood by the window and drank a cup of coffee. Then he waved to the crowd, opened the door, and walked out. Fortified by the brandy, Brushes was getting increasingly boastful, and his love life was sounding more and more like a farce.

The last song of the night was playing, a wild, raucous song to accompany the customers as they filed out. A leather-jacketed girl was really grinding as she walked, her thin, nylon-encased legs wriggling from one end of the aisle to the other.

"What do you think of that?"

The red mole above Ma Yifu's eyebrow was twitching.

"Look at her, would you. Like she's humping some guy . . . I'll bet she'll be out selling it in no time!"

Huiquan scooped up the last bite of salad and shoved it into his mouth. He didn't like hearing Brushes talk like that. The girl had pretty good rhythm, as far as he was concerned, and he'd never have the guts to carry on like that.

"Let's get out of here."

Huiquan rapped Ma Yifu on his lecherous head, but Brushes was too busy undressing the girl with his eyes to notice.

5

The days passed uneventfully, albeit they were more orderly than before, and that was an improvement. Huiquan had made considerable domestic progress, even becoming a pretty good cook while he was at it. He had bought a copy of *Popular Cooking* at a book stall, and it was soon grimy and grease spattered. He had milk delivered and drank it just before going to bed at night, having read in the *Newspaper Digest* that it provided more nutrition when drunk that way. He bought all sorts of reading material, from *Soccer News* to *The Boundless Universe*—anything that struck his fancy. Sometimes he even read *People's Daily*, with which he was already familiar, having heard it daily in camp—an hour had been put aside every day for someone to read it aloud, the reader changing on a rotating basis. He didn't mind the paper, even though nine out of ten of its stories bored him to tears. His favorite sections were sports and the law. *People's Daily* was an eight-page paper nicely printed on good newsprint, ten cents a copy. Thumbing through it while waiting for customers was a good, sometimes even educational, way to kill time. At home his reading tastes tended toward booklets with titles like

Crime Digest. For some reason his favorites were exposés dealing with victimized girls, especially things like gang rapes. Reading them drained him emotionally, as though he were the culprit. He kept these booklets under his pillow so no one else would see them.

Bright and early every morning he went jogging, one and a half turns around Temple of the Sun Park, and then stopped for a breakfast of soybean milk and butter cakes at a local café, frequently returning home just as Uncle Luo was heading off to Standing Waters Bridge or Tyrant West or someplace like that to do some fishing. Always full of pep in the morning, Uncle Luo would promise to bring Huiquan a nice red carp. But all he ever caught were bigheads and silver carp and sometimes nothing at all. On the rare occasion when he managed to bring home a good catch, he shared it with Huiquan, who learned how to cook a mean braised fish once he got the wine and sugar quantities down. He must have been the only person who didn't think Uncle Luo was crazy to go fishing all the time; he figured it must be a lot more fun than tending a stall day in and day out.

His mood varied as he pushed his three-wheeler out the gate each morning: on some days he was too lazy to do much of anything, whereas on others he was in such a good mood he treated everyone he saw like a long-lost friend. But when he came home at night, he was always in a bad mood, no matter how good a day he'd had. He tried to change this pattern, but nothing worked. The two-room home his mother had left him felt increasingly empty and restrictive, and the ubiquitous quiet at bedtime was becoming unbearable. Life had deteriorated into a meaningless succession of yesterdays, todays, and tomorrows, none of which brought him any joy.

At nine one morning he'd sell a skirt to some girl; at nine the next morning he'd sell something else to another stranger.

Sometimes he'd barely earn the cost of a bowl of noodles; sometimes he'd make enough to buy a roast duck. He had only to spread his fingers for the little bit of money he earned to gravitate toward someone else, and he couldn't escape the feeling that although nothing he did was of any consequence, life held the promise of an important mission for him somewhere down the line. What that might be he didn't know.

After spotting an ad in the paper, he lined up late one night at the symphony hall to fork over two-fifty for a concert. At first he thought he was the only one pretending to enjoy it, but before long he was convinced that everyone in the audience was doing the same thing: swaying with the music while suffering terribly deep down. He never went back—he couldn't bear to. But he did go to the art museum, twice, strolling past each painting until he had grown weary. Then he went into the waiting room, sat on a sofa, and smoked cigarettes. In the end he spent more time smoking than looking. Some of the things he saw in the paintings provoked envy; others depressed him. He bought catalogs and programs, then paced the gallery in a new windbreaker that had set him back eighty yuan. His melancholic look gave him a cultivated appearance. He stood before the colorful canvases, looking without seeing; he even stared at a painting of a pretty girl without harboring a single lewd thought. Although his mind was murky and confused, one question was clear: Is life worth living?

He was twenty-five years old. Once more around and he'd be fifty. Then seventy-five. Time flew by, lightning quick, and he realized to his dismay that he was on a fast track to extinction, as though by tomorrow he would cease to exist, and there wasn't a thing he could do about it today. At times like this life lost its appeal. He grew weak, his spiritual malaise affecting him physically. A vague sense of despair quickly led to self-pity.

He shunned human contact. When Luo Xiaofen returned from viewing the ice sculptures in Harbin, they met once in the compound. He greeted her coldly and moved on. He was pushing his three-wheeler at the time; she was drawing water at the tap, a slender, obviously well-bred young man behind her—her fiancé, by all indications. Huiquan suddenly hated his rickety three-wheeler, his padded overcoat, and his face, which was burning up. His greeting was correct but terse as he headed down the path toward home, forestalling her attempt to make introductions. Two old friends no longer had anything in common. She was a graduate student; he was an ex-con who peddled goods from a pushcart. And even though she spoke to him, she must have harbored only scorn for him, and that prospect was more than he could bear. Although he noticed that she had filled out a bit, the subtle changes in her face escaped him. The tearful girl waiting to be consoled as she stood at the edge of the athletic field, her hair in a puny, lackluster pigtail, no longer existed. She had been succeeded by a young graduate student whose role in life was to mock him.

Life had even arranged for the sophisticated fellow standing behind her to mock him as one of society's outcasts. Indifference was Huiquan's only defense. Maybe that particular form of incivility would correspond to the view of him that others held. No one, with the possible exceptions of Auntie and Uncle Luo, could possibly have a good impression of him. He always seemed caught up in that pensive moment before a fight. He didn't have to be told he had a mean face; he wore it as a shield, removing it only in the privacy of his rear-compound rooms.

In early April a letter from Spike arrived. There was no denying its authenticity, given the sloppy nature of the handwriting and the incomprehensibility of half of what was written. Nowhere amid the scant, dry, utterly emotionless sentences was there any indication that he was happy or sad or anything. Still, Huiquan read the letter over and over to extract from it what little warmth it contained.

His friend's uncomplicated descriptions dealt exclusively with the enmity between inmates from Beijing and Hubei. Either he had nothing else to say, or he had trouble finding the words. His final comment, surprisingly, was "Eat good, take care of body!" Impossible to tell whether he meant himself or his reader, but Huiquan understood his friend completely. He had eaten well enough since getting out and wanted to write back to say so. He needed human contact—badly—but the people he wanted to be with were far away or no longer walked the earth.

Sometimes, absorbed in his thoughts and feeling a need to put his desires into words, he stared at a photograph of his mother. That need to express himself both stimulated and alarmed him. In his dreams he had done the deed with someone who had a blurry face but a clear, distinct body, so clear, in fact, that even after he awoke, he could recall every detail, every comment made, and every action undertaken. His fantasies brought him freedom and relief, and he sometimes imagined that jogging in the morning, manning his pushcart all day, drinking milk at night, and life's other little monotonies were just part of his fantasies. If only the rest of the world could be transformed into fantasy, his cares and worries would be over. He knew that was impossible, at least for the time being, but it might happen someday. He wasn't really fated never to know happiness, was he? But what is happiness, anyway?

At the very least, he thought, happiness should play a role in changing his life. One of them was too intractable—life or him. His life was a reflection of his inner being, and he could no longer tell which nurtured or obstructed the other, the being or the image. He went to concerts, and he cruised art galleries; in some of his lonelier moments he even went to the bird market in West City, where once he very nearly bought a dove. Not one of these activities accomplished a thing. When life resists change, human effort is futile. Maybe something would happen tomorrow, but he'd have to wait till then to find out. Tomorrows are many, but people who are truly contented with their lot are few.

He saw Ma Yifu a couple more times, once at the club and again at the stall at Eastbridge. The chubby girl wasn't with him either time. Yifu said their relationship was pretty rocky, since she thought he was too free with his money and struck her less and less like a solid citizen.

"Complaining about being tightfisted is one thing, but how can anybody be too free with his money? A few cups of coffee . . . some neckties—is that being too free? Life's hard enough as it is!"

Yifu painted himself as the victim, but Huiquan knew there was more to it than that. If he had been in the chubby girl's shoes, he'd never have fallen for someone like Brushes. All this talk about being free with his money was a smoke screen.

Yifu said the fellow Cui had asked about his business.

"What does he want to know for?"

"You got me, but it's nothing to worry about. There's no bad blood between you, is there?"

"Maybe not, but he doesn't seem like the type to ask idle questions. You know him, so tell me everything, or get the hell out of here!"

"I really don't know him very well. I'd know his whole name if I did, wouldn't I? Cui's no punk troublemaker, so why worry? Give him a chance. Every new friend opens up one more road."

"If you're going to play games with me, don't start whining

if I forget you're a friend. I've seen too much to be fooled by the likes of you.''

"Take it easy! You should know me better than that. This is everything I know. I met him a few years back at the Cultural Palace dance hall. I didn't know his full name then, and I don't know it now. But he asked if I could get him some silver dollars, and when I scraped up twenty or so, he bought them with foreign-exchange certificates. After that he acted like he didn't know me, and the subject never came up again. If we've got something cooking between us, you can use your rolling pin on me, and I won't raise a hand to protect myself. What harm can it do to be on the good side of someone with his contacts?''

"What did he want to know about me?''

"He asked why you'd served time, and I told him. By the sound of his response, I'd say he was impressed. He'd like to talk to you . . . Didn't say what about.''

"Has he been at the club lately?''

"Haven't seen him in over a week. Probably out of town. He's always off somewhere. He's been all over the country. As soon as he gets back, he'll show up at the club.''

"Why?''

"He can't wait to see a singer they're supposed to be hiring one of these days. Back in the dance-hall days he never showed up without a looker on his arm, and never the same one twice. He's cleaned up his act lately, maybe losing his nerve in his old age, but he's still got a dick, and he keeps asking when this girl's going to start.''

"Is there anything you don't know? I wonder what you tell people about me.''

"What kind of pal do you think I am? You're kidding, right? I don't talk about friends behind their back. If you're not interested, to hell with it. But if you are, leave everything to me. You

won't regret it. But you're still the worst businessman I ever
saw.''

"Why are you so concerned about my affairs? I advise you
to mind your own business and not get mixed up in things that
don't concern you!''

After putting Brushes in his place, Huiquan picked out a
white silk scarf and told him to give it to his girlfriend. Ma Yifu's
unhappiness at being ridiculed quickly turned to embarrassment.
He accepted the scarf and stammered something about the shoes
he had taken the last time. But he shut up when he saw the
menacing glare in Huiquan's eyes.

Huiquan had never had many friends, but his loyalty to the
few he had was absolute. Basher Li lived by one principle: he
would die for a friend if necessary. Ma Yifu might prove to be the
exception, since he appeared to have willingly relinquished his
manhood. Huiquan felt sorry for the chubby girl, for even though
he was a past master at belittling himself, he didn't doubt he was
a better man than Ma Yifu and his ilk would ever be. Maybe the
silk scarf was a gesture of consolation, who knows?

At a little after nine o'clock on the last Saturday evening in April,
Li Huiquan went to the club to spend an evening. Ma Yifu wasn't
there, but that was to be expected: he was always hard up by the
end of the month, since payday at the Jeep factory was the fifth.
Huiquan knew he wouldn't see him again until then.

He spotted Cui's beard as he walked through the doorway.
The man looked a little like Friedrich Engels. He greeted Huiquan, who was very guarded, and scooted over to make room.

Huiquan sat down but didn't begin a conversation right
away. An all-but-empty magnum of champagne sat on the table.

Two moist lips showed through the beard. Cui handed Huiquan a cigarette.

"What's your name?"

"Li. What's yours?"

"Cui."

"I'm Li Huiquan."

"Champagne or brandy?"

"I'll order my own."

Huiquan ordered some Bulgarian ham and a large brandy and began eating diffidently. Never much of a talker, he didn't make friends easily, and in the old days if a fight were brewing or peace talks were called for, someone else did the talking. He was always ready for action; in fact, violent action was all he could ever offer. He wondered what his tablemate had on his mind. Was he looking for an enforcer or an avenger? Neither seemed likely.

"Pretty rough inside, I'll bet. Three years is a long time."

"I managed. You've never been busted?"

"I've been lucky. Besides, I make sure that whatever I do is safe, and I don't make things hard on myself."

They were speaking softly. Whiskers was being very non-chalant. A ballad was playing, soft and monotonous. No one went up to the microphone to sing. Familiarity breeds boredom, if not contempt.

"You went to Sixty-eight Middle?"

"Right."

"Did you know Hairy Ape?"

"Heard of him."

The fellow called Hairy Ape had been executed the year of the earthquake. He was several years ahead of Huiquan, who had heard of but never met this schoolmate who wound up in the wrong place at the wrong time doing the wrong thing. Caught rifling a knitting-mill safe during the chaotic aftermath of the earthquake, he probably never dreamed he'd pay for the act with his life. It was all over a dozen or so hours after the ground shook. He was the butt of all kinds of jokes.

"We were pals—used to hang out together. A smart guy who made a mistake, a very big mistake. But if he was still alive, you can bet he'd be doing better than me."

Why is he telling me this? Huiquan was thinking. "My hands have never been dirty," he said.

"Really?"

"Blood but no stink!"

"Bully for you!"

"I like to keep clean and do things straight on."

Afraid he might not have been understood, Huiquan stared into the bloodshot eyes above the beard. They gazed back without blinking.

"My name's Huiquan. What's yours?"

A pause. Waiting for the ballad to end?

"Yongli—Eternal Blessings. Anything else you want to know? You've got sharp eyes, you know. Me, I've had too much to drink. Get me a cup of coffee, no sugar . . ."

Cui Yongli? Eternal Blessings? Probably not his real name.

Huiquan bought Cui a cup of coffee. While wary, the two men maintained a friendly facade. People were watching them. Cui banged his glass loudly—a little tipsy.

"I've seen your stall. The pants, the shoes—all pretty ugly. I don't see how you can make a living on that stuff."

"All I need is enough to keep my belly full."

"I don't believe you. You don't like money?"

"Would it like me if I did? I've got food, smokes, and a little spending money. What else do I need? The big money doesn't have my name on it."

"You'll never know till you try."

Huiquan sipped his brandy as he tried to figure out exactly what that meant. His patience was running thin.

"I'm not as brave as I was three years ago. Haven't got it anymore. I stay clear of fights and get weak-kneed if I see a cop . . . I'm finished, I'm a joke! Don't have what it takes."

"You got me wrong . . . I'm not trying to make you look bad. You've got more guts than me. I've never had a fight in my life. What do you say we order some litchi nuts?"

Cui Yongli wore a calm, inscrutable expression, and Huiquan was worried he might have talked too much. He was sure the guy wanted something, and he was prepared to say no. The prospect of beating someone up or getting beaten up was not appealing. No funny business for him. He'd done enough stupid things for one lifetime.

Cui went over to chat with the manager about a car crash that had occurred a few days earlier near Six-Mile Villa. The manager, a gaunt man in his early forties, had a warm, genial face but crafty eyes.

"Brains splattered all over the place!"

"They couldn't peel his face off the steering wheel."

Cui and the gaunt manager exchanged the gory details with gusto. Meanwhile, Huiquan's salad began to taste funny, sort of like transparent or milky-white brains. The gaunt manager laughed lustily. A little later, when Huiquan got up to leave, he waved to Cui, who was leaning against the service window, staring drunkenly at the air conditioner above as though trying to comprehend its inner logic. His eyes were so glazed he probably couldn't see a thing. Once again Huiquan was reminded of the Wire, the middle-aged man jailed for selling funerary urns. What could be going through the minds of people like that? He was drawn to Cui by the man's disarming optimism and carefree attitude. Some people managed to go through life relaxed and confident. He wondered how they did it.

On his way out Huiquan noticed a sheet of yellow paper posted on the wall by the take-out section. The word NOTICE at the top in red letters was followed by several conspicuous exclamation marks. The text was a combination of large and small print, and Huiquan had to read it twice before he realized what it said. The third-prize winner in the B group of an amateur pop-singer contest sponsored by the Cultural Palace would be performing at the club from eight to ten every evening for two weeks beginning the twenty-ninth of April. Not very exciting news, hardly worthy of all those exclamation marks. The 3 in "3rd" even looked as though it might have been a 2 that was reluctantly changed—the calligraphy didn't quite match. Maybe even third was stretching the point.

The singer's name was Zhao Yaqiu. The announcement referred to her as "Ms.," an affected term of address that fit nicely with the Western items on the menu—sandwiches, spaghetti, and brandy. "Fuck her!" Huiquan grumbled under his breath. She must be feeling pretty smug over being called "Ms." Probably one of those girls who wiggles her ass and throws kisses all around—assuming that her audience is a bunch of idiots enchanted by her presence. A lot of karaoke singers were like that. They didn't know the first thing about singing but were captivated by the sound of their own voice. They writhed like little sexpots, having picked up all sorts of tricks from professional singers, which only made their affectations more obvious. They were often so moved by their own performance that when they finished, they couldn't talk for a few moments, as though their tongue had melted or they were spaced out or something. But they were no more disgusting than their sisters on TV, and maybe even slightly less pretentious and less affected. There they were—*Ms!*

Zhao Yaqiu. He read the name again. The twenty-ninth was the day after tomorrow. He didn't have anything better to do that night. He expected her to be a girl with long, flowing hair, one who pouted and sighed as she sang, her lips pressed against the microphone, a husky, breathless song oozing from the speakers. Maybe, maybe not. He'd see for himself.

The twenty-eighth was a Sunday. A light rainfall began before dawn, and when Huiquan returned home from his morning jog, his shirt and shorts were soaked, his running shoes covered with mud. After changing into dry clothes, he decided to take the day off. He would throw on his raincoat and go to the post office for some newspapers, which he would read in bed as the rain fell outside. It was a comforting thought. While he was at it, he'd buy some minced pork to make fried meatballs. They had fallen apart the last time—not enough cornstarch.

He didn't make it out the door, though. Auntie Luo, umbrella in hand, dropped by to tell him that the sectional sofa Xiaofen had ordered at an Eastbridge furniture store was ready to be picked up. Xiaofen and her fiancé would be setting up house in a married-students dormitory at Little West Heaven following a simple ceremony at the university on May 1. Auntie Luo invited Huiquan to the ceremony as she jabbered on and on, not saying much of anything. Meanwhile, Huiquan was calculating the distance between Eastbridge and Little West Heaven—in the rain.

"I'm not busy. I'll give her a hand with the sofa."

"She just called from the furniture store to see if you were home. It's pouring out there . . . Protect yourself against the rain. I don't want you to catch cold. I'd feel terrible—"

"Enough of that talk! You think a little drizzle scares me? See if you can find a sheet of plastic to cover the sofa . . ."

The furniture store was practically deserted. From their vantage point under an awning, Xiaofen and her fiancé were thrilled to see him, thrilled and enormously relieved. Several three-wheelers stood idle, their beds covered with tarps, their aging drivers squatting beneath the awning, smoking cigarettes. The patter of rain on the tin awning was loud and persistent. The rain was picking up.

Huiquan rode up to them. Not knowing what to say, he said nothing. Xiaofen was wearing a pink plastic raincoat and soft purple high-heeled rain boots. Strands of hair peeking out from under her cap, washed by the rain, shone as though oiled. Her skin was fair; her lips were red, although Huiquan couldn't tell if she was wearing lipstick. She puckered her lips in the direction of her fiancé, who quickly dug out a pack of cigarettes and some matches, which he offered to Huiquan.

Even as he smoked, he said nothing, concentrating instead on inspecting the five sectional pieces. He spotted a missing castor and a hole in one of the cushions, from which the cotton was poking out. Xiaofen reacted as though she had been swindled.

Huiquan helped her pick out a new set, but instead of thanking him, she just grumbled about her fiancé, who looked pained.

"A big help you are! Look what you picked out . . ."

"Thank goodness Little Li was here . . . Shall I take the first leg on the three-wheeler?"

After fastening the sofas, the men jockeyed to see who

would do what. Sensing that Xiaofen was waiting for him to take charge, after a brief pause Huiquan said, "My brakes aren't so good, and you might have trouble on the overpass. I can manage . . . You two wait for me at the normal college."

"The east gate, west side of the street . . ."

Xiaofen was embarrassingly demonstrative in showing her gratitude, probably because of how dangerous it would have been for her fiancé to pedal a three-wheeler in the rain. And by asking Huiquan to help, she was showing they were still friends. What did she expect, he wondered—his thanks?

She and her fiancé walked to the bus stop.

Huiquan hadn't gone more than a few feet when a corner of the plastic cover came loose, so he took off his raincoat and covered the exposed spot. The sofas weren't bad looking, but the backing was skimpy—a sheet of gauze stapled to the frame. You wouldn't catch him buying shoddy merchandise like that if he ever got married. The college assistant is an asshole! The graduate student is also an asshole! They didn't mind spending six hundred yuan on a set of sofas but balked at parting with ten yuan to hire a three-wheeler. Talk about bargains: free delivery in a rainstorm without a murmur! Huiquan could have kicked himself.

At the Chaoyang Gate overpass he turned west, negotiated the incline, and pedaled into the bicycle lane on Loop Two Road.

In a few days Xiaofen would be a bride, and eventually she and her husband would be associate professors, then professors. People change so fast. They start out walking hand in hand, but somewhere along the way they split up, with one taking the high road, the other the low.

Once, back in the third grade, a yellow butterfly had flown into the latrine while Huiquan and Xiaofen were playing in the yard. As it perched on a wad of filthy paper, they tiptoed in after it, with Xiaofen jumping in front of him at the last minute, just as the startled butterfly flew off. When she reached out for it, she slid in up to her waist with a scream. The muck slurped, and a potent stench hit him in the face.

After Auntie Luo stripped her naked, she stuck her under the tap and washed her off. Back then Xiaofen was taller than he and sort of chunky. He secretly and nervously watched from his hiding place by the walkway. Her pale little rear end with the red marks where Auntie Luo had spanked her left a lasting impression on him, but not as lasting as her screams. She was so embarrassed she wanted to crawl into a hole and hide.

"Don't you dare tell anybody!" she warned him on the way to school the next morning, looking at him with her sad little eyes.

He nodded, still able to smell the pungent stench of excrement. He never told a soul. They were close in grade school, but after they entered middle school, they ignored each other when around others, although they still spoke at home. In high school he was assigned to a bonehead class; she went into an accelerated program. Then it was college for one, unemployment for the other, and the relationship ended altogether. How can today compete with yesterday? If a tragicomedy like that can determine one's fate, he wished that he had fallen into the latrine instead of her.

By now he was soaked to the skin, his pant legs covered with mud thrown up by the chain of the three-wheeler. The rain was heavy one moment, light the next, and the clouds were a mixture of white and gray, soon turning black. He stomped down on the pedals angrily, feeling a surge of indomitable strength.

He hummed a Russian march as he rode along. He recalled how he had nearly melted from the sight of the naked, smelly Xiaofen, and this memory tempered his current discomfort with a sense of intimacy. There was a tacit understanding between him and females, however fragile. Sometimes, he felt, you just had to feel sorry for them. But how did they feel about him?

A drenched Huiquan rode past Desheng Gate, keeping his spirits up by humming the military march; he was ignored by the umbrella-wielding pedestrians he passed. They were no more interested in him than they were in the sofas he was delivering. While he was bestowing sympathy on his childhood playmate, her latter-day sisters refused to afford him the same courtesy. He stomped down on the pedals to speed up, raising his buttocks up off the seat, and with his raincoat currently being worn by the sofas behind him, he looked for all the world like a typical operator of a three-wheeler for hire. With jutting cheekbones and thick, dark lips, he had the appearance of a man who would just as soon fleece you as look at you. The rain was chilling him—one of those cool spring rains.

6

On the evening of April twenty-ninth there was a bit of a stir at the club on Mill Road. The seats were all taken, many by high school students who hoped their cup of coffee would last the night. The waitresses added a dozen or so chairs in the take-out section and left the door open so everyone could catch a glimpse of the microphone at the far end of the aisle. The sidewalk was packed with teenage boys resting on their haunches, cigarettes dangling from their lips. A few were strumming guitars.

Since he arrived late, Huiquan had to sit in the take-out section on one of the folding chairs. Zhao Yaqiu was already into her third number. Heads were bobbing in the smoky haze, the blackness of the hair disturbing him for some reason. Since his view was blocked, he closed his eyes and listened to the mellow, throaty sounds.

"For my next song I'd like to do 'I Love You, Ito.' Thank you."

"Love ya!"

The echoing shout came from the pack of young ruffians outside. Huiquan turned to look and was eyeball to eyeball with several faces flushed with excitement. As she began the rhythmic Japanese pop song, some boys out on the darkened sidewalk began to twist and sway. Huiquan ordered a brandy.

"Sorry, only coffee and cola tonight. Manager's orders."

The girl craned her neck to look inside as she apologized. One of her sister waitresses threaded her way into the take-out section and was astounded to see the doorway filled with people. She pointed behind her.

"Did you see the way she's made up? She must have taken lessons."

"How old is she?"

"Nineteen. Failed the music-academy entrance exam and has been looking for work for six months. Or so the manager says."

"Nice voice. But not much in the looks department."

"Shoot, she'd never make it as a professional singer with that voice. Her looks are so-so . . . Too bad she has one single-fold eyelid and one double fold. But she's got that look—"

"You sure didn't miss anything!"

"But she draws a crowd . . . Eight cases of Coke already! Can you believe that?"

The waitresses' tongues were wagging. Meanwhile, Huiquan was reminded of how much he disliked the medicinal taste of Coke. But he went ahead and ordered two bottles, sipping the drinks the same way he did the hard stuff. So she was only nineteen. The announcement had listed her as Ms. Zhao Yaqiu. A chump! Third place, B group—still an amateur. "A real chump!" He tensed when he realized he was talking out loud. Fortunately the music drowned out his grumbling. Why was he acting like this all of a sudden? He should be trying to crowd up front to get a better look. What was it he expected, some sexy older woman? Some kind of turn-on? After all, he'd got a haircut and shined his shoes that day, just like a man with a hot date. What difference did it make if she were a mere girl or some vamp? He was acting like a jerk, making such a big deal over it. Everybody else took things like this in stride, but not him. While they were having a grand old time, drinking, eating, and clapping and yelling after each song, he was as tense as he'd been at the concert hall. He couldn't escape his belief that he was superfluous. Happiness was in the cards for those punks in the doorway, but not for him.

Xiaofen had revealed his origins to him when they were in the third grade.

"I heard my mom say so to my aunt. Don't you tell anybody!"

He had nodded somberly, betraying no surprise, as if he already knew. Maybe his father had mentioned it when he was too young to grasp the significance of the revelation. His father could have told him lots of things when he was drunk. But whether it was old news or new, instead of going straight home from school that afternoon, he followed the subway-construction route toward Beijing Station. The ditches along the way were inviting. He had nine cents on him, so he bought a large ice for five, a smaller one for three, and ate them as he went.

He suddenly jumped into a ditch and ran at a crouch, as he'd seen soldiers do in the movies. After hugging the side for a while, he fell across a pile of dirt as though he'd been shot and lay there for a long time. His "death" brought him enormous comfort. Rather than go to Beijing Station to try to find that particular underground-cable ditch, he clutched the remaining coin in his hand as he weaved in and out of the crisscrossing ditches along the construction route until night fell, and then he went home.

He had already begun to consider himself superfluous way

back then. That mental certainty was now his emotional haven. He could put in there at a moment's notice. When a teapot becomes superfluous, its shape, color, value, and quality are of no consequence, and smashing it is irrelevant. People are like that, too.

Zhao Yaqiu's songs were so sublimely simple they made his heart ache. She had a tender, sweet voice that was devoid of coquettishness—like a girl softly confiding in her parents and her siblings about the pain in her heart. Suddenly overwhelmed by a desire to look at her face, Huiquan knew he had to move fast. He stood up, pretending to be looking for someone, then squeezed into the lounge, angering the people in the doorway on his way through. It was standing room only, and he found a spot against the wall. People were scrutinizing him. He blushed and self-consciously cowered up against the wall, casting anxious looks toward the far end of the aisle. Zhao Yaqiu, her back to the audience, was turning slowly to the beat of the music. She lowered her head and picked up the cord of the microphone.

Her song told of the plight of an unemployed girl being scolded by her parents—sprightliness tempered by melancholy. The melody sounded familiar, but the lyrics were new, probably made up as she went:

> *Tomorrow's my birthday*
> *I'll be twenty tomorrow*
> *I'd like to sleep in tomorrow*
> *If my gift isn't changed*
> *Daddy's scolding me*
> *Mommy's scolding me, too*

She had rosy cheeks, and drops of sweat glistened on the pale skin at her temples. An average face—the look of a shy and not very intelligent little girl. If a grown-up told her to sing, she sang, giving it everything she had. Her look of innocence hardly matched the song's melody or its message. Huiquan watched, transfixed. His mind was a blank.

> Today's my birthday
> I'm twenty today
> I'd like to sleep in and not get up
> Because my gift wasn't changed
> Mommy's scolding me
> Daddy's scolding me, too

Her eyes weren't large, but they were captivating when she batted those long lashes. Her mouth and nose were on the small side and set in a round baby face. She had shiny shoulder-length hair with bangs that covered her eyebrows. That night she was wearing gray slacks and a maroon tunic, with the sleeves rolled up to reveal a large black digital watch. On her it looked heavy.

On any given day at Eastbridge at least fifty girls like her walked past Huiquan's stall, filled with themselves even though they probably had barely enough money in their pockets to buy an ice cream. This girl's attraction lay in her shy, innocent look and in her voice. Definitely not pretty, and without makeup she would be as common as they come. Huiquan noticed that her teeth were slightly crooked, and she had a jutting forehead. But none of this disappointed him; in fact, it excited him. He clapped when everyone else did.

"Bravo!"

He regretted the shout the moment it left his throat. Every eye in the place was fixed on him. Zhao Yaqiu looked at him and smiled, bowing slightly in his direction.

"Thank you!"

"You're welcome."

The audience roared. As his face turned scarlet, he glared venomously at the gawking faces. The laughter died out quickly. It was then he spotted Cui Yongli in the front row. *He* wasn't laughing. Apparently just now noticing Huiquan's presence, he waved his fork—a piece of ham stuck on one of the tines—in greeting.

Zhao Yaqiu began her final song of the evening, a ballad. As she sang, she held a hankie to her face, and at each break in the lyrics she wiped her face and her neck grandly. Finally she folded the hankie and tucked it away. None of these movements distracted from the song, but Cui was too busy stuffing his face to pay attention to it. Drops of whatever he was drinking clung to the whiskers around his mouth. Huiquan shifted his gaze to Zhao Yaqiu's digital watch. Her wrist was round and fleshy and, from all appearances, soft. She was young but busty. A button was missing from her tunic. She probably didn't know it, and someone ought to tell her. Huiquan, absorbed in his thoughts, was oblivious to the song she was singing.

As the applause was dying down, the manager took the mike, said all the expected nice things, and led Zhao Yaqiu down off the stage. The patrons made room for her to pass. *Click, click!* The swivel chair was banging up against something. The raucous crowd in the doorway raised a twitch on the manager's gaunt face.

Huiquan followed the singer with his eyes as she passed. He watched her rest her hand on the back of a seat as she paused briefly. Her tiny nails, painted red, seemed blood spattered. She lowered her head, and her nostrils flared almost imperceptibly. Downy hairs, moist with perspiration, quivered on the nape of her neck and above her upper lip. She looked tired and tense, almost pouty, it seemed to him.

Cui Yongli was shoving a piece of ham into his mouth.

The manager led Zhao Yaqiu into the storeroom-office be-hind the sales counter in the take-out section. Students began filing out of the lounge, littering the tables, chairs, windowsills, and any other convenient place with empty coffee cups. Others slipped the cups into their pockets. The crowd on the sidewalk wasn't so quick to break up. Flashes of yellow lit up the sky around them as matches and lighters touched the tips of ciga-rettes, briefly illuminating one young, vacant face after another. Someone cracked a dirty joke, too abruptly for any reaction. A dozen guitars were being strummed simultaneously; the same number of throats were ejaculating their own noises. People inside listened diffidently to the sounds beyond the plate-glass window. Brandy and Western snacks had made a reappearance. Closing time was still four hours away; these were the club's golden hours.

Li Huiquan was stung by the song being sung outside, as though someone had dredged up his past:

> We have no father
> We have no mother
> We have no brothers
> We have no sisters
> We have no money
> We have no illness
> We have no joy
> We have no pain
> We have no tears
> We have no semen
> We have no tongues
> We have no . . .

The caterwauling was accompanied by guitars that sounded like rusty saws cutting through rotten wood. The lyrics became more and more obscene, but inside the club they fell on deaf ears. At least one couple in a booth was kissing. *Slurp!* Copying the sound from some foreign movie. Cui Yongli beckoned to Huiquan, who walked over to him blankly as he tried to sort out the lyrics of the song outside. Following "We have no blood" and "We have no cells," the "we" vanished into thin air and became nothing. People who have nothing, not even their own bodies, ultimately have it all. The universe is theirs; everything good and beautiful belongs to them.

That this coarse ditty was actually a paean to optimism came as a revelation to Huiquan, who had never been able to relate to anything but the first two lines:

> *We have no father*
> *We have no mother*

The story of his life. But in the mouths of the people outside it became a declaration of liberation. There was no melancholy in their voices. They obviously had parents, the little impostors!

Huiquan sat down and smiled at Cui Yongli.

"I got here too late to get a good seat."

"I thought she'd be a hot item, not some ugly little piece of bean curd. How bogus!"

Huiquan frowned. Hearing Zhao Yaqiu demeaned like that grated. Then Cui surprised him by leaning over and whispering salaciously, "I like the mature ones!"

Huiquan didn't understand.

"The older ones are safe. Mess up one of the tender young ones, and you got trouble!"

Assuming that the uncomprehending look on Huiquan's face was an act, he patted him on the shoulder and cackled. Huiquan found the display of intimacy puzzling. They had barely met, and it was far too early to start opening up to each other. Was he drunk? He didn't look it. Just what did he mean by *safe* and *trouble*? He'd never witnessed such an open absence of shame in anyone.

Cui pointed out the window.

"Donkeys in heat!"

Through the open door Huiquan was watching the activity in the take-out section. Zhao Yaqiu hadn't left yet. Maybe she was still inside counting her take. Why waste her talent in a place like this? His thoughts drifted to the downy hairs on the nape of her neck and above her upper lip. He was emotionally drained. Others must have noticed the same things, and that thought depressed him. He wished she'd hurry up and leave.

Cui Yongli had something altogether different on his mind. He had a solemn look but seemed chummy enough. With his arm around Huiquan's shoulder and the smell of tobacco heavy in his mouth, he said, "It's ten o'clock. You busy later on?"

"No . . . What's up?"

"I'll take you someplace if you're up for it."

"Where? What kind of place?"

"A good place; don't worry. What're you so nervous about?"

"It's late . . . What's there for me?"

"What do you think?"

"I haven't a clue."

"Sure you do. I can see it on your face."

"I doubt that."

"Ninety percent sure. I can see what's missing in a person by reading his face, and I can see what he needs by looking into his eyes. You want to hear me say it?"

"That's up to you."

Seeing the disagreeable look on Huiquan's face, Cui smiled and let the matter drop. Huiquan assumed that whatever Cui had to say would undoubtedly be seedy. Sure, seedy thoughts popped into his head once in a while, too, but not now. There was nothing for Cui to read on his face or see in his eyes. He was thinking only of the girl, and as far as he could tell, there was nothing unpleasant about her. Of course, by then he was already infatuated with the fine, shadowy hairs above her upper lip. The only crude thought in his head—and it was well defined—was that he'd like to stroke the nape of her neck, just to touch the delicate, curly hairs there. A fleeting thought, and not a very realistic one, it was gone in a flash.

He glanced again toward the take-out section. "You're pretty moody," he said.

Cui Yongli was suddenly a different and very solemn person. "I used to be moody myself, but I wised up when I realized that anger is bad for you. Let others get angry. People like you and me should have our hands full just having a good time."

Huiquan wished he hadn't given Cui the opportunity to carry on with his arcane philosophizing.

"I've got some stuff I'd like to show you, that's all. I rent a couple of rooms in a farmhouse not far from here. Ever hear of Sha Family Inn?"

"Yeah."

"Head east down Gold Terrace Road, past the old temple. You can't miss it. A red brick wall, pepper plants around the outside. We can go anytime you want. Just don't tell anyone."

"Not tonight."

"That's up to you. I don't go there often myself."

"What kind of stuff?"

"You'll know when you see it." Cui inspected his finger-nails and then added, "Don't worry, it's not girls."

"So what if it was?"

"I'm just kidding."

"I'm not."

"Come on, get off it! Some clothes, just some clothes—you know, the stuff you sell. If you're interested, I can let you have it. If not, I can always find someone else. That's all. You don't mind if I ask if you're married, do you?"

"I'm not."

"That's what I thought . . ."

Huiquan reddened, but Cui looked away. A young couple was talking in hushed tones and giggling. The girl was pretty. Cui glanced aimlessly around the room. It was all an act, Huiquan was thinking.

"When do you want to go?" Cui asked abruptly.

"Tomorrow . . . No, after May Day."

"How about the afternoon of the second?"

"Okay. What'll I bring?"

"Just your three-wheeler and some cash. Not too much, but not too little, either! Strictly business . . ."

Before getting up to leave, Cui repeated the directions for him. The beard masked the look on his face. Huiquan knew he couldn't trust the guy and that he'd have to be very careful. Cui was too slick for him.

The noise level rose abruptly in the take-out section as the manager and a waitress walked Zhao Yaqiu outside, where she received scattered applause—probably the students having some fun at her expense. All Huiquan saw was her hair. It was dark and glossy. A quick glimpse and it was gone. Would he be disappointed if she never showed up again?

He had already formed a mental image of her baby-doll face.

He and Cui Yongli said good-bye at the door under recently installed neon lights—reds, blues, and greens—which flickered gaily. The slightly parted curtain allowed a glimpse of the patrons inside. Someone was already up and singing. The ruffians who had assembled outside were long gone, having given the sidewalk over to parked bikes and motorcycles. The faint twanging of guitars drifted on the air.

The neon lights turned Cui Yongli's beard into a rainbow as he turned to greet a friend who had just arrived. He and his friends, both male and female, always treated each other with courtesy.

Huiquan didn't know whether to stay or to leave.

Just then someone came running toward them under the bright streetlights. Huiquan stepped into the shadows as whoever it was slowed down and looked back to see whether anyone was following. It was the girl. She'd run over from the housing project across the street. In that maze of narrow paths either there were no lights or the lights were very dim, and she must have run into some sort of trouble. But that was none of his business. He lit a cigarette and went looking for his bicycle. Someone had moved it.

"Manager Han, could you come out here, please?"

Her voice was different, sort of shrill.

Cui Yongli was talking with his friends, but Huiquan couldn't make out what they were saying, something about "the goods." Their conversation was muted and animated at the same time.

The gaunt manager nodded as he listened to Zhao Yaqiu

tell him what had happened. Meanwhile Huiquan stuck his key into the bicycle lock, but it wouldn't open. He was close enough to hear the gist of her story. The pack of students had followed her, scaring her by yelling and singing, so she had run back here. She spoke shyly, haltingly.

Huiquan's forehead was beaded with sweat, but the damned lock wouldn't open. He felt like kicking it but stopped himself.

Zhao Yaqiu was acting like a spoiled brat. Girls always make mountains out of molehills.

Having gravitated toward the manager's side, Cui Yongli was eyeing Zhao Yaqiu dispassionately. Huiquan tensed. But Cui didn't seem like someone who got his kicks from tormenting girls. What could he be thinking?

The assembled faces all had a strange, eerie cast under the neon lights.

"Which block do you live in?" Cui asked her.

"Four."

"Li Huiquan! Little Zhao here lives in block four. Why don't you walk her home? You live on Spirit Run Street, don't you? What's wrong? Lock broken? Or is it the key?"

Cui walked up, a cigarette dangling from his lips. Huiquan's hand shook as he fiddled with the lock. Block 4? Not even two stops on the bus. At the far end of the housing project. But the bus took the long way round, so they'd have to walk. Should he do it? Would she object? Was he obliged to protect her?

He didn't dare look up. "Must be the key."

The words were barely out when—*snap*—the lock popped open. A faint sigh was released behind him. Who was it? It couldn't have been the girl, since she was gazing at him blankly.

"Ten cases, don't forget!" the manager reminded Cui.

Was there anything the man couldn't get or any connection

he couldn't make? The manager was apparently more concerned with his ten cases than with the girl's safety, since he was handing her over to a patron he barely knew rather than take the responsibility himself. How much had he given her to sing eight songs? Five yuan? Ten? For which she'd had to endure those stares and strange looks, not to mention the intimidation. Was it worth it?

Even though he felt like talking, Huiquan didn't open his mouth the entire trip; he just couldn't.

They passed several apartment buildings, Huiquan walking his bike ahead of her. She shortened the distance between them where there were no streetlights, nearly crawling up his back, but as they approached the lights, she dropped back until she was a good five yards behind him, by the sound of her footsteps. At intersections she gave directions before he could turn around: "Turn right here."

Huiquan turned when she told him to, finding neither the courage nor the opportunity to say anything. In his mind's eye he saw the downy, incredibly soft hairs on the nape of her neck. Her slightly crooked teeth and jutting forehead only enhanced her charm. He desperately wanted to scrutinize her features when she wasn't looking, for although she wasn't pretty, she had a certain appeal. Those long eyelashes—they were real, weren't they? Why was he so interested all of a sudden? He leered at pretty girls on the street all the time, but this time he didn't feel like doing that. Why? he wondered.

They didn't encounter the young students who had terrorized her. Not that he was eager to use his fists, but he couldn't help thinking he was missing a chance to show what he was made of. He might not get another, and how else was he going to show her how he felt? That was the only way he knew. One can't be a gladiator without an arena. Still, seeing blood no longer seemed so natural to him, and he'd rather take the defensive than throw down the gauntlet himself. It would be a spirited fight, he was confident of that, one that would impress anyone who saw it.

Black voids separated the buildings; few lights showed in the windows. The footsteps behind him stopped, and Huiquan spun around. She was standing on the lawn in front of a stairwell.

"This is where I live. Thank you."

". . . You going back tomorrow?"

He had managed to say something. The question had been on his mind all the time they were walking, but he was genuinely startled to hear his own voice.

"Sure, I'm going. I've signed on for two weeks."

"That's a bogus joint! You should stay away if you can."

"Is your name Li?"

"Yeah, Li Huiquan."

"Where do you work?"

"I've got a pushcart. I sell clothes . . . I go to the club a lot, so I know the place. You're still young, and you should stay away from there if you can. Can't you sing somewhere else? They're bad people . . . but on the other hand . . . anyway . . . I talk too much . . ."

"I need the experience, and besides, I have to eat. There's no need to worry. Except for walking home alone at night, I'm not scared of anything. Were you the one who yelled 'bravo' after I sang 'The Birthday Song'?"

"Yeah."

"You looked so mean I didn't think you'd want to walk me home. That's why I was so quiet. I'm really sorry. How do you like my singing?"

"It's pretty good."

She smiled to cover her disappointment. She seemed to have more spunk than he had imagined.

"I have to go in now. Thank you. Thank you very much!"

She took a few steps, turned to wave, and then walked into the old building. Panes of glass were missing from the door, the stairwell was dark, and the banister was made of concrete. Even after she had disappeared into the building, he kept staring blankly at the spot where she had stood. As she walked through the doorway, he'd noticed she was wearing flats with cloth tops and straps. Girls rarely wore shoes like that anymore, but they looked great on her. He thought of her baby-doll mouth.

One of the windows went dark. The light in another went on. Huiquan wondered which room was hers. He turned and walked off, committing the location and appearance of her building to memory as he pushed his bike along. All the thoughts running through his mind were submerged by the image of soft down, which gave off the sweet redolence of new grass.

He turned north at Eastbridge and made a sweep around the Workers' Stadium. It was eleven-thirty by the time he was back at number 18, East Lane, Spirit Run Street, so he carried his bike down the pathway to keep from making any noise. The dreamy feeling hung on even when he was confronted by the greasy, smoky kitchen odors of his home. He lay down in the dark, fully dressed, and began to smoke cigarettes and guzzle water.

At that moment he didn't think much of himself and wished he could see himself through her eyes. He wanted her to notice and respect him, for her plain face supplied the answer to his longings. The appearance of this lovely angel in his life vindicated the reluctance to interact with women that he had felt till now.

Of course, he had to admit that considering her a lovely

angel was slightly perverse. Where did dumb thoughts like that come from? What was his problem exactly? Once Hobo had told him about a pretty girl he and Spike had seen in Yongan District. Instructing Hobo to "watch and learn," Spike had walked right up to her.

"Say, baby, how about a kiss?"

"Where?"

"Anywhere."

Hobo watched them walk into an apartment building, where Spike led her up to the fifth floor and back down again, then up and back down several more times. Afterward he told Hobo he'd got exactly what he wanted. But when Hobo wanted to try his luck, he couldn't spot a likely candidate and was afraid of screwing up, so he just sighed. Huiquan had called him "a horny ass."

Huiquan knew his problem wasn't that simple. What should he do? He had dirty thoughts but no dirty intentions. Or, more accurately, he had dirty thoughts, but none he wanted to translate into action. Excited by his fantasies, he felt as if he were about to explode; but he hated the idea of doing it.

Luo Xiaofen would be getting married on May Day. A few days before the wedding Auntie Luo had found a girl for the beat cop, Liu Baotie, and it looked like a decent match. "You're next!" she'd said.

Was he really? Of course he was! Huiquan fell asleep in the fetal position, a look of sheer agony on his face, his mouth twisted horribly.

7

The construction of high-rise apartments had begun on a large open space south of Sha Family Inn. The green limbs of cranes and orange girders sliced up the gray sky. Standing in various stages of completion, the high rises resembled stacks of toy building blocks. The fetid air held the persistent odor of concrete and quicklime. An ancient brick temple north of the dirt road rose to the height of nearby willows. The pepper plants, covered with a layer of dust, occupied only a tiny area. The smell of manure hung in the air.

Huiquan located the farmhouse Cui Yongli was renting. It consisted of three rooms in a row to the north, plus a kitchen, an outhouse, and a water faucet in the yard. Since the landlord and his family lived in another compound, the place was hushed.

A girl with an out-of-town accent opened the gate for Huiquan. Cui Yongli, slippers on his feet, stood in the entryway beside a couple of motorcycles and an assortment of cardboard boxes.

"I said I'd come, and here I am."

Cui led him inside with little apparent enthusiasm. The girl from wherever she called home, wearing a pink blouse, went into the easternmost room, where the curtains were drawn. A door linked the two western rooms, the outer one serving as a living room and the inner one most likely serving as a bedroom. The furniture was no great shakes, and the rooms were cluttered. A dozen or more cardboard boxes lined up against the wall were stamped with the words TOY CARS. But liquor bottles and phony trademark stamps poked up between the flaps.

Seven or eight cartons of top-quality cigarettes lay on the desk, all of them open. Cui Yongli unwrapped a pack and offered Huiquan a cigarette. As he was lighting up, he noticed a foreign picture magazine lying open on a tea table. The colors, in geometric patterns of yellows, pinks, and whites, were starkly appealing. The paper was slick and glossy.

Someone brought in tea—another girl, pretty in a rustic way. Cui smiled at her.

"Everything ready?"

"Just about."

A southern accent. She smiled easily. Huiquan nervously patted his pocket.

"I brought the money."

"How much?"

"Seven hundred."

"Good. Actually, five hundred would have been enough. We'll start off small. Plenty of time later for bigger deals. I don't want to force you into anything—"

"Just what is it we're talking about?"

"I told you—clothing."

Huiquan laid down his teacup and moved the magazine. The shapes changed. Now he could see it was a Caucasian woman's bottom encased in lace-trimmed panties. The opening in the crotch was also lace trimmed. He wondered how they'd taken the shot.

Cui Yongli leaned over the desk to write a list, a receipt. He wrote, "various outfits and underwear . . . five hundred thirteen yuan and eighty cents." An odd figure, for the sake of appearances. Even he couldn't keep from chuckling.

"For tax purposes, just in case."

"Is it an out-of-town receipt?"

"Doesn't matter where it's from. After all, you're selling on commission, so what's there to be afraid of?"

Nothing. He was afraid of nothing. He picked up the receipt and read it over, trying hard to look unconcerned.

The seal read, "Overseas Chinese Fashion Company, City and County of Yongfeng, Fujian Province." Huiquan had never heard of the place or the company; they probably didn't exist. He folded the receipt. Had Cui stolen it? Made it himself? Was he a con man? He fished out the money with an expansive gesture.

The girls tossed five nylon bags onto the bed of the three-wheeler, which he'd parked by the doorway. Since Cui hadn't offered to show him the merchandise, he didn't ask, not wanting to seem petty.

"One hundred per bag, and that's a bargain."

"As long as you trust me, that's all I ask."

Cui hadn't expected that remark, as Huiquan could see. Cui was caressing the nylon bags as though they were human.

"I wouldn't have invited you here if I didn't—you can be sure of that. I'm a good judge of people. Everyone says Basher Li puts a lot of stock in loyalty, and that's all I need to hear . . . Let's not haggle. I can tell you're a loyal friend."

"Don't worry, money doesn't mean that much to me."

"Those two girls work for me. Been with me for over a year.

They cook, watch the place, take deliveries . . . They're not trash, if you know what I mean. They do what they're told—"

"Stuff like that doesn't concern me. I trust you."

Huiquan mounted his three-wheeler. "I'm not here very often," Cui Yongli muttered as he patted him awkwardly on the shoulder. "I live somewhere else—"

"I know."

"I'm off to Harbin in a couple of days. Are you in the market for some Korean ginseng? There isn't much else worth buying there."

"No."

"Well, see you at the club. I'll drop by as soon as I get back."

"I'm there every night."

"Li Huiquan . . . get a good price."

"Don't worry."

There was nothing left to be said. Huiquan's unsmiling face was matched by the somber expression on Yongli's. The sale had gone smoothly, but both men were feeling awkward. Theirs was a tense relationship. Neither could figure the other out, and both were wary. Friendships like theirs can be exhausting. The scowling Cui Yongli stood in the gateway until Huiquan skirted the pepper crop and rode up onto the path leading to the highway.

Each time he was tempted to stop and see what he'd bought, he fought off the urge. Once he was back home on Spirit Run Street, he tossed the bags onto his bed, unzipped them, and removed their contents, one article at a time: a pair of pajamas, a jacket, some bras, panties, scarves, vests, jumpers, soccer socks, a girl's canvas shoulder bag, even a tailcoat. The nylon bags were like cornucopias, spilling out one unexpected item after another. The styles were new and fresh, but the goods were all secondhand, and they had a musty odor. They also smelled of mothballs. Huiquan found a coin in the pocket of a pair of wool pants; it had an eagle on one side and the bust of a head on the other. Everything had foreign labels, except for some panties and camisoles. It was hard to tell whether those items were made in Hong Kong or Taiwan or were local knockoffs. There was a blood stain on one of the jacket sleeves. Strands of hair—some long, some short—were caught in the rolled-up scarves. The buttons on the tailcoat didn't match. The soccer socks had sweat stains that apparently wouldn't wash out.

The room stank.

Secondhand imported goods, all of it. Actually, *secondhand* was a bit too elegant a word, since the stuff looked like junk picked from a trash heap and smuggled willy-nilly into the country. But he'd make a killing on it—no doubt about that. The nearly transparent panties were the size of hankies, and he wondered whether he could get two-fifty a pair for them.

A bag of candy and a pack of cigarettes lay on the table—wedding treats that Auntie Luo had brought over the night before. He hadn't touched them. What was Xiaofen doing now? What were all his former classmates doing? What was the convict Spike Fang doing? Could there be another person anywhere in the world doing what he was doing—digging through a pile of foreign junk and carefully calculating the price each item would command? That magazine model in the open-crotch panties—where was she at this moment? What was she doing? What was she thinking?

As he sat on his bed, surrounded by cotton goods of every kind and description, Huiquan seemed mesmerized. He just smoked and reflected, his eyes closed as though he were a Buddhist idol, his thoughts chaotic, serious ideas all mixed together with frivolous ones. He wasn't sure which of them represented his mood.

This wasn't the way he had planned it. The foreign model and Zhao Yaqiu were linked in his mind, and the depravity of that mixture of thoughts disgusted him. He assumed Cui Yongli took turns sleeping with each of the two southern girls. Was he jealous? Did he envy the bearded man or hold him in contempt?

He stuffed the clothes back into the nylon bags carefully, to keep from wrinkling them even more. This would be his first and only transaction with Cui Yongli. No sense courting danger over something like money. He made enough to live on. Let Cui and the others play their cat-and-mouse game.

He would have to sell this stuff in the late afternoon to avoid being noticed by the market supervisors. And he couldn't sell it too cheaply, since doing so would raise suspicions. The bottom line was that he'd have to clear this junk out fast, with no sympathy for the gullible customers. People in search of the latest fad deserved to be swindled. Let them strut around town in their secondhand threads! This stuff was made for them.

That evening he went to the club for some of the Japanese wine he'd got to like, a green, heavy wine with a wallop.

Zhao Yaqiu didn't show up. He hadn't seen her since the night he walked her home. Had she taken his advice about not returning? He didn't dare ask around for fear that someone might think he was up to something. An experienced eye might detect a telltale sign in his eyes, whatever that might be.

A high school student clumsily holding a cup of coffee stopped a waitress and asked timidly, "Pardon me, is Zhao Yaqiu coming tonight?"

"No."

"May Day's over. Why isn't she coming?"

"The shows at the Cultural Palace won't be over till after May Fourth—Youth Day. Come back on the fifth."

The youngster nodded, slurped down his coffee, put down

the cup, and left. His school insignia showed he was from Hu Family Tower High School; he was dressed too simply to be one of those playboy types. An amateur music fan? If he had known Zhao Yaqiu wouldn't be there, would he have bought that cup of coffee? At two-fifty a cup, it was the same price as a concert ticket.

Huiquan left the club and rode to the housing project across the street. But he never found the building he was looking for. He recalled there being a grassy area in front but discovered there were lawns in front of nearly all the buildings. Hers had a cement banister, but all the ones he looked at had wooden banisters. She had taken her building into hiding with her.

Her delicate face was growing hazy under the assault of his fantasies. Believing that all he had to do to recall her face down to the last detail was to lay eyes on her building and its seedy stairwell, he suddenly found everything immersed in darkness. The moonlight on that May night was hazy; the grass was black, and so were the trees. He couldn't find her doorway. Sounds of every imaginable kind emerged from windows all around him; loudest and most persistent of all was the bawling of a baby. Scared? Hungry? He left with great reluctance.

Physical stirrings woke him that night. He was drenched; his underpants were wet and sticky. He remembered his dream but couldn't identify the person who had shared it with him. Dreams and reality were fighting over him. He had to admit that reality had brought him precious little happiness, but the net effect of his dreams was intensified agony. His dreams were too scary to dwell on. In the darkness the girl's smiling face decorated the ceiling; her downy hairs brushed his skin. He shuddered.

Auntie Luo informed him the following day that the price of milk was going up, but the newspaper said the price of eggs was going down. Still, he needed their nutritional value. Tomorrow he'd buy a braised chicken to replenish what his body had given up. He would also buy some lotus seeds for his porridge. That was something he'd read about in the paper. He learned a lot from his evening paper, which he preferred over all the others. It was the one that revealed people's deepest, darkest secrets.

Some guy born into a privileged family was going around cutting girls' pants and jackets; a forty-year-old man was found to have been born with a uterus and Fallopian tubes; a four-year-old boy fell from a fifth-story window and walked away unhurt; a pair of twins were struck by different cars at the same time and died at precisely the same moment; the five children of a retired worker all graduated from college, and had even gone on to complete graduate degrees or to study abroad. A treasure trove of stories.

About the only other chance he had to talk or learn about things during the day was when he had a customer. So his newspaper was an additional window on the outside world. Reading it was like having a companion to talk to. It showed him how rich and varied life could be, how some people lived well whereas others were always down on their luck. Still, he didn't know what fate held in store for him, since the experiences of others were not particularly revealing where his life was concerned. But seeing that some people were worse off than animals cheered him a bit. There was even one guy from the Rockview Mountain area who had a thing about following women at night and kicking them in the rear. Rather than do something worthwhile, he went around kicking women's bottoms. The paper said he was sentenced to three years of hard labor. Huiquan couldn't understand why a jerk with a dopey fetish like that received the same punishment as he—three years of hard labor. People like that, he believed, should be shot. How would that man be able to live among normal people when he got out in three years?

Huiquan did not consider someone like that his equal. He had done his three years, and now he could live in society without making any excuses, except maybe to his mother, who had already passed on and was resting in an urn—an urn like those containing ingredients that might soon be used in making Chinese medicine. He had touched those ashes once: incredibly light and airy, they rustled when he shook them, like footsteps on a cinder path. The urn, wrapped in red satin, was stored in a dresser drawer that also held a pair of his father's leather sandals that his mother had been unwilling to throw away.

They had been bought only a year before his death, and Huiquan's father had scarcely worn them. But Mother had polished them yearly and told Huiquan he could have them when he was grown. Well, he was grown now, but he didn't like the style and he couldn't tolerate the smell of the shoe polish: it seemed to reek of death. They had already begun to mildew and to merge with the shoe box, alongside which rested the woman who had cared for them. He hardly ever opened that drawer, afraid that he might be tempted to throw the sandals away. But more than that, he was shaken by a sense of loneliness whenever he saw the urn holding his mother's ashes.

Maybe he pored over the evening paper so earnestly because he was looking for a story similar to his. Could there be another orphan somewhere in the world (dare he contemplate even the same city?) who shared his life with the ashes of his mother? If the evening paper ran a story about it, he might learn what to do in moments when he was bored to tears. But there were limits to the kinds of stories the evening paper favored. An orphan like him was either unique and therefore unnoticed by others, or so common that no one cared. He had no idea how others viewed him. As long as he lived, he would have to figure things out for himself. No one would come forward with advice on how to dispose of the lot of used clothing he had bought. Even less likely was the prospect that someone would teach him how to court a girl like Zhao Yaqiu, no matter how richly he deserved to know.

As a burst of brilliant light filled his head, Huiquan sensed that his latent desires were being rekindled. The illustration in that foreign magazine was a flower in full bloom, filling the air with its perfume.

The next day he sorted the clothing and stuffed it into plastic bags, entering prices in a notebook, carefully calculating each one. He settled on 2.65 for the panties with the Chinese labels, 113 yuan for the tailcoat. It was tiring, this game of price-fixing, and it turned the merchandise into an abstraction.

He hung this batch of goods inside the awning so as not to draw too much attention to it, knowing that someone in the market for bizarre clothing was blessed with more patience and acuity than the market supervisors were. That was the kind of customer he was waiting for. Sooner or later such customers would pop out of the flow and prostrate themselves before the god of foreign junk.

The tailcoat was bought by a young man with a northeastern accent. A middle-aged woman bought six of the silk scarves, which worried him: what if she shook out additional strands of hair or something else clinging to them? After the sun set, a crowd of girls gathered round his stall. They had their sights set on the panties, which were no larger than the palms of their hands. They had probably spotted them earlier but lacked the courage to pick at them until after dark. One by one the undergarments were lifted up by dainty fingers and examined meticulously, inside and out. He realized he'd priced them too low. The less they covered, the greater their appeal. He hadn't even considered that. If they had been no more than some string and a piece of material the size of a coin, he could demand any price he wanted. Things that had been worn by foreign floozies were now bringing glory to the pushcart at South 025 at Eastbridge— bought and carried off to cover the voluptuous body parts that lie at the core of fantasies.

With a perpetual sneer Huiquan took his customers' money and made change. As he was closing up for the day, a portly woman ran up and between gasps demanded a refund for her two-sixty-five purchase, which she was carrying in a plastic bag. She probably lived nearby, and Huiquan suspected she'd already tried the panties on, since she said they were too small. Most likely, she'd been chewed out and called shameless by her husband—justifiably, as far as Huiquan was concerned.

He refunded her money.

"Stinking whore!" he grumbled under his breath, displaying his usual hostility toward women who were so keen on dolling themselves up. His inability to explain the source of this hostility did not lessen his disgust for the woman. She and the angelic creature with the delicate, innocent features were as different to him as night and day. Could it be that he held others in contempt *because* of her? He had to see her.

Zhao Yaqiu reappeared at the club on Mill Road at eight o'clock on the night of May sixth. In the second row, contentedly sipping a cup of Maxwell House instant coffee, sat Li Huiquan. Somehow he had managed to wait her out.

She smiled warmly. She'd spotted him. Obviously the smile wasn't for him alone, but when she looked down at him, there was no denying the tenderness in her eyes. Did anyone else see it? He doubted it. Poor Huiquan didn't know it was a gimmick all singers used.

She sang the same songs as before, but with more confidence and greater ease. Around the first of May the weather had turned warm, each gentle breeze carrying a hint of summer. Zhao Yaqiu, dressed in a blue jumper over a pastel yellow blouse and wearing a pair of canvas flats, seemed guileless, somber, and tranquil. Each time his eyes met hers, Huiquan lowered his head again and sipped his coffee. He couldn't make his eyes linger on her face. The flavor of the coffee was lost on him.

During the break in her set, she went up to his table. Eyes followed her every move as he scooted over to make room for her. A waitress brought her a complimentary soft drink and some cold cuts.

It wasn't hot inside, so why was he sweating? His palms were sweaty, his collar sticky. His smile, like everything else about him, was unappealingly stiff.

"Back again, I see?" she said brusquely.

"I'm here every night."

"I haven't been here for a week."

"You performed at the Cultural Palace over the holiday."

"How did you know that?"

"Everybody around here knew."

"Just for kicks, that's all."

"I like the way you sing."

It sort of slipped out. She took a hurried sip of her soft drink, almost as though she hadn't noticed his comment.

"Really?"

"You've got a . . . great voice!"

"Gee, I've heard that a hundred times. But my voice stinks. Honest. It's nowhere near great. No professional singer has ever complimented me on my voice. But I'm pretty good at covering other people's songs. Have you heard the way I make my voice sound a little raspy?''

Two male patrons in the booth opposite were staring at them openly. Zhao Yaqiu's lively, artless airs carried a measure of pride. Her expression was frank and innocent, without a trace of anxiety. The performances over the holiday had given her experience and confidence. The awkwardness of her first show was only a memory. She now seemed more worldly than he.

"Can you walk me home tonight?''

"Sure. It's on my way home,'' he quickly added.

"Let's see, your name is Li Hui—''

"Huiquan. Li Huiquan.''

"That's right, now I remember. I won't forget it the next time. Singing in this place gives me the creeps, and knowing I have a friend in the audience helps. Little Li . . . you don't mind if I call you that, do you?''

"No.''

He was at least five years older than she. Was that her way of showing off? She ought to call him Old Li, or comrade, or something like that. After all, she was only a girl. But that didn't alter the fact that he was captivated by her. Out of the corner of his eye he glanced at the golden down above her upper lip. In the artificial light it looked softer and gentler than he thought possible. He wanted to take a closer look, but when she moved her head it seemed to vanish, leaving in its place only pink skin.

"I've got four more songs. Don't forget to applaud.''

"I don't have to be told. I know what to do.''

"Not too loud, though.''

"Don't worry, I won't.''

With a parting glance, a strange one at that, she walked up onto the stage to begin the second half of her performance.

Several times during the show she glanced down at him, but he always averted his eyes and rested his head against the back of the booth. He looked slightly tipsy or slightly disoriented. What he was trying to do was comprehend the lyrics, as a show of respect. But as the volume increased the words became harder to understand. That was typical of pop music. He knew it was part of the act, so why make an issue of it?

As they walked out of the club, the waitress's looks made Huiquan feel as though he were doing something he shouldn't be doing. Yet even that didn't dispel his powerful sense of good fortune. Why had he, and not someone else, been given the duty of seeing Zhao Yaqiu home? Coincidence? In earlier times the greater the distance between him and girls, the more urgent his longing for them. Now, tired of deceiving himself, he was translating his feelings into action, and only he had the power to determine the course that action would take.

Everything about the girl intoxicated him: her looks, her voice, the way she talked. While he was unsure of the possibility of success, he was emboldened by the bright prospects that seemed to appear from time to time. Just walking with her brought immense satisfaction. Dare he dream of actually possessing her someday?

Their feet scraped along the concrete walk under the dim lights of the housing project. She was a mere step ahead of him, walking crisply. He plodded along behind, walking his bike.

Her father was deputy secretary of the labor union at Cotton Mill 6; her mother, a retired mill worker. She had taken the music-academy entrance exam but failed, and she didn't want to fill her mother's slot at the mill. So she was forced to join the ranks of the unemployed until she could retake the exam. Meanwhile, if a theatrical troupe showed interest in her, even if it wasn't a local one, she would sign on. The stage was her calling, her great dream. Her remuneration at the Mill Road club was six yuan a night, but she'd have sung for nothing. Her great desire was to have her own fans. A singer's success was linked to her fans, a point stressed over and over by her teachers at the Cultural Palace. She was confident she could win her audience's heart.

All this she told Huiquan as though letting him in on a grand strategy. He listened quietly, gradually realizing the gulf that lay between them. To her he was just another fan, a loyal, volunteer bodyguard. Under that childishly innocent exterior lurked a mature woman. She could not possibly help him realize his romantic dreams, for they shared no common ground.

When it was clear she was waiting for him to volunteer something about himself, he said softly, as though fearful of shocking her, "I'm an orphan."

She just looked at him.

"I've only been out a couple of months."

"Out of where?"

"Paradise River. I did three years of forced labor . . ."

Her eyes widened. The streetlights illuminated her blue eye shadow and the streak marks left by her carelessly applied eyeliner pencil. He stared at her; she stared back—an unintended confrontation.

"What for?"

"I stabbed a man but didn't kill him. I used to fight all the time. They called me Basher Li."

His voice began to crack. She paled, and her lip curled into a pout. Either she was contemplating what he'd said, or she was truly shocked. Why had he lied about the incident? Was he trying to frighten her or impress her? No, it had just come out, to his chagrin. The interesting part was that he no longer cared how she might react. He would say whatever popped into his head and watch her changing expression with a contempt of which even he was unaware.

Quickly lowering her head, she picked up the pace. Her long legs peeking out beneath her skirt turned blue gray under the streetlights. If he were Spike Fang, would he embrace her in that alcove between the buildings up ahead? The place was nearly deserted. Or would he take her on the grass? Would she resist? Would she scream? Or would she let him have his way? His thoughts, obviously unhealthy and spooky, seemed to be those of a dispassionate observer. Still, it didn't take him long to feel ashamed of them.

Zhao Yaqiu stood in the stairwell of her building, still the innocent, lovable girl. The light shining down on her revealed a tranquil expression that exuded warmth and harmony. She was smiling broadly.

"Do you have many friends?"

"Hardly any."

"How about a girlfriend?"

". . . I . . . don't like . . . am not used to being around girls. I'm a loner, no girlfriend . . . a girl in school . . . a neighbor girl, but that doesn't count as a girlfriend . . ."

Why spout all that nonsense? He was fuming at himself.

"I have lots of friends, boys *and* girls. I don't think you can have too many friends. Friends can help each other in lots of ways . . . Well, good night. My mom's probably frantic waiting for me to come home."

She was in the door and out of sight in a flash. The lack of emotion in her voice had hit him hard. Upon seeing his emotions, she had thrown up a barrier to ward them off. She was obviously a girl with courage and experience in warding off advances by men and boys. She wasn't even twenty. He was already twenty-five, and in many ways he was unworthy of her. His admiration for her was ridiculous and utterly worthless. His fantasies regarding women were nothing but emotional garbage, and she was helping him sweep them away. He was the sort of person who gained an understanding of himself only through the intervention of others, and that, unfortunately, seldom occurred. She could never fall for him, and he lacked the ability to love her. This was the latest message life had revealed to him.

Several panes of glass were missing from the door to that building whose banister was made of cement. Zhao Yaqiu passed through it daily, in and out. As far as Huiquan was concerned, the seedy stairwell was more blessed than he.

In the shadows of the alcove he spotted a familiar figure leaning against the wall. It was the student from Hu Family Tower High School whom he had seen at the club. He didn't try to hide or get away as Huiquan walked toward him. The look on his pasty face was one of sheer agony.

Huiquan thrust his clenched fists into his pants pockets. His back muscles were cramping up, the warning sign of an impending fight. He pinched himself on the thigh.

"Who told you to follow us?"

"I'm following her, not you."

"What for?"

"No reason—"

"Does she know you?"

"I know her, but she doesn't know me. We were in the same school. She was two grades ahead of me. I wrote to her, but she ignored me, and I wanted to ask her—"

"Ask her what?"

"I'm not sure."

"Then ask her. Why sneak around like this?"

". . . I don't know."

"Dumb shit! You're a dumb fucking shit! You stay away from her, or I'll make you wish you had . . ."

The high school student didn't move. Something flashed in his eyes. Huiquan often saw this brooding boy at the club. He must be neglecting his studies something awful. A tragic case of lovesickness. If he'd been his brother, Huiquan would have slapped him.

"Get the hell out of here! You call yourself a fucking man?"

Huiquan patted the boy on the shoulder. His comment was meant for both of them. He was much less troubled when he climbed onto his bike, his movements suddenly free and relaxed. The foolish boy was a warning. He mustn't take girls too seriously. They lacked understanding. For Zhao Yaqiu to ignore a schoolmate who had written her love letters showed how callous she was. Someone like that was incapable of being taught. Did she have it in her to become a wife and mother who would take care of things in the rear compound at number 18, East Lane, Spirit Run Street? This wasn't the first time this question had crossed his mind; at one time it had even excited him. What a joke! Fate would never make a grand mistake like that.

Sooner or later he would marry a woman as ugly as he, someone who would endure his faults, past, present, and future, someone who would drive away his loneliness and bring him joy, who would instill in him the confidence and know-how he needed to go on living. He doubted that such a woman had been born yet, so he would have to wait. What was the difference between the happiness brought to a relationship by an ugly woman and that brought by a pretty one? He, for one, didn't know.

In his dreams he continued to struggle with the woman he could not identify yet who seemed so familiar. His desires were simple and concrete, an extension of reality just beyond his grasp. He didn't know what to do with himself. At critical moments he tried to run away, as though he were a shivering little coward.

But where did he hope to hide?

Where *could* he hide?

8

Liu Baotie, the beat cop, was all spiffed up. His shoes were shined, and his collar was spotless, but most significantly, he had quit smoking, so the nicotine stains on his fingers were just about gone, and his teeth weren't nearly as dingy as they had been.

Huiquan smoked alone as he awaited the questions.

He was sitting in front of a table in the Neighborhood Committee office, where he was required to go from time to time to report on his ideological progress. This was the sixth time so far. From the beginning Liu Baotie had treated him well enough, and in the past one or the other had supplied the cigarettes so they could smoke as they chatted, usually wrapping things up by the time they'd finished one cigarette. This time the cop sat there sucking on a hard candy, running it noisily and attentively over his teeth.

"Sure you don't want a cigarette?"

"I'm sure."

"Why not?"

"I'm determined to quit."

118

Huiquan had seen the beat cop's intended: a tall, unsmiling sourpuss, not the sort of woman people like to be around. He had seen them together in the lobby of the Zhaotong Temple Cinema. Apparently irked about something, she had turned her face to the wall as the beat cop, dressed in civvies, stood behind her, looking quite perplexed, a soft drink in either hand. Huiquan didn't disturb them, but at the first opportunity, he commented to Liu Baotie, "She sure is tall!" The cop smiled bashfully.

Liu Baotie liked her, ugly or not. Why else would he have quit smoking? She ran him ragged, and Huiquan felt sorry for him.

The cop unwrapped another piece of candy and popped it into his mouth.

"Anything unusual happen lately?"

"Nothing to speak of. Same old grind."

Huiquan clammed up about his dealings with Cui Yongli. No one was hurt by them, not really, and mentioning them wouldn't do anyone any good.

"No new friends?"

"No. I saw a Beijing representative from Xinjiang about taking some leather coats on commission, but we couldn't agree on terms. I forget his name . . . He looked me up."

"Be especially careful these days."

"Why?"

"Incidents are on the rise. Don't get involved in any."

"I take my pushcart out every day, and that's about it. I'm staying out of trouble. Even if I wasn't, I'd stay off your beat."

"That's what you say."

He sucked unhappily on his candy.

"How's business?"

"Okay, I guess."

"You can trust me. I'm not on the take."

"Don't be offended, but how my business goes is nobody's concern but mine."

"Don't get so huffy! I work like a dog day in and day out, and if you add it all up, wages and bonuses, I make less than the loose change you pull in. I'm not offended. Why should I be?"

"What good's money? All you need is enough to live on."

"That's easy for you to say."

"Okay, let's swap, what do you say?"

"I'd jump at the chance."

"Standing there all day long, gawking at people, sometimes I feel like coming home and hanging myself. I keep asking myself how long I'll have to stay with it . . . You think you've got a boring job, well, mine's worse. Try it if you don't believe me."

"It's boring because you're alone. Why not let Auntie Luo find you someone? If you had a woman to look after you, my job would be a lot easier."

They laughed. Huiquan was blushing slightly. He was filled with good feelings toward the young cop as he left the office. The image of him standing in the cinema lobby holding two soft drinks, looking vulnerable and incorruptible at the same time, persisted. He saw him as yet another unfortunate human being who would spend his life with a sourpuss and love her in his own way. The thought saddened him.

You can't run away from miseries. Like bicycles clogging up traffic as they dart this way and that, they're everywhere. Miseries are a necessary evil that attach themselves to people who go looking for them. They're a part of life.

One morning shortly after Huiquan had set up his stall, Ma Yifu—whom he hadn't seen for a long time—materialized in front of his three-wheeler as though he had popped up from beneath the sidewalk. He giggled bashfully as he helped Huiquan get ready for business. He was thinner than before, and the mole over his eye seemed larger as a result, his errant tooth sharper, and his skin metallic looking. He had dark circles under his eyes—he looked like death warmed over, but good news tumbled from his mouth. His American boss at the Jeep factory had given everyone a raise and a promotion, and his brother had been assigned living quarters by his work unit, so Yifu's brother and his wife and their son were moving out. Yifu would now have a room to himself at home. Meanwhile, he and his girlfriend were getting along beautifully and, as a matter of fact, were going to tie the knot around the first of October. His future mother-in-law was helping his mother make the arrangements.

The frown on his face seemed out of place with all that cheerful news. After taking the cigarette Huiquan offered him, he squatted beside the three-wheeler to smoke. Huiquan had a pretty good idea what his friend was up to. He didn't have much money on him, and the bankbooks were home under the mattress. He opened his cashbox and counted the change. Yifu was getting jittery.

"We're not getting married for months yet, but I'm beat from all this running around."

"You asked for it."

"There's a Sharp cassette recorder she likes—"

"You mean one *you* like, don't you?"

"C'mon, don't make fun of me . . . I can't scrape together enough for the Sharp. She's afraid the ones made in Japan are going to keep getting harder to find . . . If she—"

"If I hear another word about what *she* does or does not want, you can just get lost! How much do you need?"

"Three hundred. A little more wouldn't hurt."

"Watch the stall for a few minutes."

Huiquan went home, took out one of the bankbooks, and went to the bank on Outer Chaoyang Gate Boulevard to withdraw four hundred yuan. Ma Yifu was speechless as he took the money. He'd never expected it to be *that* easy.

"I'll pay you back soon, next month if I can. Having to borrow like this makes me sick. I'm beyond salvation . . ."

He helped Huiquan put up the clothes rack, straightened the price tags on the merchandise, and then policed the area around the stall, throwing the garbage into a nearby bin. He would have gladly turned handstands to please Huiquan. Obviously all the other people he'd approached had turned him down. He was a high-risk borrower, and Huiquan was the only lender with a heart.

Huiquan felt sorry for his friend. That's what a woman can do to a guy. Poor Brushes, such a pathetic figure—in every way.

"Keep it. I'm not so hard up I have to worry about a few yuan. Buy what you need, and forget about the rest."

"I said I'll pay you back. What kind of friend would I be if I didn't? Basher, I know I'm not in your league, but if you ever need me for anything, man, I'll be there. If not, I'm a no-good son of a bitch!"

Uncharacteristically caught up in his emotions, Yifu was breathing hard, and the hand holding the money was shaking. He walked off, reeling down the sidewalk like a drunk. Whatever was bothering him had him in its grip and wouldn't let go. Maybe she had laid down the law: *If you don't do this, then you can't have that! Since that's the way it is, that's the way it's going to be! This is no good, that's no good, so tell me, what is it you want?* Stuff like that. They got off doing things like that.

She had him on a short leash, and he didn't dare say a word. And she wasn't pretty; Huiquan was adamant on that score. Fat and retiring, no one would give her a second look out on the street.

What about Zhao Yaqiu? What was the source of her magnetism? They hadn't spent more than a few hours together, yet he felt as though he'd known her for a long time. He was drawn to her each time she faced the back wall of the club, mike in hand, then slowly turned toward her audience. Time and space ceased to exist for him; by now he had convinced himself that he had brushed his lips against the downy, heart-melting hairs above her upper lip. The deed was stamped in his memory. An indivisible bond between them had formed in his fantasies even before he'd met her. She was just the kind of girl he was looking for. But was any of this logical?

Maybe her songs had taken him back to his school days, or earlier, causing him to mistake her for the girl with whom he had grown up and fallen in love, only to be rejected by her once they reached maturity. There are plenty of idiotic music fans like that, but he told himself he wasn't one of them.

He liked her, that's all. He had given her a few more looks than usual, as he would any pretty girl; he was attracted to her for the same reasons all men are attracted to pretty girls. He wasn't the first man to have his head turned by beauty. With some, that can lead to rape or adultery, as it had with Spike; for others it is the first step on the path to marriage. Beauty makes worriers out of some and gawkers out of others, men whose eyes light up around a pretty face or a pair of captivating eyes. He had little in common with men like that. In fact, the only similarity between him and them was in the ineffable sense of disappointment with which they were left.

Just the sight of her gave him an empty sensation in the pit of his stomach, as though something had ceased to exist or had been taken away. It was the subtle feeling that all was lost, the result of a collision between hope and despair. It was the same feeling he had experienced at the age of six or seven, when the *chop chop chop* sound of a cleaver woke him, as though it were hacking at his neck. Sometimes the chopping was replaced by a strange sawing noise, and at such times he wished he could stay in bed forever.

When he saw Zhao Yaqiu, his thoughts turned unspeakably chaotic. He talked to no one, not even to himself; his face, devoid of expression, looked like a human caricature.

At the club he sipped costly French brandy from a snifter, each drink costing as much as a pound of pork or half a pound of cured beef. During those days he nearly lived for brandy.

Zhao Yaqiu sang on, seemingly without a care in the world, as sweetly and innocently as always. Fewer youngsters gathered in the doorway, for the novelty had worn off. Zhao Yaqiu had a new companion: a sissified, fair-skinned boy who never showed up without his guitar. Sometimes he accompanied her on the instrument, and once in a while he joined her in a duet. But most of the time he just sat around waiting for her break so they could share complimentary soft drinks and talk in hushed tones. He was her new bodyguard, whose only other function was to see her home.

"I can't keep imposing on you. My schoolmate here can see me home from now on . . ."

That was how she broke the news to him.

"You here again?"

From then on, she greeted him brusquely, and his response was equally casual, sometimes a mere nod, as though he couldn't be bothered with her.

The club was enjoying a brisk business. A citation from the district catering company hung conspicuously in the take-out section, and Manager Han was forever polishing the mirror. Zhao Yaqiu was given an extension on her contract and, apparently, a raise. Each night her voice filled the smoky air of the club. She once asked that smoking not be permitted, but the manager never got around to honoring her request. By now she displayed such skill and ease that she sometimes sang a foreign rock-and-roll number in that raspy voice of hers, to the sheer delight of her audience.

At times Huiquan, who never smoked while she was singing, felt like going up and choking the little assholes who constantly smoked, ate, and drank during her performance. The only thing that kept him from making them put out their cigarettes was his fear of making a fool of himself. Besides, she didn't need him to come to her aid.

After each show Pretty Boy walked her over to the housing project across the main road, frequently with Huiquan following at a distance. To his surprise the anonymous student from Hu Family Tower High School was still dogging them, stubbornly, almost dementedly.

Over time Pretty Boy was replaced by a youngster with long hair and rings on his fingers. This latest companion was the son of one of her mother's co-workers, or so he was told. During the month of June a total of four or five young men took turns seeing her home, each more solicitous than his predecessor. She responded by gracing them with her friendship. They gazed at her with cautious optimism, all the time harboring the knowledge that their optimism was futile. They all looked weary from pursuing her; and though she never openly rejected them, neither did she give them the answer they sought, leaving them hanging in the limbo between dread and weariness.

Whenever she offered one of them her glass or patted him on the arm, flames of jealousy raged inside Huiquan. But there was nothing he could do about it. Her indiscriminate affection may have flowed naturally from the warmth of her being, but it sometimes seemed suspiciously manipulative.

When she sang, however, she was like a child. Throaty, nasal—it didn't matter if you couldn't understand the lyrics, for the performance was always playacting by an angel who could be forgiven anything.

"Whore child!" Even as he cursed her under his breath, his thoughts were focused on the act of nuzzling that spot above her lip—a pipe dream, and he knew it. As his thoughts turned more frequently to Spike, he began to create in his own mind a number of ways to conquer women. But then, mortified by his own debasement, he knew he would rather die than carry out most of the things he had dreamed up. He imagined that the heads of men everywhere were filled with similar thoughts. The boys who took turns walking her home gazed at her with wolfish looks; they all wanted the same thing, but she wouldn't bestow it on any of them.

"Whore child!"

He angrily recalled the nearly naked model who lay obscenely in the photograph on the magazine page as though she were unwilling to emerge into the real world. He fantasized ripping her off the page. He needed a woman now more urgently than he had at any other time in his life. The problem was, Where was she? He was twenty-five already and couldn't keep putting off the inevitable. His fantasies were getting out of hand and beginning to scare him. He feared he might do something terrible someday.

On the night before their graduation from high school, the monitor of his bonehead class had been savagely beaten. While lining up at the New China Bookstore he had rubbed up against the girl ahead of him—his intentions were transparent—and when her boyfriend realized what was happening, he lit into him without saying a word. The monitor, a glib boy, always tried to look progressive, and if his schoolwork had been a little better, he'd never have wound up in a bonehead class. He was the school clown, frequently surprising and delighting the other students with his antics. Always the horny one, he left school after that, and no one ever saw him again.

Now, all these years later, Huiquan sympathized with the monitor. Rubbing up against that girl must have tormented him to the point of madness, until he was no longer responsible for his actions. Huiquan felt that he, too, was falling victim to the same allure.

He couldn't put it off any longer.

Auntie Luo introduced him to a girl who sold tickets at the Purple Rays Public Bath. Twenty-six years old. Lived on Broad Avenue in East City. Father a gateman at Workers' Stadium, mother a fishmonger at the public market. One older brother, two younger sisters. Not great looking, but—and this was critical—an agreeable disposition and a whiz at housework.

"I brought a photo. Where's yours?"

Huiquan handed Auntie Luo one of the snapshots he'd taken for his vendor's license and took the one she handed him, shoving it into his pocket without looking at it. He didn't want to be too obvious.

"You just give the word, and I'll do whatever you say."

He didn't dare look at Auntie Luo's smiling face. The old lady's jubilant airs threw him into a deep funk. Without having to ask, he knew the kind of woman she would introduce him to. He went into the bedroom, but instead of looking at the photo right away, he first studied himself in the wardrobe mirror. He had to do something about his fragile self-confidence.

He took out the photo and gave it a quick glance. His anxieties immediately disappeared, along with his nervousness. The reflection in the mirror didn't seem that bad all of a sudden. Although lackluster, his eyes were large; his lips were on the thick side, but his teeth were straight and white. He had nothing to apologize for.

They met in mid-June. Auntie Luo and another woman brought them together and then left them alone to stroll for over an hour along the road north of the washing-machine factory. It was nighttime, and the street was crowded, so he barely glanced at her and hardly spoke. The curious expression on her face made him feel as though he were being carefully scrutinized. She didn't say much more than he, because she was either shy or disappointed, but her features were constantly changing, like someone in a mountain gully who didn't know how to get out. Her neck was dark, her face pale—she wore too much face powder. She had a startlingly flat profile, and when she smiled, her mouth broadened considerably and her eyes virtually disappeared. When she wasn't smiling, her eyes were wide and staring, but her mouth formed a thin line. Her face, changing from light to dark and back again under the streetlights, seemed somehow insubstantial, like that of an animated cartoon character. Yet she appeared smug, for she knew about his past and was not happy with his looks. He knew. He could tell.

This was the first real date in his life. He knew he could never love someone with such a flat face—like a flat cake just before it's tossed into the oven—but love had really never been at issue here. She was a woman, and she could do housework. That would take care of most of his problems. The fact that she wasn't pretty was actually a relief, since she'd have no cause to treat him with contempt. Being the object of a woman's nit-picking is humiliating, and the thought of it made him uneasy. In her case there was nothing to worry about, given her family, her profession, and her flat-cake face. He didn't foresee any problems. As for her smugness, he just wrote it off as a character flaw common to all young women. He treated her courteously the whole time, even though his doing so didn't seem to have much of an effect on her. That may have been where he went wrong. If he had been a bit more cavalier, he wouldn't have been so vulnerable when the ax fell. He wished he'd forgotten Auntie Luo's coaching altogether.

"What's your phone number?"

She shot him a quick glance and then looked away.

"What's the best day to call you?"

". . . Is that really necessary?"

Like a pile driver. He was barely able to keep from spitting in her flat-cake face. She wasn't human; she spoke the language of demons. Whoever married that half-baked woman was in for a lifetime of trouble. Whoever became her old man would beat her for sure. If she had any sense at all, she'd know that no man in the world could ever fall in love with her. Where did she get off acting like a princess? "Is that really necessary?"

Huiquan nearly laughed in her face, but turned and walked off instead. "Flat Cake," he felt like saying, "who the fuck do you think you are?" But he didn't.

His first-ever date, and he had never expected it to turn out like this. It made him sick. Nauseated him. As if he were drowning in a puddle of dog piss. He felt like puking; he felt as though his bowels were about to burst. That's a date? That's what they call a dress rehearsal for love? He'd only asked for her phone number, but she had acted as if he had tried to rape her. As if she could stir up his desires!

"Is that really necessary?"

It still rang in his ears. It might not have hurt so much if it had come from the lips of someone like Zhao Yaqiu, but in the mouth of Flat Cake it cut deeply. If even a homely woman like that disdained him, where would he find anyone to accept him?

He had sunk so low that a woman no one could ever love could not force herself to love him; even people whom others pitied laughed at him behind his back. Once again he was aware that the rest of the world had nothing to do with him. His thoughts were drawn longingly back to that underground-cable ditch: he imagined himself lying in it; he imagined the look of stupefaction on Zhao Yaqiu's face when she saw him there. He fancied her jumping in and lying next to him, both of them to be buried by dirt that fell like the multicolored confetti of exploding fireworks. The blissful comfort he derived from the thought of such a death was immutable and eternal. He was incomparably happy at that moment, imagining that he saw large, glistening tears roll down her soft, delicate face. He would have given his life to win just two of those teardrops.

It was agonizing to watch his dream disintegrate, reappear, and then disintegrate again. The Zhao Yaqiu of the club, however, was as cheerful as always. She ignored his torment. If he were to die tragically in a car crash, she might heave a sigh, but that would be the end of it. His death would be of no more concern to her than was his existence. His loneliness meant less to her than the lyrics of one of her songs. People understood her lyrics, but no one understood his loneliness. No one cared. His loneliness meant less than a dog turd. There could be a thousand unhappy men in the world to whom a thousand women said, "Is that really necessary?" and his misfortune would still be unique. Only his misfortune was immense. He felt sorry only for himself.

It had been a week since Auntie Luo's last visit. The case for rejection made by the girl's family was that Huiquan was too old (thirty, at least), too coarse, and uncouth. Auntie Luo was fit to be tied.

"What is she, after all? A ticket seller at a public bath. She looks down on us? Well, we look down on her, with that face of hers, as flat as a dried persimmon!"

Forgotten were all the nice things she'd said about her at first. Huiquan suspected she was putting on an act for his benefit. What had she told them about him? How much of the saga of Li Huiquan had she related to the local clutch of old ladies?

"You can't pick up any old kid off the street. If you get a good one, fine and dandy, but what if you get a freak or some idiot? Why, in our rear compound . . ."

He had overheard Auntie Luo's comment in his high school days, back when he was a real troublemaker and had already been detained in the station house once. He never told a soul and, for Xiaofen's sake, never tried to get back at Auntie Luo, whose so-called concern for him was rooted in pity. Deep down she didn't like him and congratulated herself for the good fortune that he was somebody else's child and not hers. She could never really care for him. But what about his mother? Had she still loved him after all the misery he caused her, all the trouble? How did she feel when he was sentenced to hard labor and taken away? It must have broken her heart. Did she wish she'd never agreed to adopt him in the first place?

He was someone who didn't deserve to be loved.

As he sat in the club on Mill Road, enchanted by Zhao Yaqiu and moping over the sight of her exquisite face, one simple statement kept running through his mind: he didn't deserve to be loved by anyone.

Nearly everyone was superior to him. He envied Xiaofen and her husband; he envied Zhao Yaqiu and her retinue of young men; he even envied Cui Yongli for his unflappable nature.

What did Cui do when he was having a good time with women? Stroke his beard with one hand and stifle a yawn with the other? Or giggle like a kid playing a game? Thoughts like these always gave Huiquan sweaty palms.

He saw Cui only once during the month of June, a casual encounter at the club after Cui's return from the Northeast and just before his planned trip to Guangzhou. No one knew what kept him so busy. He appeared travel weary and full of pep at the same time. Beneath his calm exterior hid a shrewdness most people could only guess at.

He casually called attention to Zhao Yaqiu's companion.

"Who's the pretty boy?" he asked Huiquan.

"He's in the chorus at the Cultural Palace."

"Is he with her every night?"

"No, but if it's not him, it's someone else. She's lined up a whole squad of them, and they take turns seeing her home."

"No kidding. Didn't you used to do that? Let me think; when was that . . . I'm sure you . . . Tell me, is she on the level?"

"Hard to say. I can't tell."

"She looks like she's grown up since the last time I saw her. Shit, I thought she was so tender you couldn't lay a hand on her . . . Why the hell don't you make your move? If you want to see her home, do it!"

"Anybody who wants to see her home is a slug!"

Cui Yongli noticed that Huiquan's chin was quivering, but he just smiled and dropped the subject. Huiquan expected him to mention their business transaction again, but he seemed to have forgotten all about it—as though it hadn't even occurred. Cui was the type who always left himself a way out of things.

Could he be waiting for Huiquan to bring it up? That's what you'd normally expect, especially if he'd made a killing on the stuff or had been busted trying to sell it. But Huiquan didn't want to say anything, and it was Cui who finally broke the ice.

"Everything go all right?"

"What could go wrong?"

"Then it was worth doing."

"Are there things that aren't worth doing?"

Cui laughed nervously. "You, my friend, don't understand me . . ."

Huiquan didn't reply, and Cui lowered his head in thought. "I just want us to be friends, that's all."

"That's not the way I figured it. I figured you were worried about getting stuck with those goods, so you got me to dispose of them for you. But five hundred yuan is penny-ante shit—"

"Of course it is! Five hundred? I wouldn't bat an eye if five thousand or fifty thousand passed through my hands! That batch of used clothes was an incidental piece of business, not the real thing. Whether you made a bundle from it or got fined and came looking for me wouldn't have had much of an effect on our relationship. You know what I mean?"

"Why would I come looking for you? Even if they fined me everything I owned, it'd be my business, nothing for you to worry about."

"I guessed right."

"But from now on give your business to somebody else."

"Right again! Now you're acting like a friend . . . Have another drink. This brandy tastes like licorice."

"It tastes like beaver to me!"

"Wouldn't know; I've never tasted beaver." Cui laughed so hard the people in the next booth turned to look at him.

Zhao Yaqiu, who was on a break, was leaning back in the

swivel chair and studying the mural on the wall behind her, a painting of a black bull and a fair-skinned nude woman, whose arms were wrapped around the animal's neck; its eyes were as large as the woman's breasts.

Cui stopped laughing long enough to wipe his beard with his handkerchief. The black whiskers were shot through with light strands, like reeds that have started to wither.

"I'm pretty good at sizing people up, and I can see what a good friend you'd make . . . You're an orphan, aren't you?"

"How'd you know that?"

"I'd be a fool not to know things about people I want to call my friends, wouldn't I? But I don't divulge my sources." Cui laughed again. He was playing the fool.

"Brushes must have told you."

"Brushes? You mean that pal of yours named Ma? He's a loser! A born loser! And you can tell him I said so. He was born under the sign of the rat, which makes him a sneak and a coward. He's going nowhere fast."

"He's honest enough, and he's loyal to his friends."

Huiquan spoke with such earnestness that Cui was taken by surprise and, it appeared, somewhat touched.

"You never have bad things to say about people, do you?"

"Never learned how."

Cui Yongli was momentarily at a loss for words.

"What . . . what do you think of me?"

"Too early to tell. It all depends on how you treat me. But it seems to me that you like to work alone and not let others know what you're up to. If you ever decide to go into partnership, you'd better find somebody pretty dense. Anyone as shrewd as you could be trouble. But that's just my opinion . . ."

He took a sip of brandy and looked away. Zhao Yaqiu,

holding a cassette, was saying something to one of the waitresses, who nodded in response.

Cui appeared deflated, to Huiquan's secret delight.

"Was I right?" Huiquan asked.

"Right on the button, . . . but don't get me wrong."

"Don't worry."

"Friendships are no laughing matter."

"I know. I met most of my friends in fights. I know—"

"There's a little left in the bottle. You drink it. My head feels funny. The licorice taste is too strong."

Cui lit a cigarette and gave Huiquan a friendly pat on the shoulder as he pointed to a bunch of long-haired fellows in the corner. Huiquan recognized them as regulars.

"See them? They deal in motorbikes, normally a couple a month. They'd cut your heart out for the right price! You see the one nearest us, the one with the scar near his eye? He'd cheat his own mother if he had to. Hell, he'd *sell* his own mother or his kid sister if he felt like it . . . That's why I say that making friends is serious business. If you're not careful, your best friend could turn on you one day and throttle you."

"That's news to me."

"When you've been around a while, you'll know what I mean."

"I just want to make enough from my stall to put food on the table."

"Maybe so, maybe not . . ."

Huiquan let the discussion drop there. Zhao Yaqiu was singing again. In another half hour it would be ten o'clock. He shifted in his seat so he could rest his head against the back of the booth. What absorbed him this time was not her voice but something else. Two children running through the grass. When the girl gets tired, the boy carries her piggyback, and they vanish into the tall grass. He had never seen grass like that in real life, but this was a recurring daydream. The scene was probably from a documentary or something like that, maybe one about Inner Mongolia. The girl looked a lot like Luo Xiaofen. Back in elementary school he had carried her home piggyback when she said her feet hurt. Afterward she complained to another girl, "It was all his disgusting idea!"

But she let him repeat the disgusting activity, since they lived a long way from school, and her legs tired easily. They were about the same height at the time, and Xiaofen might have weighed a little more, which meant he had to strain to keep moving, especially with her arms wrapped nervously and tightly around his neck. He enjoyed it, though. And she enjoyed seeing his face turn red and watching him thrust his neck forward. Females need this sort of gratification.

The girl in his daydream had no name and no distinguishing features. She was just a blurred silhouette with short hair and red clothes. The melancholy it produced grew stronger each time the dream recurred. He wished he could see the girl's face and hoped it might be that of Zhao Yaqiu. But the girl concealed her face from him, making the daydream so wearisome, far more exhausting than the dreams that came at night. He would have gladly died for the girl. The grassy scene inspired him.

Zhao Yaqiu paced the stage, her mouth opening and shutting as though she were an actress in a silent movie. A middle-aged customer across the aisle broke a coffee cup, the pieces floating to the floor without a sound after sailing gracefully through the air. The booth in front obscured a girl's back, but a fair, sleek leg stuck out into the aisle, the skirt hitched way up to reveal a leg in all its fullness, long and lovely, with a smooth, rounded calf—a human leg, a woman's leg.

Huiquan felt like biting it. Only the taste of blood would satisfy him. Then the owner of the leg stood up and turned toward him as she walked out. She was a woman in her forties, with wrinkles all over her face, old and repulsive. Curiously Huiquan's desire was not diminished a bit.

The shadowy upper lip floated like a cloud on the strains of the music. Huiquan cocked his head and saw Cui wiping his pant leg with a handkerchief. He was trying to remove a stain.

"Leaving?" Cui asked.

"You go ahead . . ."

When he heard his own voice, Huiquan knew he'd had too much to drink. But he picked up his empty glass, wishing it were full.

Even cold water would do.

9

Huiquan traveled to Changping County, where he bought two hundred plaid shirts from the Sunshine Clothing Factory. They were all the rage, partly because they were so cheap. He left them in the factory guesthouse and then boarded a bus to the Great Wall.

Not once in all the years he'd lived in Beijing had he been to the Great Wall. For all he knew, his parents had never gone, having more important things to worry about. Then, by the time there were no more important things to worry about and they were free to go, it was too late. Death had claimed them.

The Great Wall, aswarm with people, straddled the mountain ridges with no visible beginning or end. Dense wooded areas paralleled the wall on both sides, and when he stood inside the Western Beacon Tower, the highest point in the area, and looked northward, he saw the Guanting Reservoir, a tiny, dazzlingly blue lake. Cars and pedestrians crawled along the nearby highway like little worms and ants.

For upwards of two hours, Huiquan lay on a grassy slope, letting the tourists on the wall peer down at him. Clusters of them were picnicking not far away, the sounds of their talking and laughing shuttling through the trees. Food smells floated on the air currents. The ground was littered with wrappers, paper cups, tin cans, even lengths of sausage and loaves of bread. Human beings and their disposable ways.

He wasn't thinking about plaid shirts as he lay there; there was no need to. They were good for a twenty-percent profit, easy. This was the uncomplicated side of life, for he had already estimated the income they would produce. After selling the shirts, he would do all the required calculations—actually, even that wasn't necessary—and he would know precisely what was coming to him. In the final analysis that shitty little bit of money wasn't worth worrying about.

His mind was occupied with a jumble of unrelated stuff, like memories and dreamscapes and real-life reflections, all tumbling around inside like potatoes falling off a truck. In camp once he had single-handedly unloaded seven truckloads of potatoes, his shovel moving through them like a mower through grass, creating hillocks of potatoes plus a rhythmic thudding sound. Political Instructor Xue had criticized him in front of the entire brigade, since potatoes with bruised skins did not store well over the winter. That's why he'd done it. In those days his hatred had known no limits.

Had that changed? Who did he hate now? The foreign tourist gaping at him from the wall? He sneered at the foreigner, who whipped out his camera.

As he lay near a pine grove beside the Great Wall of China, which snaked through the rugged terrain for thousands of miles, he was obsessed with the same old questions: Why is life so empty? What's the point in living? He refused to believe he was the only person in the world who agonized over these issues, the only one who was banging around like a headless fly. Yet everyone he saw seemed happy. The wall hummed as though a flock of chattering birds were perched on it.

He was a man now, and his days of searching out a good fight were gone forever. He had learned how to think things through. No, he had been *forced* to think things through. A raging tumult filled his head, and he could do nothing about it. He was so tired.

Death seemed to be the starting point. It was the summer of his first year in middle school, a rainy afternoon. Forced to stay inside, he went to bed early. He slept in the inner room; Mother, in the outer room. She was coughing; the rain was falling noisily. He was thinking about his long-deceased father: Father propped up in his hospital bed, ignoring everyone, mad at the world. Now he was dead, and no one in the world, except maybe Mother, still carried his image around. Then his thoughts turned to Mother, to his teachers, to Luo Xiaofen and his other classmates, and finally to himself. What linked all these thoughts was death. If everyone had to die someday, sooner or later his turn would come.

The first time this thought invaded his peace, he found he couldn't get rid of it. It kept him in its terrifying grasp for a very long time. The patter of rain and Mother's coughs were harbingers of death, sounds from another world. Was Father there in that other world? Could he speak? Would he recognize his own son? Why did people have to get sick? If they didn't, then they wouldn't have to die, would they? And if everyone has to die sometime, then what's the point of sickness? Life on earth—what's the point?

He spent that year tormented by a host of silly questions. It was the year his grades took a nosedive and he turned into a taciturn, morose "little old man." His classmates began pestering and teasing him: they drew animals on his back with chalk, they spit on pieces of paper and stuck them to his clothes, they called him the Cantonese, and they shot spitballs at him in class. Some of the boys in class gloated over the downward spiral in his grades. He had no idea what was going wrong. At night he'd sit down to do his homework, but his mind kept wandering. If he was doomed to turn to ashes or dust someday, what was the point in working at this stuff? He was puzzled that no one else seemed to think as he did. Needing to talk to someone, he brought up the matter with Xiaofen on the way home from school.

"What do you think's better, being alive or being dead?"

"What's the matter with you?"

"Are you scared of dying?"

"Me? . . . I never thought about it. We're just kids! Why talk about dying? There are lots of things we haven't seen yet, lots of good food we haven't tried—"

"Good food?"

He was at a loss. Then in the first semester of his second year in middle school a breakthrough occurred in the strange thoughts careening around inside his head. It was during gym, a game of dodgeball. When it was his turn to be it, the kids missed him intentionally, until one of them threw the ball right at him so hard it bounced way up into the air. He retrieved it, and the same thing happened again. After a while they stopped throwing the ball at him altogether, to make him drop his guard, and then they aimed it at his head when he wasn't looking. The episode was masterminded by a kid named Wu, the biggest kid in the class. He had always intimidated Huiquan.

How far is he willing to take this? he asked himself. When he fetched the ball this time, he picked up a broken brick, which he laid on the ground next to his foot as a silent warning. The laughter petered out in a hurry, and everyone waited to see what was going to happen. The kid named Wu was slightly red-faced.

Now we'll see what he's made of! A silent incantation.

The next time Wu hit him on the knee, everyone—boys and girls alike—snickered, not to be mean but just because it struck them as funny. In that split second Huiquan picked up the brick and charged like a cat streaking across a rooftop.

It took three stitches to close the gash on Wu's head, for which Li received a reprimand. A notice was posted in the glass-encased bulletin board by the front gate of Middle School 68. For Huiquan it was a release, since the incident liberated him from the strange morbid thoughts of death that had gripped him.

On the way home from school he grabbed another of his tormentors by the collar and showed him the brick. Now that death had lost its sting, there was nothing left to fear.

"Give up?"

"I give up!"

"Say 'uncle'!"

". . . Uncle . . ."

Never one to mock people, he relaxed with a sigh and shoved the frightened kid aside. From then on his erstwhile enemies fell all over themselves trying to be friendly. He was shorter than most of them, barely five feet tall, but they were afraid of him.

It was quite a bit later that he began using a rolling pin in fights, and by then he had grown to about five foot eight, not tall, but not short either. He earned a reputation as a fighter who would never back down. By placing no value on his own life, he was freed from having to value the lives of others. He fought like a demon, and it was sheer luck that he never killed anyone or wasn't killed himself.

The rush of anticipation before a fight and the satisfying

high that followed it drove the fear of death right out of him. He was fifteen at the time.

Not counting the humble circumstances of his first few weeks of life, that rainy night ten years earlier, when his thoughts were wildly confused, marked the beginning of his troubles. That point was driven home once more as he lay on the grassy slope beside the Great Wall. A group of college students came down the slope and walked right past him. He remained motionless, the grass beneath him like a soft blanket. They glanced down at him as they passed, and one of them, a girl, must have thought he looked like someone who had swallowed poison and was struggling to stay alive. She was barely able to keep from screaming.

He sat up. Off to the south he saw banners flapping in the breeze and some shifting white dots. The dots were the caps of tourists who were meandering down the slope beneath the red flags.

A fellow inmate at camp, a former lathe operator, was known for always saying, "My mind was poisoned by the diabolical Gang of Four," at thought-reform sessions. He was serving time for child abuse, having sexually molested his foreman's eleven-year-old daughter. He was a notorious snitch, reporting everything from dirty jokes to masturbation. And always his refrain: "My mind was poisoned by the Gang of Four."

"Did the Gang of Four tell you to molest that little girl?"

Everyone in the dormitory loved to ridicule him. When you've sunk so low as to molest a child, you're better off smashing your head against a wall and being done with it.

Huiquan never had much to say during the thought-reform sessions. He wished he could talk about that rainy night years earlier but was afraid of being laughed at. He had poisoned himself. Reasonable or not, he simply couldn't articulate his feelings.

People are strange animals.

An old man in his seventies walked toward him, gasping for breath and smiling foolishly. A little girl in a pink frock was squatting down, peeing, leaving a bright yellow puddle on the steps. Her mother stood nearby, fanning herself, waiting for the girl to finish. A foreign teenager chasing his friend down a steep section of the wall stumbled and fell head over heels. He struggled for a good ten yards but couldn't stop tumbling. His misadventure was followed by hundreds of smiling eyes, both Chinese and foreign.

A peasant girl was hawking socks by one of the exits. All she had were those gaudy nylon things you can buy everywhere, but damned if she hadn't drawn a crowd. A middle-aged man dropped an entire ice onto the ground. It snapped in two but didn't shatter. He froze for a moment, then bent down, shoved half of the thing into his mouth, and held the other half in his hand.

Yes, people are strange animals, all right.

For a while Huiquan watched the comings and goings of the tourists from his vantage point under one of the gateways; then he headed to the snack bar on the southern edge for something to eat. Feeling more relaxed, he spent the night in Changping. Hazy images of Zhao Yaqiu disrupted his sleep. His blanket stank of dirty feet. After they were married, he was thinking, he would take her to see scenic marvels far more impressive than the Great Wall. Of course, he would have to start putting some money aside if he were going to carry out his ambitions of touring. Naturally, the wife he imagined wasn't Zhao Yaqiu. But why shouldn't it be? His mood swung back and forth between joy and sadness, and he couldn't tell whether he was awake or dreaming.

Back home on Spirit Run Street, Auntie Luo said someone had been by to see him. It was Political Instructor Xue, the last person in the world Huiquan expected. He had left a note and a thin book, the note folded neatly, the book wrapped in newspaper. That was Political Instructor Xue, all right, neat and tidy. He tore open the note.

I'm on my way to a meeting at the Ministry of
Justice and stopped by since it was on my way. The
Neighborhood Committee says you're doing OK.
That's good to hear. You haven't written for a couple
of months, and I was afraid you were in trouble again.
Now I know I don't have to worry. I wanted to buy
some good books for you, but they're all too
expensive, and I didn't bring much money along. I
flipped through this one, and it seems OK. Read it.
Don't forget to write, since I worry about you.
Comrade Luo says you're an honest young man, but
she only sees one side of you, and we both know you
have another side. Don't get impatient with women,
since that usually leads to trouble. That's what
worries me most. You have to work at it. Of course,
everyone says you're doing OK. Have you been
practicing your calligraphy, like I said? Don't forget
to write.

The note covered both sides of a sheet of notebook paper. He wondered where Political Instructor Xue's ramblings would have headed if the paper had been larger. Calligraphy practice was a great way to straighten a guy out, or so Political Instructor Xue had written in an earlier letter. To prove his point, he included an item he'd clipped from a newspaper. It had made no impression on Huiquan, who wanted to do something worthwhile but not practice calligraphy. Besides, it was too late for someone his age to be studying anything new.

"He had a kind face," Auntie Luo said. "Called me Elder Sister. I could tell by looking at him he was a good man."

"Next to you, he's the kindest person I've ever met."

"If you keep doing what you're supposed to do, everybody will be on your side."

Auntie Luo must have told Political Instructor Xue about her matchmaking attempt, and that bothered him. Political Instructor Xue probably knew more about the whole incident than he did. There must be lots of girls who would refuse to meet anyone who had done time. Auntie Luo knew that, and he wished she wouldn't go around telling people, especially people he respected. Why should other people need to know these things if he didn't? That disgusting bathhouse ticket taker, reeking of soap and water, represented a large group of people who stood before him, ugly, robust, and smug. Fuck 'em all!

Huiquan tore off the newspaper wrapping. The yellow-covered book had cost eighty-five cents. He wasn't thrilled by the title: *Youthful Ideals and Perspectives on Life.* One of those books that put you to sleep before you've read a page. They make you feel as though you were in the presence of a hypocrite who stops you from relieving yourself and then takes a leak right in front of you. But maybe, just maybe, it was worth reading. Political Instructor Xue was certainly no hypocrite. Huiquan read the opening paragraph and promptly laid the book down. Then he wrote to tell the political instructor that he was getting along fine, his neighbors treated him well, he would work hard, and there was nothing to worry about. He didn't mention his love life, suddenly realizing his heart held many secrets about bachelorhood that he could never reveal. Not everything you feel is for public consumption. You can't walk naked down the street. The only way to keep Political Instructor Xue from worrying was to say, "Everything's fine." And to tell him, "I'm looking forward to reading the book . . ."

Huiquan knew he was the hypocrite.

As June gave way to July, the days grew sweltering. The asphalt exhaled suffocating fumes; there was absolutely no wind. Branches weighted down with dusty leaves sagged, and the colors of flowers faded as though made of wax. People showed as much skin as possible—arms, chests, legs, even midriffs—just about everything but their faces, which they covered tenaciously to keep them from baking in the blistering sun. Elderly bodies wilted; young figures blossomed. Soft-drink stands popped up all over the place, selling homemade thirst quenchers that were either so yellow they seemed green or so pink they seemed purple. But the crowds swilled them down even though they had all the appeal of tepid food coloring.

Huiquan's stall at Eastbridge was not in a good location. Being backed up to the road wasn't a problem, but having to look straight into the sun was disastrous. The Eastbridge Department Store blocked the sun midway through the parking lot, but that was several yards from where his awning began. He was directly under the baking sun. Draping the cloth he used as a rear curtain over the awning and moving the clothing racks to the sides helped, but there were no breezes, and the fumes from the hot asphalt floated up unimpeded from the rear.

The Management Office hooked up electric outlets for each stall. Since they were no longer required to share the light or the costs, the vendors could now stay open as late as they wanted. A retired worker sat on a stool and recorded the amount of electricity each vendor used.

Huiquan began doing business at night, since the crowds

seemed to be denser then than during the day. The intersection was a favorite gathering place for people looking for a bit of cool air. Most of them were just browsing, however, and business suffered.

A week had passed since his last visit to the club.

Then, one evening, Liu Baotie, the beat cop, appeared out of the blue in front of his three-wheeler. Seeing the cop there gave him quite a start. There was a serious, even tense, look on Liu Baotie's face.

"We need to talk."

"I . . . What's wrong?"

"Can you close up? I think you'd better. We can talk while we're walking. This isn't the place."

"What have I done?"

"Take it easy, it's not about you."

Liu Baotie smiled, but the look was obviously forced. He helped Huiquan pack up, as though trying to put him at ease. The other peddlers watched nervously until they saw the cop hand Huiquan a cigarette.

They walked together to the entrance of a grocery store, where Liu Baotie stopped. The store was closed, and the two men rested on their haunches in the space between two sets of steps.

"You know someone named Fang Guangde, don't you?"

"Spike Fang? What's wrong with him?"

"What's your relationship with him?"

"Why ask? You already know. It's in my dossier. What's up?"

Huiquan was clearly annoyed. Liu looked him straight in the eye, and the scrutiny was insulting. It must be serious business, and he was a suspect.

Liu Baotie spat. "He ran away from Qinghai."

"He broke out of camp?"

"Let's just say he ran off . . . Was sent to the train station to load coal and hitched a ride. They didn't catch him, so he either got through or jumped a train along the way . . . Just received a telegram."

Liu Baotie looked at him with genuine feeling in his eyes. "Now you see what I mean?"

Huiquan was speechless. His first thought was that Spike was done for this time. Leave it to him to screw up—a coward who winds up stabbing someone; a ladies' man who forces himself on a thirty-year-old peanut vendor; a guy who writes to say he's trying to get his sentence reduced and then pulls a dumb stunt like this. What the hell was he up to?

Huiquan squatted there, virtually stunned. Liu Baotie's expression softened. He patted Li on the shoulder.

"Why get involved with someone who's got shit for brains? How many times did you write?"

"I—"

"Don't worry; we've already been to his house. We're waiting for Qinghai to send what they have, and I wouldn't be surprised if your letters were included. You didn't throw his letters away, did you?"

"No, I've got them."

"How many?"

"Four, I think. They're all there. You'll see when you read them. There's nothing in them—"

"He's not *that* stupid."

"You people think I'm involved, don't you?"

"If we did, I wouldn't be talking to you like this. Bring the letters over tomorrow. And if anything should happen, such as he comes looking for you or you see him somewhere, you know what to do, don't you? You've got my phone number, or you can call the Criminal Investigation Division. Just make sure you don't help him get away or hide him out. Of course, if you catch him, that's even better . . . I doubt if it will come to that. But be on your guard, just in case—"

"I know."

"Huiquan, my boy, make sure you do the right thing!"

"I will."

Liu Baotie left him to go find a girl called Parakeet who had spent a night with Spike. She lived in a dormitory near the railroad tracks at the end of the West Lane of Spirit Run Street. She had a child now and was behaving herself. Huiquan had seen her at the vegetable market and at the milk stand. Would Spike be dumb enough to look her up? No way, and he wouldn't look Huiquan up, either. Not unless he wanted to get his friend into trouble. The cops were overreacting on this one.

Huiquan stopped at the smoke stand to buy a couple of packs of Phoenix cigarettes. With the lights on in Spirit Run Street, the rooftops looked higher and more imposing, and there were more dark corners. Behind a tree, at a bend in the wall, in a shadowy gateway—at any minute someone might spring out at him.

Spike's not that stupid, is he?

After turning into East Lane and walking only a few steps, he spotted a familiar figure. His heart raced and then slowed down. He was standing beneath the light across from the gate at number 18, reading a book. The face was all but identical, but it was only Spike's kid brother. He had grown half a head taller in the six months since their last meeting. Huiquan knew why he'd come. He rang the bell of his three-wheeler, and Little Five's handsome, schoolboy face jerked upward.

"It's about time. Do you know how long I've been waiting—"

"What's that you're reading?"

"English. My mom sent me—"

"Inside. We'll talk inside."

"No, I have to get back to study. Exams coming up . . . My mom wanted me to tell you : . . My brother ran away!"

"You're too late; the cops already told me."

"No, what my mom means . . . After all, well, if my brother comes back to Beijing, he might look you up, and if he does, she hopes you'll help him . . . He's really in hot water now."

"He's goddamn finished, that's what he is. I can't help him. If I tried and got caught, I'd be finished, too."

"No, that's not what my mom means. If he comes looking for you, she wants you to talk him into giving himself up, and if he won't do that, she wants you to turn him in. After all—"

"What else did your mom say?"

"She said . . . she's afraid they might kill my brother. The police are armed these days. She's done nothing but cry the last two days."

"Killing him when they arrest him or executing him later— it's all the same. He's a goner either way. Go home and tell your mom that if he shows up, I'll tie him up for her, and she can come get him to turn himself in."

"You're pretty funny." Little Five had a good laugh over that. He couldn't care less what happened to his brother. All that concerned him was his English exam. "I've gotta go. The exam's in a few days . . . Mom's worried sick, but what good does that do?"

"Do you miss your brother?"

"Nah, he's a jerk who got what was coming to him."

"You look like him, a lot like him."

"That's what the neighbors say. My aunt says my eyes are better looking than his . . ."

He was clearly proud of that, and a little embarrassed. The

fair-skinned brother with the pretty eyes disgusted Huiquan, who felt like kicking him.

But in the end, Spike's mom had reacted like a mother. After all those years of refusing to acknowledge him as her son, not even sending him a letter in prison, she was beginning to worry about him. The love was still there. Either that or she realized he had run away because he missed his family and his home. She would have been right to think that.

In every one of his letters Spike had asked how his mother and father were, and since Huiquan couldn't go into any detail, he just replied that they were fine and then encouraged him to worry more about himself and less about his family.

What had gotten into Spike? What was he thinking when he hitched a ride on that train? Where was he now? Maybe lurking in the shadows nearby! What the fuck was he up to?

Huiquan hadn't the foggiest idea. Since no two people are alike, it's futile to try to figure anyone else out. The mother doesn't understand the son, and the son doesn't understand the mother, so what chance does an outsider have? And if he couldn't solve someone else's riddle, his own was even more elusive. If Spike Fang appeared in front of him at that moment, what would he do with his longtime friend? Knock him senseless and turn him in? Hide him and then report him? Or just tell him to get lost? Still no clue.

Little Five swaggered off, looking just like his brother, taking advantage of the remaining light to study his book. A good student with no capacity for sympathy. He'd go far.

Huiquan smoked a cigarette as he stood next to his gate, lost in thoughts of his friend. Spike did what he did because he was tired of living. There's nothing you can do with someone like that. If dying is what he wants, you might as well accommodate him.

The handsome, girlish face of Huiquan's friend materialized in his mind, however faintly. The inside of his head was like
a wasteland in which Spike's figure careened desperately, like a
starving wolf with nowhere to go, on the verge of collapse.

"Huiquan, your three-wheeler's in the way!"

It was Uncle Luo. A bighead carp weighing several pounds
lay over his bicycle rack: his best catch ever. Air whistled
through the dark gaps between his few remaining teeth, a smug
sound.

"I'm going to throw it in the fridge. Come over and cut off
a piece if you'd like some."

"Where'd you catch it?"

"Ocean Reservoir."

"Nice going!"

"I'm going back tomorrow . . ."

They lived in two different worlds. In Huiquan's world his
friend was on the lam somewhere, and Huiquan was terrified he
would come looking for him. He felt sorry for Spike but had no
intention of helping him out.

The next day he took Spike's letters to the station house.
Liu Baotie introduced him to the chief, who was too busy to talk
at that moment.

"You're at the crossroads between meritorious service and
criminal activity."

A comment he would do well to remember. On his way out
Liu Baotie grabbed him by the sleeve.

"Don't lose your nerve. Just do what you have to do."

He wished he could, but he didn't know how. Figuring he
ought to go to work, he loaded up his three-wheeler but then
promptly unloaded it. Today all he wanted to do was stay home
and do nothing. He stared at the bare walls and listened to the
cicadas outside, feeling confused and unhappy. But when he

went outside, the stream of pedestrians seemed to conceal the very person he wanted not to see. He was frantic that Spike would sneak up behind him and smack him on the shoulder. Anything was possible.

He took a streetcar to the lake at North Sea Park and rented a rowboat. He'd been there before, after learning that singles—male and female—liked taking refuge on the lake. It was exciting and calming at the same time. That could be a sign of loneliness; it could also be a sign of elitist pride. Rowing a boat alone on the deep, blue water can turn the ugliest duckling into a swan. Huiquan rowed the way he looked at the paintings in the art museum: with no particular objective in mind. He just wanted to relax a bit.

He tried to row over to the botanical gardens on the far shore but kept going around in circles, so he took a turn around Jade Island, rising and falling on the swells, his oars slapping the surface of the water awkwardly. The island's white pagoda seemed to be tipping precariously, as though it were about to topple into the lake. The surrounding trees propped it up.

"Let the fucker come if he wants!" he mumbled from the bench of the rowboat. The blinding sun made the water's surface sparkle. A boat glided past. In it was a lone girl in a white skirt. He squinted—he liked what he saw.

Go after her. Strike up a friendship. Why not?

The girl's face was marked, but he couldn't tell whether it was freckled or pockmarked. She was a virgin for sure—an aging, unwanted virgin. He decided to go after her, not to get a closer look, and certainly not to strike up a friendship, but just because he felt like going after her. The tragedy was that he couldn't stop going around in circles.

If he were Spike Fang, he would be able to seduce her easily.

There in a metal boat in the middle of the lake at North Sea

Park, Li Huiquan suddenly felt an overpowering desire for a woman. Grabbing his oars, he stared up at the blue sky. Even the white clouds and the blue water were unspeakably lewd.

Other people out on the lake wore expressions like his. Probably those on the shore did, too. And outside the park. They were everywhere. No two people are exactly alike, but sometimes people are remarkably similar.

"Fuck!"

He spat the word out. What he meant he didn't know. What he was thinking at that moment he didn't know, either. He wore a tranquil look. Tranquillity: mysterious and inscrutable. People sometimes find mysterious, inscrutable faces scary.

People on the shore were staring at him. He stared back. Actually, they were probably staring at someone else. Anyone who seems interested in others is really interested only in himself.

The pockmarked girl had rowed out of sight.

10

Open-air refreshment stands sprang up outside the club on Mill
Road. Bamboo tables and rattan benches were set up beneath
mushrooming umbrellas, all painted white. People stayed home
during the day and came out at night. The curtain across the
plate-glass window was not drawn, so customers sitting alfresco
could watch the performances inside even when the door was
closed because of the air-conditioning. With no sound escaping to
the outside, it looked like a mime show, and Zhao Yaqiu was its
star. She paraded across the stage, mike in hand, looking far more
natural and at ease than ever. Preferring slinky motions to grinding ones, she appeared at first glance to be reading a notice or
giving a speech, except for the way her lips twisted. Pedestrians
frequently stopped to gawk.

"Down in front!"

Customers nursing soft drinks beneath umbrellas weren't
pleased about having their view blocked, and as the curious
sidled out of the way, other passersby looked over their shoulders
at the plate-glass window, attracted by the sight of Zhao Yaqiu
inside.

Huiquan was sitting under the southernmost umbrella, the one closest to the front door and directly opposite the stage, a vantage point from which he could see Zhao Yaqiu's every gesture without moving. He ordered three scoops of ice cream, two of which melted before he had finished the first.

His face was red; he was, in fact, bathed in red. The streetlights had been supplemented by red neon lights installed near the honeycomb screen of the air conditioner—Ordinary, nonflickering lights in the shape of four very interesting words: FIVE GRACES FOUR BEAUTIES.

The gaunt Manager Han was a shrewd character. By immersing the tiny stretch of street in the soft, cleansing rays of red, he added a layer of somberness to the lively atmosphere and made it more elegant. And he could not have chosen a more appropriate advertisement than this popular political slogan, which stressed such notions as decorum, good manners, proper hygiene, and the beautification of mind and behavior.

He bought all his merchandise at cost, although no one knew how he managed it. Cui Yongli had arranged to sell him ten cases of Hundred Springs cola, which had just come on the market and for which the manager had to be obligated somehow. A great deal more went on here than met the eye.

Inside the club a smiling Manager Han was seeing some patrons out as Zhao Yaqiu held the mike up to her lips as though it were a drinking glass. Pretty Boy, her choral classmate, was singing along with her. He was a frail little thing whose expressions were effeminate, or perhaps they were more coquettish than effeminate. A fellow in one of the booths, either drunk or asleep, was pillowing his head on his companion's leg. She could have been his wife, his girlfriend, his mistress, or a casual lover.

The waitresses had begun wearing miniskirts, and when they leaned over to clean the tables, you could see pretty much all the way up. Did even their panties come with the uniform? Another of Manager Han's ideas? The outfit made it easier for him to cop a feel beneath the bar or in the storeroom or behind his desk in the office. He was a bad sort. Anyone who sold coffee for two-fifty a cup had to be.

The plate-glass window was an enormous viewing screen. The people inside looked like caged wild animals moving slowly and gracefully, conserving their strength while they waited for their chance to break free and return to the wild.

Huiquan was shocked when he saw Zhao Yaqiu up close. She was wearing a low-cut black dress that showed plenty of skin, including cleavage. The bodice of the daring dress squeezed her breasts together to create a dark shadow down the middle. In back it revealed her shoulder blades and her spine. Her skin, glistening like shiny porcelain, was made even fairer than usual by the blackness of the dress.

He hardly recognized her. No longer the naive little girl he had once known, she was now the embodiment of self-assurance. But her hairdo was all wrong. She shouldn't have worn it swept back like that. Without bangs her forehead was too conspicuous. And she was wearing too much lipstick, which made her mouth look larger and her teeth more crooked than they actually were. The low-cut, backless dress didn't become her. Anyone as young and innocent as she ought to be more sedate. She should sing with energy, not languor. She wasn't one of those sluts who paraded their sex when they sang.

The ice cream had melted into sticky, sweet goop that dripped through the cracks of the bamboo table and onto the ground. Huiquan would have gone inside to have a drink if the place hadn't been so crowded. Should he leave or stick around awhile? As he tried to make up his mind, he studied his reflection in the window: white shirt, gray slacks, average height, medium build, facial features that were hard to see clearly. He jammed his hands into his pants pockets and shifted one leg to a jaunty angle. Not too bad.

People were looking out the window, but they probably couldn't see anything. He would have been invisible to Zhao Yaqiu if he had stood right next to the glass. Still, he wished she could see him.

Finally he squeezed his way into the take-out section and stood behind a dozen or so people holding soft drinks in their hands—a bunch of head-wagging, self-absorbed pop-music fans. Was the student from Hu Family Tower High School there? Bending slightly at the waist, he searched the corners with his eyes. No, he wasn't there.

"Good to see you! Sorry there aren't any seats. What would you like to drink?"

"Coffee."

"Cream?"

"No."

The waitress smiled. He couldn't remember her name, but she was the first one at the club who ever served him. If he'd been someone else, he might have whispered, "How about taking a walk after you get off?" or, "I could use a new friend, what do you say?" He had seen some of the other regulars flirt with her like that. If they "accidentally" tripped her, she giggled and pummeled them as though she were a spoiled little girl while their hands roamed freely. He'd seen what went on beneath the tables. But she probably wasn't what you'd call a proper girl before she came to work here, anyway.

"Here you go."

"Thanks."

She elbowed her way past him, her skirt brushing against his leg. She had long legs with several nasty-looking mosquito bites above the high heels whose spikes looked as if they might snap at any moment. Another of the manager's ideas? His waitresses' appearance must have been very high on his list of priorities.

The manager is a low-life slug, he concluded.

He looked up just as Zhao Yaqiu glided past. White flesh, black dress—much prettier than the girls who worked there, a thousand times prettier than any other girl he'd ever seen. He gazed at her longingly.

She seemed tired, and the down above her upper lip was damp with perspiration. She had nice, rounded shoulders, and he wondered whether her breasts were holding up the dress. What was she wearing underneath? Panties no bigger than the palm of her hand? She was gorgeous, so nicely filled out—cleavage a foreign woman would be proud of. Is that what she was trying for?

Huiquan was burning up. There was so much sugar in his cup he couldn't taste the coffee. Zhao Yaqiu began her final number:

> The blowing rain wets my umbrella
> My umbrella is a weeping flower
> The mud has dirtied my shoes
> My shoes are sinking boats . . .

Huiquan laid his cup on the windowsill and walked out. The moon was large, round, and bright yellow; there were hardly any stars in the night sky. Pine trees lining the sidewalk rustled softly in the gentle breeze. Shirtless men sat beneath streetlights, playing chess. The world hidden beneath umbrellas now belonged to lovers—no more old folks, no more children. A shout-

ing match erupted in the housing project across the road but soon
died out. He heard a shout but couldn't tell where it came from
or whether it was an angry shout. People sipped their soft drinks
quietly; young couples spoke in muted tones. The boy said something and the girl nodded, or the girl said something and the boy
nodded. They were probably all saying the same things:

"I love you."

"I love you, too."

"Do you really love me?"

"I really do, I love you so much."

"Me, too. I've never loved anyone but you."

"I'll love you forever and always."

"I'm crazy about you."

Was that what they were saying? He'd heard stuff like that
before. No, he'd *read* it—in books. In all kinds of different books
male and female characters engaged in the same dialogue. Over
the past six months or so he'd read several books like that.
Authors of romances didn't have much imagination, but the
plots always provided him with a fresh experience. Someday, he
hoped, he could play a role in such a drama, for he had nothing
against those dry, insipid declarations. Certainly he had never
uttered anything like them—not even once.

How he envied all those lovebirds, who shared so much joy.
To unhappy people their joy was a mockery and an insult. He
loathed them. But only momentarily, for joy is a powerful force,
and in the end it won him over. No one can deny the lure of
happiness. But what is happiness? Is it a kiss?

A couple was doing it out in the open.

He was twenty-five already, yet he had only seen it done:
in a book, in a movie, out in public. His own lips were virgin. He
trembled slightly, a sign of the malice building inside him.

A kiss. She tilts her head way back. He touches her hair and cradles her head in the crook of his arm or between his neck and shoulder. A kiss.

Huiquan turned away, walked over to a poplar tree, squatted down behind it, and lit up. Zhao Yaqiu was bowing now. Pretty Boy straightened out the cord of the mike for her. Scattered applause. She greeted someone as she came down the aisle, her sleek round shoulders caressed by many eyes. The recess of her cleavage was blue. Her wide black skirt swayed gently yet mysteriously.

She went into the take-out section, where Manager Han handed her an envelope across the counter. They exchanged a few light comments as she folded the envelope and slipped it into her beaded shoulder bag. She was saying something, wagging a finger to make her point. Whatever it was, it had Manager Han and the salesgirl in stitches. Pretty Boy stood behind her as if waiting for instructions, a purplish guitar slung across his back. Huiquan saw it all, and the scene set his mind racing like rapidly turned pages in a book.

She walked outside, smiled at her fans, and turned down the street. Under the blue haze of the streetlights her skin lost its luster and seemed thick and coarse. As a Nissan whizzed by, she grabbed Pretty Boy's arm, sort of romantically, and they headed toward the housing project. They walked single file down the cement sidewalk, with her in the lead.

Huiquan then did something that took even him by surprise. Flipping away his cigarette, he darted across the street and ran up to Pretty Boy, tapping him on the shoulder and asking him in a gentle tone to get lost. It was just as he had imagined it while rehearsing in front of the plate-glass window, except he never expected he would be so calm.

"I'm free tonight, so I'll see Little Zhao home."

". . . You are—"

"Don't you remember me?"

The boy was scared silly. It took Zhao Yaqiu a moment or two to recognize Huiquan. She smiled. It obviously took some effort.

"Oh, it's you! I haven't seen you in a long time—"

"I need to talk to you. I'll walk you home."

"Okay. Little Xu, you're off the hook tonight."

Pretty Boy was obviously disappointed, and his shaky nerves betrayed him as he gaped at Huiquan, who stared back menacingly. Zhao Yaqiu pulled Pretty Boy aside and whispered some sort of an explanation to him. She seemed as nervous as he was. Huiquan used the time to go over what he wanted to say to her. But as he was rehearsing his little speech, a flood of extraneous words and thoughts got in the way. Did he have the verbal skills to get his meaning across? He'd find out soon.

The other fellow walked off, looking over his shoulder every few steps.

"You gave me kind of a scare. I haven't seen you around lately. You're not tired of listening to me sing, are you?" She tried to keep her tone casual and her voice steady.

"I've been busy. I'm in a tiring business."

"Life's a tiring business. I'm tired, too." Then she added, as an afterthought, "But I'm making two yuan more a night than before. Did you know that?"

She looked so proud of herself, just like a little girl. Huiquan's throat was bone-dry. The streetlamp shone down, revealing the fine hairs in the shallow furrow that ran the length of her back. She must have those fine hairs all over her body.

"Little Zhao, I think . . . I think you're real special . . . I think . . ."

"I feel the same way. We may not know each other very

well, but you seem sincere and trustworthy. I used to think that life was pointless, but not anymore. Just knowing there are so many people who care about me makes me happy. I mean that—"

"I think—"

"Go ahead, say what's on your mind."

So straightforward—no surprise, no wonder. She'd probably been exposed to this sort of hemming and hawing before and had most likely got used to it. By encouraging him to speak up, she was making it virtually impossible for him to do so. There was a hint of impatience in her aloofness: the fruits of experience. She was clearly a practiced hand at situations like this. Men had spoiled her.

Huiquan's courage began to melt away.

"You don't know what suffering is all about. You're too young—"

"I'm twenty!"

"You used to dress nicely. But I don't much care for—"

"It's too revealing, isn't it? I only wore it to get my mom's goat. But so what, it's just a dress! People look a little more, that's all. It doesn't hurt me. And it's so comfortable in this heat . . ."

"And I'm surprised you'd do your hair like that. The way you used to wear it made you look like the girl next door. It's a pity you had to go and change it . . ."

His heart suffused by a warm current, he wanted to show his gentle side. He was touched by his change in attitude, and he hoped she was, too.

"Really? No one said anything . . . A pity, you say? Okay, I'll change it back . . . You're very observant."

Uncertainly she touched the hair stacked up on her head.

Her shadow on the sidewalk looked as though she were carrying an upturned flowerpot on her head.

The scraping of their feet on the concrete sounded like the maracas on the club synthesizer.

There was even a layer of fine hairs on her forearm.

"You're still young, but you ought to try to be a little more reserved. One mistake can ruin everything. Don't be too trusting. With all the cheats and liars out there, if you're not careful, you could find yourself in big trouble."

". . . I know."

"Whenever you feel that life is pointless, bear up and get past it, no matter what! Don't turn out like me, muddling along, not paying attention to anything. That's why my life is such a mess . . . Don't laugh at me."

"I'm listening."

"You have a bright future ahead of you just as long as you work hard and keep your goal in sight. You have a nice voice—don't squander it . . ."

"I appreciate the advice. I never really thought . . . never in my life . . . really . . ."

She giggled. What was so funny? This had not been easy for Huiquan, even though it seemed to come off so naturally and without sounding threatening. He had nothing more to say. Either that or he didn't know how to put the rest of his thoughts into words.

Zhao Yaqiu was still giggling. He stopped walking. The closer they drew to her home, the less time he had to salvage his dignity. This time he didn't want to leave feeling ashamed of himself. He had spoken from the heart; there was nothing phony or manipulative about what he said.

"What are you laughing at?"

"Nothing—"

"Come on, tell me."

"I'm laughing . . . You sound like my dad, that's all. Even the words are the same."

Huiquan's heart seemed suddenly drained of everything but a residue of foolishness. He stole a glance at the fullness of her breasts and shoulders and had to admit that he liked her in this dress. What he found unbearable was the way everyone else leered at her. Waves of excitement flowed through his heart, here one moment, gone the next. He cast an agonizing glance at the slight arch of her hips, and all he could think of was how he would like to caress the furrow of her naked back. He wanted to kiss her.

Actually there were lots of things he wanted to do, and he had to keep shouting to himself inside, I'm not a phony, I'm not a hypocrite! I was sincere! But at that instant he was forced to confront his own naked desires. His palms were sweaty.

"Do you know you're being followed by a student from Hu Family Tower High School?" He took a look around.

"I know. He wrote to me in high school. At first I felt sorry for him, but then his letters started getting out of hand, like he was some kind of hooligan."

"He likes the way you sing."

"I've got lots of friends, but they're not guttersnipes like him."

That comment hit him hard. The boy's a guttersnipe because of you! he thought. He loves you. He can't think about anything but you, so he's become a guttersnipe! Dejection was setting in.

"I wonder if he's around tonight?" he asked.

"I doubt it. A friend of mine scared him away. He wouldn't dare cause any more trouble."

Huiquan opened his mouth, but no words came. How about him: was he causing trouble? Did he have any more nerve than that pathetic, lovesick little boy? If he had any backbone, he would grab her by the shoulders, pour his feelings out to her, and then kiss and nuzzle her. She needed a man who would dominate her. She was a spoiled girl in need of some rough treatment, but he wasn't the one to give it to her.

"I really appreciate the advice. I have lots of friends, but some of them are just out for what they can get. But I've got their number. I haven't been a singer all these years, including my time in school, for nothing. They don't scare me. I know it won't be easy, but I'm going to make it in this business. I won't rest until I do! . . . Well, thanks for seeing me home. You don't have to bother tomorrow. Let Little Xu do it. His feelings are so fragile he's always threatening to kill himself. I have to humor him—"

"He's too high-strung for his own good."

"I don't like his type."

"He's got a pretty fair voice."

"He has no future in this business. But he's okay as a friend . . . Well, good night!"

She nearly flew into the apartment building, the hem of her dress flapping like dark feathers. As the exposed parts of her body moved away from him and into the circle of light in front of the building, they recaptured their porcelain gloss. She was clean and fresh, like a new blossom. But she had shown a callous side, which he found scary. How many twenty-year-old girls were capable of holding someone in contempt without being obvious about it? What sort of soul lay hidden inside that seductive body? There was really no difference between her and the woman who worked in the bathhouse. All his encounters with women could be summed up in that one emasculating comment: "Is that really necessary?"

No, not really. All his muddleheaded advice had been a waste of time and emotions. He was like a clown whose purpose in life was to serve her whims. Outside of giving her a good slap across the face, tearing off her clothes, and ravishing her for his own wild pleasure, nothing was really necessary. If the world were to end today, that's precisely what he would do, just to see how fragile her regal airs really were.

As he was leaving the housing project, he remembered he had left his bicycle back at the club, so he retraced his steps. Pine trees lining the sidewalk cast rows of shadows. People sitting outside to cool off were starting to head home. Old folks were coughing. As he concentrated on his senses, he discovered lingering traces of Zhao Yaqiu: her perfume, her footprints, leaves she had plucked from branches, echoes of her voice—there but not there, real yet unreal. Reminded of the soft down above her lip, he shivered. He had lost something, lost it forever, but it hadn't belonged to him in the first place. He had made a fool of himself—again.

Was this the thing called love that he had seen, heard about, read about, guessed at, and thought about? Back home he lay uncovered on the cool bed mat and tried to sleep. But images of that face had him tossing and turning. A series of savagely violent thoughts—rape and worse—shattered his peace. He was crushed.

During the latter part of July he stayed away from the club altogether, having lost interest in the place. By now he opened his stall only after dark and for no more than four hours at a stretch. The rest of his time he spent reading, watching chess matches in the park, and attending furniture and automobile shows. He would have joined an aerobics class if it hadn't been so far from home.

Spike hadn't appeared, and there was no news of him. But

Liu Baotie was still on the case, and Huiquan saw him every time he went to the office of the Neighborhood Committee. He gave the cop an extra theater ticket once, but since he was too busy to go, Huiquan was stuck watching the movie with Liu Baotie's girlfriend, who, he noticed, didn't stop feeding her face from the time the movie began. First it was candy, then melon seeds. Huiquan thought that was pretty comical, but he never said so to anyone. This was a match made in heaven, at least as far as she was concerned. When the lights were out, she took off her shoes, and the faint odor of pickled radishes wafted up from under her seat. Poor Liu Baotie.

Ma Yifu hadn't been by to see Huiquan either. After he left with the borrowed four hundred yuan, it was as if the earth had swallowed him up. Huiquan couldn't help thinking that his friend had played him for a sucker. Consideration for one's fellow humans was becoming an endangered species, as an item in the evening paper made abundantly clear: a man somewhere had poured scalding water over his aging mother's head to show his anger over her refusal to die. Beasts in the wild don't do things like that.

Shortly after Cui Yongli returned from the free economic zone of Shenzhen in early August, he dropped by Huiquan's stall at Eastbridge to invite him to dinner at the house at Sha Family Inn. Cui's beard was as full as ever, but his face was gaunt, his skin dark and sunburned. His languid movements showed how weary he was, like a man who had just emerged from an exhausting fight.

Huiquan assumed the man wanted something from him.

He showed up Saturday afternoon. He was the only guest. The meal was cooked and served by the two girls from the countryside, who sounded and looked so much alike he had trouble telling them apart. The taller of the two kept making eyes at him, but since she didn't appear to be a very respectable girl, he didn't give it a second thought. The wine was good, the food wasn't bad, and Cui Yongli played the role of friend to the hilt, entertaining Huiquan with fascinating anecdotes about his trip. His mood seemed lighter than any he'd been in in a long time. Huiquan could tell he was no stranger to loneliness and that, like him, he had few friends.

They were about halfway through dinner when Cui dragged Huiquan into the bedroom and pointed to two cardboard soapboxes stacked against the wall. They were filled with rectangular black boxes: videocassettes, dozens of them.

"This is what you call southern water for northern fields. Dirty water, that is!"

"What's that supposed to mean?"

"They're ninety yuan apiece in Guangzhou, but you can sell them for ten times that up north in Qiqihar. What do you say to that?"

The room was furnished with a double bed that was littered with pillows in terry-cloth pillow covers. Three pairs of slippers, all of different sizes, were lined up next to the bed. A sofa had been pushed up against the wall, next to a TV stand. The rear window was sealed with bricks; the one on the opposite wall was covered with a thick purple curtain. The room felt damp and murky.

Cui Yongli was visibly excited.

"Eighty of them. Twenty originals and sixty copies. I have to get rid of them fast. These things can stick to you if you're not careful."

"So that's what you're up to."

"That and other things."

"Including secondhand clothes?"

The question was tossed off so nonchalantly Cui didn't detect the sarcasm right away.

"Not much, and most of it goes west to Lanzhou and Yinchuan. It's too risky in Beijing."

"That doesn't bother me. I can use seven or eight more bags if you've got them. I did okay last time."

"Don't give me that, man! I'm not going to let a pal of mine deal in that junk. There are other ways to make money if you've got the balls, man. All the roads are open."

"Selling used clothing is one thing, but this stuff . . ." Huiquan shook his head.

They returned to the outer room and recommenced drinking. Huiquan's eyes swept the tea table, the desk, and the windowsill. He was looking for the slick magazine he'd seen the last time. He was ashamed of himself when he realized what he was doing.

Cui lit a cigarette for him.

"Come with me next time, what do you say? Just once."

"Where to?"

"Jiamusi and places like that up north. The people there are ripe for the picking, just waiting for us to come up and relieve them of their cash. Sex goes over big in cold climates. They love these things. I know my way around there. Come along with me. You won't be sorry, I guarantee it."

"Don't you do just fine by yourself?"

"I've got too many this time, and I think my nerve is slipping a little. Things happen sometimes. I knew a guy from Zhejiang dealing in tea who was cut up bad. Just thinking about it sends chills up my spine. There are people these days who will kill you for a couple of hundred yuan, and if they see you with a big wad, they'll have you for breakfast."

"I can't go."

Cui was refilling his glass, and his hand froze in midair.

"You don't have to give me an answer right away. Think it over first."

"There's no way I can go."

"Why not? Won't you give me a little face—"

"The cops are watching me."

"Why, what did you do?"

"Nothing. A friend of mine doing time in Qinghai escaped, and the cops think he might try to look me up. They come to see me every couple of days, so I have to stay close."

"Too bad . . ." Cui sighed. "Well, there's always next time. You ought to try it at least once. Who knows, maybe we can become partners. What do you say?"

"I don't work as anybody's bodyguard."

"Who said anything about a bodyguard?"

"I like to work alone. It takes the worry out of things. If I can't figure somebody out or they can't figure me out, it just makes things hard. No, working alone is the answer."

"You're one stubborn motherfucker! Aren't you interested in getting ahead? I could make the same offer to the first person I met on the street, and he'd drop dead he'd be so happy. You can't help but make a killing on this!"

"Get someone else. I can't go."

"Shit! I would if I could. What monastery do you do your monking in?"

The booze was beginning to effect Cui, who dribbled some sauce down the front of his shirt. He kept refilling Huiquan's bowl and glass, but his words had taken on a rough edge. Huiquan was too busy stuffing his mouth with cold sliced-jellyfish salad to notice. It was a lot better than the salad he made at home.

Don't get sucked in! Huiquan cautioned himself. You don't know a thing about this guy, so there's no way to tell whether he's telling the truth or not. They were both regulars at the club, and they were both private entrepreneurs. Both liked to work independently yet enjoyed having someone to talk to when things weren't going well. That's where the similarities ended. If Cui had been cheated out of a bundle— say, twenty grand—on one of his trips and wanted to entice Huiquan into being his avenger, he was in for a rude awakening. He didn't know Li Huiquan very well if he thought he could get away with that. It was all hypothesis, of course, but it could be true. Cui Yongli's asking him to go along on the trip had the feel of beggars can't be choosers. Obviously he'd taken a beating of some sort and was in desperate need of someone to bail him out.

Don't get sucked in. Don't!

Huiquan kept drinking even after the room began to spin. Cui said it was Five-Grain wine, and Huiquan's taste buds told him it was the real thing. In this regard, at least, Cui was on the up-and-up. Full-bodied. Good stuff.

The streetlights came on as Huiquan went to the toilet out in the yard. He nearly puked. When he returned, Cui laughed, a bizarre chuckle, and helped him over to the sofa. He turned on the TV set.

Colors immediately leapt across the screen. And there was music. *Blah-blah-blah.* People talking. Laughter. Foreigners, it sounded like.

Huiquan's stomach lurched.

"Stick around. You can sleep here. I'll sleep in their room . . . Ever see one of these before?"

More laughter. Men and women talking.

"Hot shit!" Cui stomped his feet.

A scream. Heavy breathing. Mumbles and moans. The images on the screen flickered crazily.

"Same old shit . . . Horny horseplay."

Cui yawned and walked up to the TV. Static drowned out the other sounds. He ejected the cassette and inserted another one. Exotic music began, its strong beat gradually softening until it was replaced by ocean sounds and then followed by erotic mewing.

"You go ahead and watch it, I'm going to turn in. This'll run an hour. If you don't want to watch, don't worry, it'll shut off automatically . . . You look pretty turned on!"

With the lights off, bright splashes of color exploded from the TV screen, bleeding and shifting.

Huiquan felt like puking again. He had polished off a good seven ounces of strong liquor, six at the very least. It had been a long time since he'd drunk that much hard stuff.

Cui tossed a pack of cigarettes onto the sofa.

"Why don't I have one of them come over to keep you company? It's no big deal. Live a little!" He patted the bed. "Don't worry, they're clean! Pretty good, too. Give 'em a try, and you'll see what I mean. But nothing kinky, okay? Well, what do you say? It's up to you. I'm just trying to be a fucking buddy."

He staggered out of the room. He was pretty well gone, too, it seemed to Huiquan, who opened his eyes as wide as possible. Everything was still blurry. His stomach lurched. The TV images mystified him. Are these human beings?

His hearing was still functioning pretty well. The woman's moans cut like knives, making his heart throb painfully. Beauty or ugliness? He was repulsed yet perversely stimulated. All these years had he treated his body too well or not well enough? So that's how people do it. Now he knew. Up till now no matter how wildly his imagination ran, it had been nothing more than juvenile musings. Twenty-five years down the drain.

Human beings instinctively act like animals. Human beings *are* animals. That white dude with the mustache and a dick like a horse's—what was he if not an animal? Would anyone feel sorry for him if I butchered him like a hog? Huiquan wondered. The woman would probably laugh her ass off. If she didn't kill him, he'd kill her. Sooner or later that's what it would come to. Sex and violence all wrapped up in one. Their depravity transcended human nature.

But the long-legged woman was the most beautiful creature he'd ever seen. He turned to jelly, letting her conquer him.

One of the peasant girls walked in to light the mosquito coil. It took several matches to do the job. She was the taller of the two, the one who had opened the gate for him on his first visit. During dinner she had smiled at him each time she brought in a new dish. She looked so vulnerable.

Instead of leaving after pouring him some tea, she climbed into bed and began undressing.

"What are you doing?"

"Yongli told me to sleep here."

"What the hell for?"

"Bed or sofa?"

Huiquan was too confused to know what to say. She laughed lightly and lay back without another word.

Sounds continued to emerge from the TV. Huiquan walked over to turn it off but couldn't find the switch.

"Next to the red light," the girl said. "Turn it to the left."

Silence took over. The stillness inside and outside the room merged; the air was the only thing moving. The girl's skin made a scratchy sound against the mat, and he could feel it rubbing against his eardrum. With shaky hands he lit a cigarette. Now that his eyes were used to the dark, he could see the seductive outline of the girl on the bed.

He didn't think he was up to it, not even if he were sober. He couldn't do it. Maybe in his dreams he could manage some of the actions, but awake it was out of the question. He was scared. No, it was more than that—revulsion had won out over the desire swelling inside him. He wanted to do it, and he had prepared for this moment. But with a decent girl, not some cast-off bitch.

Cui Yongli's money had bought her, so let him have her.

He stood up and walked to the door, careening into the wall before he got there. The girl sat up, startled.

"Come to bed! If you don't want . . . Get some sleep, at least."

A real peasant girl. Naive, sensuous, daffy. Younger than Zhao Yaqiu, by the looks of her. Where did that thought come from? What would he have done if it had been Zhao Yaqiu lying there? Would he have been as diffident, as put off, as he was now?

He needed to get out of there fast.

"Tell Cui I don't appreciate this. I've seen . . ."

What had he seen? He for one didn't know. Feeling suddenly remorseful, he added, "You get some sleep. I have to go home . . . I'll close the gate behind me, so you don't have to see me out."

The girl sat still in bed.

Huiquan located his bicycle in the yard and after several attempts managed to open the lock. A figure as silvery as a fish in the moonlight, propelled by shuffling slippers, followed him to the gate and unlocked it for him.

"Don't you want to tell Yongli you're leaving?"

"No."

"Well, take care."

"You, too."

She flashed a smile. Was it gratitude? If not, she must have thought he was the biggest jerk who ever lived. Maybe she was right.

Fuck you, Cui Yongli!

He stumbled along, pushing his bicycle onto the dirt road, a curse on his lips. The night air carried a mixture of odors: soil, manure, crops, and limestone from the construction site. He was out of danger, but that didn't make him feel particularly good. All sorts of creatures, half-human and half-animal, were committing shameful acts under the cover of darkness; unusual sounds that made his ears burn emerged from the apartment buildings under construction and from the untended fields.

Oh, how he envied that foreign man.

11

It was unbearably hot. During the day there was no place to hide from the heat, and at night it was impossible to sleep. The couple in the west wing fought like cats and dogs, with milk bottles sailing into the yard in the morning and teapots flying at night. When they were fighting, even though the language was veiled, it was clear that the wife was no woman of virtue. While working the night shift at a dairy plant, she apparently had been caught in the locker room with a male co-worker.

"You sure can pick 'em!"

"Yeah, so what!"

"You fucking whore, I'll show you!"

"And where will you find the balls? You're the king of hot air, that's what you are . . ."

Crash! Clang! A washbasin landed in the yard while Huiquan was at the faucet brushing his teeth. That's how lots of married couples live, he thought, when love has died.

"Help!"

The pug-dog shrieked in terror as she ran down the path and into the rear compound, followed closely by a man with sleep in his eyes and a cleaver in his hand. She tore around the yard like a terrified chicken, the cleaver slicing the air behind her.

"Grab him, Huiquan!"

Auntie Luo, right on their heels, was hysterical. Huiquan's first thought was to trip the husband, but someone might get hurt, so he hit the arm brandishing the cleaver with his enamel mug instead, splashing water all over the place. The man, named Yin, was in his late thirties, and Huiquan's only contact with him had been when it was time to pay the utility bill. Now he had his arms wrapped tightly around him.

"You son of a bitch! This doesn't concern you, so butt out!"

Huiquan pinned him up against the wall. The man's face was white with rage.

"Are you going to let me go or not, you son of a bitch?"

"Who are you calling names?"

"Anybody who doesn't mind his own business, that's who!"

Huiquan released him. The "loving couple" glared at each other and then walked off in single file. What had that been about?

"Forget it—don't get mad! Just write it off as bad luck to have neighbors like that!" Auntie Luo was trying to calm Huiquan down. How could people be *that* stupid? Worse than dogs or pigs. Stupidity—it's everywhere you look. Better to let them kill each other off, since each dead one means one less to worry about.

He knew he would rather be dead than spend the rest of his life with a woman like that. Auntie Luo was still trying to find someone for him, and he couldn't help wondering what sort of woman it would be. If fate had already picked her out, what was she doing right now? Fighting and shrieking like some hideous shrew? Walking down the street sucking on an ice? Reading in bed? Receiving the accolades of her audience after singing a lovely song? Hardly.

No, she was probably strolling with someone else at that very moment, maybe even carrying on with him, at least until he tossed her aside and she waited for Huiquan to pick her up on the rebound. Man predicts, but fate decides.

He was too troubled to sleep that night; angry shouts from the front compound beseiged him, loud one minute, soft the next, on again, off again, playing a definite role in setting his nerves on edge. He was just itching to use his fists.

"I'm not finished with you!"

"Let's see what you've got!"

"I've got a life, that's what!"

"I've heard that before! If you had any balls, you'd take it out on him, not on me. Real men aren't wife beaters."

"I'll kill the son of a bitch!"

"That I'd like to see."

Huiquan soaked the bed with his sweat. He was sorely tempted to take his rolling pin out to the front compound—one good blow on each head ought to do the trick. As he imagined that scene, his mood mellowed, but what really did the trick was the thought of seeing the woman gag as he crammed his rolling pin down her throat. That's what she deserved. That's what all the shrews in the world deserved. As for Yin, he should kill his wife and then himself. Seeing that wimpy bastard puff himself up like that was more than he could bear.

Huiquan was still a bachelor, the envy of many. But lying alone on a blistering summer night to sweat and sigh and have wild thoughts was not his idea of happiness. Happy people didn't cut a sorry figure like this.

A Great Wall electric fan sat on the table. It had crapped out a week after he bought it, and now he'd have to get it fixed. That thought opened a floodgate. He would have to get someone to repair the leak in his bedroom ceiling. A TV set: should he get black-and-white or color? The consignment store had a twelve-inch set for only 230, which was plenty good for a bachelor, but now that he was out of the habit of watching TV, why should he start up again? Maybe what he really needed was a washing machine. He didn't like washing clothes but had to do it because if he didn't, Auntie Luo would, and he couldn't let that happen. If he couldn't get the ceiling repaired, he'd have to do it himself, since the leak was getting worse, and sooner or later the whole thing would cave in. But who could he get to help him? So many jobs to take care of, so many things requiring his attention. Lately he had become pretty self-reliant, and the sense of helplessness that had gripped him soon after getting out of camp was now just a bad memory.

What to do tomorrow? Jog in the morning. Then pay taxes, and see what's available at the wholesale outlet. Have soup for lunch at Dongsi, and then go to the Yuqing Bathhouse for a bath and a haircut. In the afternoon have the fan repaired and buy a magazine. Cook dinner. Set up the stall at six-thirty. Be home and in bed by ten-thirty.

Now that the next day's schedule was settled, Huiquan's worries were temporarily taken care of. All those tomorrows had matured him; one by one he'd gotten through them. They held neither fear nor joy. When all was said and done, the vast majority of days provided little that was new. For confirmation he had only to observe people during the dog days or listen to the couple in the west wing curse and scream at each other. Life—there it was in a nutshell.

Precious few tomorrows strayed from the norm.

One August afternoon it began to rain, so Huiquan stayed

home. By eight o'clock the storm had passed, leaving a cool night in its wake. After flipping through the newspaper for a while, he decided to take in a movie at the Chaoyang Workers' Recreation Club, where a local soft drink he was particularly fond of was sold. He had neither seen nor heard of the movie, which was entitled *The Judge.*

It turned out to be a Syrian film and was sold out. Still, a crowd lingered around the ticket booth, where tickets that sold for thirty-five cents were being scalped for as much as sixty, even eighty, cents by people clutching wads of them in their hands. Huiquan bought one, then squatted on the sidewalk to have a smoke until the current show let out. He studied the feet and legs passing in front of him. Rain puddles on the stones and asphalt glistened like crystal. It was a fine August evening.

Suddenly he heard a familiar voice. Looking up, he spotted Ma Yifu.

"Well, yes or no? You want to see it or not? If it's too rich for your blood, make room for somebody else!"

The errant tooth made Yifu very ugly. The mole above his right eye was like a beetle that had fastened itself onto his face and was wriggling above the insolent words emerging from his mouth. He was quite a bit thinner than before.

"Brushes!"

Out of habit Yifu tried to hide the tickets he was holding, but it was too late. He shuffled over with a sheepish look on his face.

"What are you doing here?"

"I could ask you the same thing. Up to your old tricks, I see."

"What can I say . . . Got any smokes on you? What time is it? I came over right after work, without even stopping to eat—"

"You asked for it!"

Huiquan handed him a pack of cigarettes. Yifu lit one and tucked a couple more into the pocket of his T-shirt.

"Broke again?"

"You know how it is. I'd rather not talk about it."

"You're supposed to be getting married on October first, and you're still out scrounging money? Why not call it off for now?"

"Already did—"

"You've lost weight."

"I've got one foot in the grave. How's business? I didn't have the nerve to go over there empty-handed. I'm surprised to see you here . . . Pay you back . . . later."

"Fuck off! Who said you had to pay me back?"

"That's not right—"

"Get rid of those tickets. Here, sell mine, too. Hold on to a pair next to each other, and we'll watch it together."

"You go ahead. I'll be selling these right up to show time. The longer they wait, the more it costs them. The sluts love to be kissed and felt up in the dark. It beats the hell out of the park . . ."

This he said in a raised voice, drawing giggles from the other scalpers. But there was pain in his eyes; his cheerfulness was all an act.

Huiquan had never dreamed that the prospect of marriage could have such devastating effects on a person.

"How's your friend?"

"Same as always. She said she saw you once at Eastbridge."

"What are her tastes in clothes? Tell her to come see me."

"She's too fat to look good in anything. You still alone?"

His casual question stung like a whip. No one had ever asked him this before, and just hearing it felt strange. Was there really any need to ask? He smiled.

"So, you *have* got someone!"

"I haven't got shit!"

"Well, if you don't have anyone, I'll see what I can do. That's what friends are for. Have a little fun, and see where it goes. Don't make life hard on yourself, not at your age—"

"Go fuck yourself! The show's out. Can't you find something else to do? This sucks!"

"Don't get me started. I know what I'm doing . . . Go on in. See you later. I've got twenty tickets to move . . . Tickets here, eighty cents apiece . . ."

The crowd surged around him. The recreation club was a sea of heads, inside and out.

"One yuan apiece! Take it or leave it! One yuan apiece! They're going fast. One yuan . . ."

The movie was boring and insipid. The print was in terrible shape, and the actors' weeping was like that of Chinese actors— phony and creepy. But the young couples went ahead with what they'd come to do or hoped they could get away with. Every once in a while there was some scattered applause—a display of contempt for the plot.

Huiquan left before it was over, and as he squeezed down the narrow aisle, he had to negotiate his way past the tangled limbs of young lovers, like the exposed roots of a tree. Some had even draped their legs across vacant seats, making the scene look like a logjam. This wasn't the first time he'd seen something like this, but for some reason it irritated him more this time. Lust weaved in and out of his heart. He felt like lashing out at someone. He was feeling that way more and more often these days. Always looking for an excuse.

Yifu was resting under the marquee, smoking a cigarette. Both men tensed.

"You still here?" Huiquan said as he walked up to him.

"I went out and had a couple of bowls of wontons. I need to talk to you about something. I've been waiting an hour—"

"The movie was boring. What do you want to talk about?"

"I guess it's best just to tell you the truth."

"The truth about what?"

"That money you loaned me . . . I lost it."

"Lost it?"

"Gambling. I really was going to buy a cassette recorder, but then I ran into someone and figured that the most I could lose was four hundred, and maybe I'd win. But I lost it and then made things worse by trying to win it back . . ."

Mystified, Huiquan could only stare at him.

"How much did you lose altogether?"

"Over six hundred, not counting yours. I've paid back a hundred by scalping tickets. I'm really in a jam now!"

"Who'd you lose it to?"

"Some guys I met playing poker at Temple of the Earth."

"Where do they live?"

"All over, and the games are held in various places. You don't snitch on these people."

"Then why tell me?"

"Because I need to tell somebody. They come after me every couple of days for their money. I sure can't say anything to my girlfriend, and I don't dare tell my dad. I can't pay them back, and I'm afraid I'll get hauled in for scalping . . . I've really had it this time . . ."

He squatted down and buried his face in his hands.

"Scalping tickets to pay off a debt is better than gambling. Are you still at it?"

"I . . ."

"I asked you a fucking question!"

"Go ahead, Basher, kick the shit out of me . . . I won't

gamble anymore, I won't, okay? You can ask around. I won't gamble anymore, I won't, okay?''

"Do you gamble away the money you get from scalping?"

Yifu nodded. Huiquan reached down and grabbed him and then started dragging him toward the Workers' Stadium. Breathing hard, Yifu was soon sobbing. He fell apart altogether.

"Your so-called October first wedding is all a pile of shit, isn't it?"

"Yeah."

"You were hooked on gambling when you borrowed that money from me, thinking you could get away with treating me like some kind of idiot, didn't you?"

"I don't deserve a friend like you—"

"You want me to bail you out again, so you can pay off your gambling debts, isn't that right? You get a kick out of pissing my money away, don't you?"

"If you help me this time, I'll never forget you—"

"Cram it up your ass!"

"You've got to save me!"

"I said, cram it up your ass!"

"Yell at me, hit me, beat me half to death if you want to. But you've got to save my ass. I deserve it, I admit it! I've got no pride left . . . Hit me, go ahead . . .''

Yifu was standing on his tiptoes so Huiquan wouldn't rip the collar of his shirt. Basher's hand was shaking like a leaf. He was having trouble breathing, and that scared the hell out of Yifu, who wiped his eyes and looked up. His protruding tooth sparkled in the soft overhead light.

Crack! Huiquan punched him in the face. The sound echoed through the pine grove with eerie power in the rain-swept air of that summer night. Yifu landed in the mud, his back smacking into a metal barrier that surrounded a grassy knoll. He said nothing but stopped crying.

Huiquan bent over and hit him again, but Yifu warded off the second blow with his arm. "Ouch! Not in the face. I have to work tomorrow—"

"You lied to me!"

Huiquan backed up. His hand ached. After years of staying out of fights, the pain felt strange and unfamiliar. Brushes was his friend. How could he hit his own friend?

But his friend had lied to him! What was he supposed to do? He had no honest-to-goodness friends.

Yifu rose to his knees, rubbing his face, and then stood up shakily. Bicycles whizzed back and forth beyond the pine trees; someone was having a conversation on the sidewalk. Water dripped from the branches of the trees.

Huiquan was thinking back to the time several years before when he had hit Ma Yifu the first time. One swing of his rolling pin had brought out the white flag, without a trace of embarrassment: "I give up! I give up!" Ever since then Brushes had treated him well enough. Having been a coward for as long as he could remember, he had joined the gang for prestige. Like him, Brushes was going nowhere fast; they were two pathetic men who would never amount to anything, no matter how long they lived. Gambling is the best possible way for a so-called clever guy to show just how stupid he really is.

Yifu held up two fingers. Huiquan tossed him the whole pack. As Yifu lit up, Huiquan saw trickles of blood and a cut lip.

"How much can you give me this time?" He finally got around to asking the big question.

"Two hundred. Not a penny more. And you pay me back within a year. Not a penny less."

"You got it."

"And if I catch you gambling again?"

"Whatever you say. Middle finger, right hand—"

"You said it. If you gamble again, don't wait for me to chop it off, do it yourself. If you think you can make a sucker out of me again, you're in for a rude awakening!"

"The money—"

"Pick it up at the stall tomorrow night."

Inexplicably Yifu's shoulders began to heave, and he was sobbing again. Huiquan turned and walked off, saddened by his friend's plight and upset at having been deceived.

Thunder rolled in the distance, but you couldn't tell where it was coming from. The dark night seemed to be in motion. Huiquan suspected Yifu might be putting on another act. If he tricked him once, what would keep him from doing it again?

Yifu was probably laughing at him right now for being such a simpleton. Sometimes you have to be wary when people cry. Tears prove nothing. Brushes could have been planning his next bet while the tears were flowing.

All because of that chunky, snobbish female. But then again, maybe he got a kick out of living on the edge. Who can tell what goes on in the mind of a five-foot-tall adult male? The feeblemindedness and general stupidity of people going nowhere is as varied as the people themselves, which makes true understanding impossible. Yifu was a mystery to him, but he suspected that Ma Yifu had somehow managed to figure him out.

Maybe that's where other people were smarter than he.

They met at stall South 025 the next night, as planned. Huiquan tossed over an envelope, and Yifu ripped it open. He counted the contents twice. His gratitude equaled that of a man dying of thirst as he first catches sight of water. The swelling on his face was barely noticeable, unlike the iodine that had been daubed on his cut lip.

Huiquan set up his clothing racks.

"This time next year pay me back on this very spot."

"You got it! I'm through gambling—"

"I don't want to hear anymore of your bullshit."

"If I gamble again, I'm a slug. And don't worry, you'll be invited to my wedding—"

"I'll believe that when it happens."

"Basher, no matter what I have to do to get it, I'll pay you back, even if I have to sell my wok for scrap metal!"

Huiquan waved him off impatiently. He didn't believe a word of it. You don't trust someone who has already tricked you once. Their friendship was history. From now on, if Ma Yifu was in a jam, Huiquan would look on with folded arms; and if the day ever came when Yifu brought harm to him in any way, he would pull out all the stops in dealing with him.

Those two punches in the pine grove had probably neither clarified nor resolved anything—a case of too little too late. Huiquan knew it wouldn't take much for him to resort to his old ways. So what if he had no home, no parents, and no girlfriend? He could always find ways to cheer himself up, just as he could always find ways to make others respect and fear him: he could do what he had done when he was younger.

He still remembered the gang fight at Daxiaoting, which he had joined at the request of Spike to help out a friend of a friend. He didn't know a soul on either side but wound up the center of attention. Disdaining all their bicycle chains, lead shots, switchblade knives, baseball bats, sharpened forks, and bricks, he broke down their resistance with his date-wood rolling pin. He was an eagle spreading its wings and soaring above the crowd while his prey scurried beneath him like frightened jackrabbits. A brief but intense feeling of satisfaction surged through him until he really did feel as though he had sprouted wings and everyone was looking at him enviously. With that sort of attitude, winning a fight was child's play.

Later on he had shown up at the New Overseas Restaurant as the guest of both sides; there was dried blood on his face from a brick that had grazed his forehead—his badge of honor. He was puffed up with pride. Normally he said nothing at parties and hardly ever smiled, since he busied himself with eating and drinking. He had always been a drinker, not a talker. He particularly enjoyed that giddy buzz that preceded intoxication. He had earned the nickname Basher because he shared many of the qualities of his rolling pin: solid, unyielding, no-nonsense; and like his rolling pin he was cold, uncomplicated, and menacing. He was eighteen at the time, at the peak of his courage and power—an eighteen-year-old fighter who had run the gauntlets of hell. Having no clear idea of what he was up to, during those insouciant days he never gave a moment's thought to the consequences of his actions.

Maybe his deeds had brought him happiness, and maybe they were luring him back now. In the space between frenetic selflessness and extreme concern for his own well-being, he experienced the intoxication of freedom to do as he pleased; he knew he was incapable of controlling himself anyway, even if he had wanted to. Back then fighting had been his element, his haven from agitation, loneliness, and the dread of emptiness. But now that he was twenty-five, he could no longer find that haven, for it was submerged in a disheartening past.

He was an asshole, no question about it.

Whereas other people's quests proceeded from lives of quiet

knowledge, his was linked to violence; while other people always ended up with bouquets, he invariably came up empty-handed. The girl with down above her upper lip continued to frequent his dreams, night and day, but he did nothing to win her favor. On the surface he was free of desires and aspirations, but flowing underneath were lustful currents. Having his own approaches to autoeroticism, he remained indifferent to the temptations of the female body, becoming a paragon of passivity.

After tacitly encouraging a friend hardly worthy of the name to cheat him, he had attempted to preserve his odd sense of self-respect by resorting to the primitive use of fists. Knowing fully that the fellow at Sha Family Inn was shady, he had continued to seek out his company, as though by drinking with him he was drawing closer to the secrets of life—assuming he believed in such a thing, which he didn't.

The one thing he did believe in was a complete mystery: fate. Fate had been the cause of his abandonment, fate had made him an orphan and one of the army of the doltish. Diverting it was out of the question, and he could only follow where it led.

Only after Yifu left did Huiquan realize he had neglected to mention the repairs needed in his house. In the past he had relied on Hobo to help with things like bricklaying and plastering; now there was no one left to ask but Ma Yifu. And he was alienating even him. Who then? Liu Baotie? He was a cop, and you didn't ask cops for help.

He was like a damaged ship limping into port. He had no friends. Cui Yongli was certainly not one—he could be counted on to pile rocks in the cabin of Huiquan's sinking ship. A sinister man, Whiskers cared about no one but himself. By being a loner, he was spared the necessity of true friendships and the trust they engendered. Every pore in his bearded face oozed deceit.

Cui went by himself to the Northeast, where at a successful privately run farm in Jiamusi, he supplied spiritual nourishment to men and women with an abundance of sexual energy. He haggled with them, he played drinking games with them, and from time to time he stuck his hand in the pocket where he kept his wallet and a knife he carried for protection. At night he slept in his clothes, and during the day he was forever looking over his shoulder. That was how he lived his life; it was the only way he knew how to live it.

Huiquan congratulated himself for not going along, for Cui would surely round up a herd of hot northeastern mares and nonchalantly leave some of his wild seed behind when he left. He was not one to miss an opportunity.

Missing the opportunity to sit down and have a drink with Cui, Huiquan was irresistibly drawn to the man's easygoing manner and demonic tenacity. If he wanted to enjoy life, he'd have to be like that, too. Everything was his for the asking. Vainglory softened the sting of failure and disappointment. This approach to life had it all over violence.

And yet the lure of the fight had not disappeared. Fighting was in Huiquan's blood. For all he knew the father he'd never known had been a common street fighter or a witless bully. It was possible. In this world anything was possible. Fate saw to that.

Shortly after Cui's return from the Northeast, Huiquan ran into him at the old haunt. By then the club had reverted to the karaoke format, since Zhao Yaqiu had signed on at the Capitol Gate Hotel and Nightclub. Business was off. The weather was just too hot, and people had grown tired of pricey Western drinks and snacks. Few of them showed any interest in taking up the mike and listening to themselves sing. After being open for less than a year, the club was on the decline, thanks mainly to Zhao

Yaqiu, whose departure had soured the patrons. Many of them frequently inquired after her.

The Capitol Gate Hotel, located on Airport Road, was quite elegant, although not as large as some. Huiquan rode over there one day but was told that the nightclub didn't open until seven, and he went away disappointed. He missed Zhao Yaqiu. All he wanted was to see her again and listen to her sing a few songs. He was worried about her, though he wasn't sure why. Maybe as long as he worried about her, she fell under his protection. She needed protection. She was surrounded by dangers, and her predicament paralleled his prior to his very first fight: she could be standing at one of life's crossroads without even knowing it. Beneath her mature exterior she was incredibly naive. At the point where triumphs and failures cross, where self-respect and self-loathing merge, any false step can be disastrous. Maybe that's what worried him. But he didn't mind worrying about her. In his mind's eye he saw her in a low-cut black dress, like a thin-shelled egg he wanted to cradle. This, of course, was just another of his daydreams.

That is why seeing Cui Yongli again after such a long time really threw him, for sitting beside him was someone else he hadn't seen for a long time: Zhao Yaqiu herself. They were talking over coffee, a scene that held a significance and a connection Huiquan was at a loss to explain. His face felt hot and puffy, as though he'd been slapped, and he wished he could dig a hole and crawl into it.

Cui greeted him warmly, his beard bristling like a goat's whiskers. Zhao Yaqiu nodded and relinquished her spot next to Cui; she sat down across from them, and Huiquan imagined how foolish his smile must have looked.

"It's all set, then," she said. "I'll wait for your call."

"I'll wire you first, so you'll have time to get ready."

"My folks don't care, so don't worry . . ."

"You really need to get out and see a few things. Huiquan, what are you drinking? Why the long face?"

He didn't know what they had been talking about, but it sounded conspiratorial. She was smiling sweetly. Too bad she smiled at everyone that way. After a few moments of small talk she rose confidently.

"You two go ahead and talk. I have to be running."

"I'll call you."

"Okay. So long, Little Li. See you later, Old Cui."

Huiquan looked up. Her face was expressionless. He heard her laugh and say something to the girl who worked in the take-out section. Apparently she couldn't wait to get out of there. She had nothing to say to him but was only too eager to get involved in some scheme with a common swindler.

She was dressed in a blue skirt and a white blouse; her hair was tied up with a red ribbon. By no means was she pretty, with her uneven teeth and jutting forehead, but he couldn't take his eyes off her as she walked out the aluminum door and passed out of sight. He was crazy about her; she was the girl of his dreams. He would always be under her spell. Why couldn't she have been a little homelier? Why couldn't she have a terrible voice? That way he could stop being jealous and recapture some threads of self-confidence.

Cui ordered a cola and a snack. Huiquan settled on brandy and salad, as usual. They talked as they ate, but Huiquan's ears were ringing. Even shaking his head didn't help for long.

"I really knocked myself out this time. I need a rest."

"No trouble?"

"Nothing I couldn't handle. I told you to come along, you sap . . . Have you got the picture now? How about next time?"

"No, I'm not going anywhere."

He glared at the mass of dark whiskers on the man's chin and cheeks. Cui Yongli laughed and then started in on the slice of ham in front of him, sort of lapping up each piece with his tongue.

"I get the message . . . Let's just drop the subject. I haven't said anything, and you haven't heard anything. It's over! Basher, I don't want to offend you, but that was some stunt you pulled at my place that night, walking off and leaving her bare-assed naked like that. What was that all about? Do you get a kick out of stringing yourself out like that? You're really something . . ."

Huiquan didn't say a word.

"It's impossible to help someone who won't help himself. You ought to lighten up a bit, especially in this area. Get my drift? Have a little fun. No one loses, so what's the problem? You did three years, but did you learn anything? Did you actually reform yourself? You're still wet behind the ears—"

"That's enough."

"If you don't want to hear what I have to say, I'll shut up. I'm thirty-one, several years older than you. It can't hurt you to hear me out. I became a man at sixteen. How about you?"

Cui laughed again and then attacked his food with gusto. Laugh! Go ahead. Huiquan rubbed his temples and kept a deadpan look on his face. His ears were still ringing; he felt like driving his fist into that bearded mouth and silencing it for good.

"What were you and Zhao Yaqiu talking about?"

"You've got sharp ears—"

"Just asking."

"I need some rest, that's all, and I could use some company. So I'm taking her to Guangzhou with me next week."

"Be serious."

"I'm dead serious. I wouldn't have even considered it at first, but to tell you the truth, I find that girl more and more interesting all the time. She's ripe for the plucking, so it should be a snap. Maybe that's exactly what she's waiting for. I trust my instincts . . ."

"You're clowning around, right?"

"Sort of. I got her a recording session at the Pearl Sea Studio. They want to cut a tape with an initial printing of seventy thousand copies. She's real popular down there. So you could either say she's going with me or I'm going with her . . ."

A cold look froze on Huiquan's face. The club was nearly deserted. A ballad was playing. Someone got up, sang a couple of lines, and was quickly laughed off the stage by his friends. The mike dangled up there all alone.

"She's just a girl."

He blurted this out. Cui Yongli's smile disappeared.

"Don't touch her!"

"What's the matter with you?"

"Don't touch her, that's all!"

"I wasn't planning on making it with her, so why get all worked up? Have you fallen for her? Well, I'll be damned, it never crossed my mind . . ."

Cui slapped him on the back and barely forced back the laughter about to explode from his throat. Huiquan's ears seemed to be under attack by swarms of mosquitoes, but he kept his cool.

"There's nothing between us. Look at her, then look at me. I just don't want to see her get messed up. She's a good girl, but if she's damaged goods, she doesn't stand a chance . . . Don't do it to her!"

"Did you really take me seriously? You've had too much to drink. You let things get to you too much."

"Don't you dare touch her—"

"What if she touches me?"

It was a mocking question. Snatching Huiquan's glass out of his hand, Cui shoved him gently into the corner of the booth. Music floated in the air around him; the other customers were eyeing him. He closed his eyes and pressed his fingers against his throbbing temples. The ringing in his ears got louder, but he wasn't drunk.

"Anybody who does it to her will have to answer to me!"

"Shut up, you dumb asshole . . ."

Cui Yongli's muttered comment hung in the air as Huiquan raised his fist and let fly. Sounds of shattered crockery and frantic footsteps filled the air. Men and women were buzzing. He could hear lips smacking and knew that Cui was shoving the last slice of ham into his mouth.

He hadn't connected. Too bad.

12

In October the business tax went from 90 yuan to 120. Wholesalers were particularly hard hit, since their prices were fixed. From rural enterprises in the south to distributors in Beijing, it was getting impossible to find salesmen willing to take on additional goods; more and more cheap clothing was being stored in small suburban hotels. Huiquan rode out to one a time or two but saw nothing that might turn a profit. He picked up some fall clothing at a discount, but not so many items that he would be in trouble if the merchandise didn't move. The retail sales business was getting increasingly difficult, and several vendors at Eastbridge had already moved into other lines.

No one came to do the repairs on the house until the rainy season had passed, at which time the workers tore up half the roof. The paper had rotted away, so Huiquan bought a roll and papered the roof himself. When he asked to have the doors and windows repainted, the maintenance crew said that wasn't on their schedule, and he could try again the next year. So he bought a brush, some paint, and some sandpaper and spent two days putting a new face on the old place. It was a lot more gratifying than peddling clothes.

The smell of fresh paint, stronger at night when he was in bed than in the daytime, helped him sleep. He decided to buy some furniture before getting any electric appliances. He had already spotted the set he wanted; it included blond-wood cabinets that would fit perfectly against the wall in the outer room. It was time to put some style into his life.

His rooms were cluttered with old newspapers and magazines on criminal cases, sports, martial arts, detective stories— just about everything imaginable. But his interest in them had begun to wane, and about all he ever got out of his reading were two syllables: *bor-ing!* Once in a while he'd scan some criminal cases to see how people went about murdering, raping, and robbing and how they were caught, tried, and executed, but the novelty soon wore off. Since people were capable of anything, what was there to get excited about? The last resort for people who have reached the end of their tether is to do away with themselves. If only a few more took the plunge, the world would be a safer place.

> *The mud has dirtied my shoes*
> *My shoes are sinking boats*

Of all the lyrics Zhao Yaqiu had sung, these two lines were the only ones Huiquan remembered. We're all little boats, and we're all sinking.

New court notices appeared on the bulletin board at the head of the lane, each notice listing new and unfamiliar names with red tick marks—sentence carried out—beside them. The evening newspaper reported that in the previous month sixty-four people had died in traffic accidents, a single-month record. Day in and day out ambulances with their sirens wailing criss-crossed the streets delivering broken bodies. Some people sank more quickly than others; that's all. Their luck just ran out a little faster. And the living breathed a sigh of relief.

Cui Yongli took Zhao Yaqiu to Guangzhou. Huiquan went to Sha Family Inn to apologize to him for making a fool of himself and to see how things were with Zhao Yaqiu. But they hadn't returned to Beijing yet. Huiquan didn't know what the man was capable of, but if anything happened, he was prepared to do something about it. He certainly wasn't afraid of Cui Yongli. He wasn't afraid of anyone, however sinister or cunning he might be. He would wait for Cui to return.

Signs of autumn began to appear: trees and plants started losing their color, and there was a dreariness in the air. It was always the same few people who jogged around Temple of the Earth Park, including a ruddy-faced Albanian diplomat. Huiquan watched him emerge from his embassy compound nearly every morning and fall in behind a group of Chinese runners, always straining to keep up. Though his face resembled a red-dyed egg, he was never without a charming smile. What it signified was anyone's guess. Was there something in the air worth smiling about?

But he hadn't seen the man lately. Meanwhile the somber Chinese joggers ran as though they were wrestling with thorny problems. The Albanian had probably been rotated back home or might be ill, and Huiquan missed his alien, whose smiling face reminded him that jogging was supposed to be fun, something to make you feel good, not an obligation or some form of masochism.

Huiquan set up his stall, he pedaled his three-wheeler, and he bought food, but he wasn't happy. He felt short of breath all the time. In bed at night he would wake up gasping for breath. His body was filled to capacity with fantasies and illusions, leaving room for nothing else.

Most of his thoughts were of women, and the days were worse than the nights. That was a new twist. He wondered whether these thoughts were produced by self-pity or by self-gratification. Normally inspired by his self-denial and lack of desire, he now wallowed willingly in his own depravity. He took the women in his fantasies, one after another: bold, harsh, frenzied. But Zhao Yaqiu was not among them, for he was crestfallen every time he imagined what she had done in Guangzhou. He was certain Cui would not spare her.

Huiquan's self-esteem was at an all-time low. Yet he went ahead and began asking around about Cui. The news was disappointing. He learned that the mysterious Cui Yongli had been an ordinary worker at the Immortals Bridge Electron Tube Factory 704 up until a few years earlier, when he was fired for absenteeism. He lived near Bright Horse Bridge in an apartment for which he had paid thirty thousand yuan. It was in the first block of private housing to go up in Beijing, an experiment that was soon thereafter abandoned.

"They just built the one block. On the north side of the street," Manager Han informed him. "His wife still works at seven-oh-four. They have a son who must be about five . . . I've seen the whole family. Our friend Cui is a capable young man, and steady. He's also a loyal friend. Not just anyone can come as far as he has."

"I thought he'd spent time in prison!"

"Him? No way! He's as slippery as an eel . . ."

Manager Han smiled and shut up before letting anything sensitive about Cui Yongli slip out. Huiquan found the news deflating. The person he'd been so cautious with was nothing but a common unemployed worker who had the world by the tail without even trying. Money, women—it all came so easy for him.

Why couldn't he be like that? With that question he finally realized he was drawn to Cui Yongli because Cui had what he lacked: since he lived a life of ease and comfort, shady activities were mere games to him; for Huiquan, on the other hand, life was wearying and tedious. Did he take life too seriously or not seriously enough?

Life as a vendor was becoming drearier by the day. Fewer and fewer customers stopped, even to look. There was such hostility in their eyes that one might think they were convinced his merchandise was conspiring to swindle them. The vendors displayed even more hostility. There was no law that required people to shop, but they weren't going to get away with fingering the merchandise and then walking off without buying just because they didn't want to be laughed at. In Huiquan's view every person who approached his stall deserved nothing but terse replies to his or her questions. He loathed and despised them all. Once, when he sold an eight-yuan shirt for fifteen, he congratulated himself for his coldhearted indifference toward the sucker.

Something was going very wrong with his life, but he couldn't put his finger on it. He had for some reason felt edgy and irritable during the hot days of summer, but now that autumn was well along, his mood still hadn't improved. He felt as lost and as isolated as a leaf that has fallen from the tree. He knew there was precious little kindness to be drawn from the crowds passing before him. They didn't understand him, and he didn't understand them. Was anyone ever saddened by the pain of others? No. He was not moved by the sight of the blind street musician who had set up shop beside the bus stop; in fact, he assumed it was a sham, one of the oldest tricks in the world.

The old lady who picked through the trash on Spirit Run Street didn't earn his sympathy either. After spending all her waking hours buried in piles of garbage, she became little more than garbage in his eyes. No sympathy, no pity. Yet the absence of expression does express something—apathy. He got back the same as he gave. Was there a soul on earth who cared about the confusion in his mind when he awoke in the morning? Did anyone understand how his thoughts tormented him nightly? Surely not. If he were hit by a car tonight, he would be forgotten tomorrow. At most his mangled body would become a gory statistic and, briefly, a hot topic of conversation. People count for little in others' eyes. But when it's their turn, it's a horse of a different color. People feel sorry for themselves, only for themselves. People don't love other people; they love themselves, period. Nobody else counts, nobody.

Huiquan did not trust his own thoughts, but that didn't keep him from letting them spill out like a herd of sheep freed from the pen. He couldn't have stopped them if he had wanted to. As he manned his deserted stall at Eastbridge, his head felt like a broken-down machine, a car with a faulty cylinder; no matter what lay ahead, all he could do was sputter down the road.

The cop directing traffic was in the same predicament as he: surrounded by all those cars yet lonely. How about the streetcar conductor, the street sweeper, the busboy, the construction worker clinging to his scaffolding up there—were they any better off?

There was no end to problems. Solitary shadows flickered in every hidden corner of life. Huiquan saw himself in others' eyes. Lonely, helpless people are all alike: pale, waxen skin; dull, lifeless eyes; mouth in a perpetual droop, eyes too; dingy teeth. He saw a youngster having an epileptic fit in a parking lot one day, and when the fit was over, that was the look on the boy's face. At the time it felt as though he were seeing himself. He didn't know whether it was pity or what, but he felt something tragic yet beautiful when he saw the boy being racked with convulsions as he lay in the narrow space between two cars: a desperate struggle against something yet doomed to fail; although it could not succeed, the attempt was glorious. What, besides this, can anyone ever accomplish?

A hundred people eating ices display a hundred different stupid expressions. If ten men emerge from a public toilet, five will be buttoning their flies, and five will either have dribble spots on their pants or be grumbling because they hadn't finished—talking as though crying for help, swearing as though it were music, guzzling booze as though it were water, spitting as though coughing up blood and then turning back to look at it. As he stood behind his three-wheeler under the warm autumn sun, Li Huiquan made a series of discoveries. It was like dull required reading—every day he read a few pages in this book of personal history, even though he derived precious little enjoyment from it.

Among the people passing by his stall each day there were always several who were totally absorbed in picking their noses: old men, middle-aged women, neatly dressed young men, even modish young women. You could always count on someone to pop out of the crowd with a finger buried in a nostril. It made him want to puke. He had done it as a child, but his mother patiently broke him of the habit by calling his attention to it each time and making him understand how disgraceful it was. So he broke one bad habit, although he quickly picked up several more. The people before him with their fingers stuck up their noses could not lay claim to all his bad habits. They didn't get into fights, they were even tempered, they loved and were loved in return, and they had never spent time in a labor-reform camp. They were better than he, even as they mocked him by engaging in the disgusting activity of picking their noses in front of him. He really felt like puking.

Why not remove all the obstacles by slicing off their noses with a knife? For him it was too late to change; he would have to start over from scratch. He couldn't turn back the clock, nor could he make time stop. So what could he do?

He sometimes found himself envying the young epileptic. He secretly wished that someday he could lie on the ground like that and poke fun at life, letting out all the stops—his little joke. He'd like that.

One day in late October, right about sunset, a gentle rain began to fall, to the surprise of everyone, for all had assumed that the unseasonable coolness made precipitation unlikely. But the rain fell anyway, a gentle autumn shower that made the streets and sky shimmer wherever there was light. Huiquan went to bed and read a magazine for a while before falling asleep with the light still on. In the middle of the night he was awakened by a tapping at the window.

"Who's there?"

The noise stopped abruptly, leaving only the soft patter of falling rain. He turned off the light. The door rattled slightly. Slipping out of bed, he picked up an empty beer bottle and lifted a corner of the window curtain. Unable to see a thing, he waited quietly. Whoever it was out there was probably waiting, too.

He walked over to the bed and lit a cigarette. He was tense, for he had a premonition of what was about to happen. The name Spike Fang popped into his head, and he didn't know what to do.

A moan at the window, the sound of despair.

"Huiquan . . . Huiquan."

While faint, the call was strong enough to confirm his worst fears. He sat down and waited nervously. The person at the window wasn't leaving; he neither stirred nor spoke. Waiting, probably. A good half hour passed that way, until Huiquan's impatience got the better of him: he got up and opened the door.

Two shadowy figures faced one another in the darkness.

"Is it really you?"

"It's me, all right."

"How'd you get here?"

"I made my way over from Curtain Lane on the rooftops."

"What are you up to?"

"Nothing. Just tired of living, that's all."

Huiquan slid a chair over for Spike, who folded himself into it. There was no water in the vacuum bottle.

"Hungry?"

"No. But I could use a cigarette."

"You lied to me in your letters."

"No, I didn't."

"Then why'd you pull a pussy-fucking stunt like this?"

"Are they looking for me here? At this point who cares?"

"Your goose is cooked this time."

"So what? I'm not worried . . . How are my folks? I didn't think it would be a good idea to go see them . . ."

Huiquan lit a cigarette for him, the match illuminating the outline of the nearly unrecognizable profile. Gone were the urbane airs. The features of the gaunt face in front of him seemed too big and sort of puffy. His skin was nearly black, apparently baked by the sun and dried out by the wind. His girlish eyes were dull and lifeless, reflecting their owner's despair, even though he kept them averted. Some of that despair rubbed off on Huiquan, who sat down on the bed, hard. Should he humor him until he had a chance to turn him in? Or simply hog-tie him and lug him over to the precinct station? Neither would be hard to manage. The beer bottle was right beside his hand; all he had to do was pick it up, and the problem would be solved.

He looked at his watch. Two-thirty. Spike was safe for the time being. The stakeouts set up shortly after his escape had been called off, and even Liu Baotie hadn't been around recently. After all, Fang was no threat to public security, so why treat him as though he were a mad dog? He missed his family and was going stir crazy; he just wanted to get out to move around a little.

Huiquan handed Fang a box of fruit-filled cookies, preserved fruit, and little pastries. In no time he was treated to the sounds of crunching, chewing, and lip smacking. Spike buried his head in the box. His tongue and his teeth, showing no signs of weariness, merged with the food inside.

"How did you get by the past couple of months?"

"I spent some time in Inner Mongolia, then went to Chengde and Zhang Family Pass . . . Don't ask. I've done everything but commit murder. I hopped a ride on a produce truck from Xuanhua and hung around the farmers' market for a couple of days. At first I was going to hitch a ride south and say good-bye to this place forever. But my legs had a mind of their own. Maybe it's a mistake, but I want to see my mother again before I die. Since I can't go straight home, here I am. No one else wrote, so when your letter came—shit—I cried. Basher, our friendship held up—"

"Enough of that bullshit. What do you plan to do now?"

"Maybe head south and try to cross the border. If I can't, I'll go somewhere for a few days of sun and fun and then kill myself. What else *can* I do?"

"What about turning yourself in?"

"No way! They'll have to kill me first. About all a guy can do in there is play with himself or maybe fuck a donkey. For what it's worth, I've lived my life, and if it's time to end it, so be it!"

"Weren't you trying to have your sentenced reduced?"

"I wised up and reduced it unilaterally! What right did they have to sentence me to life? If I hadn't told them about that incident at Northern Kiln, they'd have never known. I got a bum rap."

"They said you used a knife."

"She used a belt to hold up her pants, and I couldn't get the damned thing untied. So I cut it with my knife and nicked her slightly . . . Guess what she told the cops? She said I shoved my knife handle up her! Am I that crazy? I denied it, but they interpreted my honesty as a bad attitude, and that's why they gave me life. I never had a chance."

"They should have shot you!"

"I'd have been better off."

"Dumb fuck!"

"What?"

"I said you're a dumb fuck!"

Spike froze for a moment and then put down the cookie box and wiped his mouth. There was no water, but Huiquan recalled there being a beer on the windowsill in the other room. He brought it inside and opened it. *Pop!* They winced, exchanged frightened looks, and looked toward the window as though the threat of danger had just occurred to them.

Spike took a couple of swigs and handed the bottle back. The rim had a funny smell—Spike's bad breath. When had he last brushed his teeth? Before all this happened, Spike had been the most fastidious person Huiquan knew. He never had sleep in his eyes or food between his teeth or dirt under his nails. In the

summer his face was never sweaty, since he carried a handkerchief everywhere, and he never looked rough in the winter, since
he used a costly skin lotion that kept his complexion rosy and
moist. These ablutions were intended to attract girls. Now his
breath stank badly, and he must have been aware of it.

"Let me lie down for a while, okay? I'm dead on my feet—"

"When do you plan to leave?"

"Let me get some sleep first, will you?"

Spike shed his rain-soaked jacket and climbed into bed.
Huiquan, who was sitting up on the bed, pushed the pillow over
to him and covered them both with the blanket as he listened
nervously for sounds outside the window. He smoked furiously,
his gray matter congealed, his hands and feet ice-cold. A chill
rose from Spike's body. He was quaking and having a terrible
time getting to sleep.

Huiquan sighed.

"What do you expect from me?"

Fang shifted his weight and grunted. He gurgled as though
a lump of mud were rolling around in his throat.

"I asked you what the hell you expect from me!"

". . . One day—that's all I ask. You can accommodate an
old friend for one measly day, can't you? You haven't got the
balls you used to have."

"What good does having balls do if all it gets you is an early
grave? I'm doing just fine here. Then you come weasling your
way back into my life, and what am I supposed to do?"

Fang didn't reply right off, and from the way he was pant-
ing, Huiquan assumed he was frightened.

"Don't worry, Huiquan. If you let me get some sleep, I'll
be out of your hair. I don't want to get you involved—"

"Guangde, it's all over for you."

"I know."

"Your folks are fine. Your kid brother's a good student. He's turning out better than you—"

"Is my mom's hair gray? I dreamed about her in Qinghai, and she was completely gray. I don't think anything ever made me feel worse . . . I really want to go see them, but I'm scared I'll get them in hot water. What a mess!"

"You miss your mom, don't you?"

"I don't know why, but she's the only one I really do miss. Sure, I think about my dad sometimes . . . like some snot-nosed kid! I don't think I can take it much longer—"

"You're afraid of getting your family into hot water, but it doesn't matter what happens to me, right?"

"I really owe you this time. I haven't been able to talk to anybody for months. If somebody merely says hello, I nearly jump out of my skin. You're the only one."

The room was stifling, with smoke filling the darkness. Outside the rain swirled. It was a cold, bleak night.

"You know plenty of people. Why not look up one of your lady friends?"

"Them? They'd sell me out before I got a foot in the door. I hear about stuff like that happening all the time."

"Well, I'm no different, Guangde, I'm no goddamn different."

". . . If that's the way you want it. But that's not the kind of person you are, not the person I knew, anyway. If you did that, you'd run out and hang yourself!"

"This is no joke."

"Come on, let's talk about something else. How's everything with you? Planning to get married? I smell fresh paint—"

"Fuck you!"

They lay side by side in bed, smoking and coughing as they

droned on in low voices. Light began to suffuse the room. Like a man who has escaped from hell, Huiquan, his eyes bloodshot, said things even he didn't understand. His somewhat unreal sense of reunion had him saying things he'd never said to anyone before. The man beside him may have been an escaped felon, but he was also his friend, really the only one he had. So he'd have to choose between pouring his heart out to an escaped felon and saying nothing. There was a bond between him and Spike. Their lying together under the same blanket reminded him of how close they had been as boys. Spike had lit his first cigarette for him.

"Give it a try; I stole it from my dad. Nifty smell, huh?"

"Yeah, nifty!"

Even in the midst of his coughing fit he derived pleasure just from looking at Spike's girlish face. They had cut class to go bird trapping behind the Temple of the Reclining Buddha. And they had fought together: Fang with his sharp tongue, Huiquan with his pile driver fists. They were buddies.

"Life sucks!"

"You said it!"

"So what do you do about it?"

"Eat, drink, and stay merry!"

"I can't do that, since my days are numbered."

"You never did learn how to have fun. Why not get yourself a woman?"

"Can't do it."

"How do you know if you don't try?"

"No, no way!"

As high school graduation drew near, they had walked the streets together, cigarettes dangling from their mouths, talking about things like this until they were bored to tears. They were open books to one another: he knew Spike liked to snuggle up to girls; Spike knew he liked the notoriety that came from being a fighter. Spike envied him and had never once intentionally hurt his feelings by bringing up his problem with girls.

Fang Guangde was his friend. He kept telling himself that, and it helped shake loose some of the pain in his heart. Did he feel better now? Yeah, a little.

"He took her to Guangzhou—"

"Shit! How could you let that happen, you dumb asshole?"

"If he deflowers her, he'll have to answer to me. I've already thought it out. I'll kill the son of a bitch!"

"What good would that do? You really like her?"

"Yeah."

"So someone finally pressed the right button! Why didn't you make your move?"

"A slob like me?"

"Who isn't a slob? As long as that tool of yours works!"

"You don't understand—"

"You're right, I don't . . . It's almost light out. Let me get some sleep. I'm beat."

"We'll see what happens when they get back from Guang-zhou."

"What's there to see? He's not screwing your old lady or anything. No slut's worth it. Look what happened to me if you don't believe me."

Five o'clock. Huiquan moved the boxes and assorted junk off the single bed in the inner room. Then he adjusted the door and window curtains so no light could get in and surveyed the place to make sure everything was okay. He told Fang he could sleep there in safety.

All those familiar faces when he was jogging and buying food suddenly made him nervous. He bought ten oil fritters, and it wasn't until he was nearly home that he realized he might have screwed up by buying so many. His heart began thumping wildly. What if he ran into Auntie Luo? Had anyone seen Spike darting across the rooftops in the dead of night? He so rarely lied he didn't really know how. He was terrified of giving secrets away. The last thing in the world he wanted was to go to jail for harboring a fugitive. But he didn't want them to nab his friend either. Spike was weary and frightened from being constantly hounded, and Huiquan was beginning to believe that he could find a way to save his friend's hide.

Before going to work, he placed a vacuum bottle and some oil fritters by the bed and then slid the bedpan under it. He knew this was serious business and that he was risking a lot. But what were his options? Slinking over to the precinct station wasn't one of them as far as he was concerned. You don't betray someone who trusted you. At least he didn't.

He thought it would be a good idea to tell Fang he was leaving for work.

"Don't make any noise. I'll be back at noon."

Fang was so tired he could barely open his eyes; he was obviously resigned to his fate, whatever it was. After double-locking the door, Huiquan pushed his three-wheeler out the gate like a man weighted down with troubles. He couldn't help wondering how things would turn out.

This was your idea, so don't blame me for what happens. He hated himself for thinking that kind of thought. Even though he still had no idea how he was going to save his friend, he could think up plenty of ways to save himself.

At noon he bought some sliced beef, mule steaks, a cooked chicken, some beer, and stuffed buns. Spike was still asleep when he returned, oblivious to the dangers all around him. His new undershirt and shoes were probably stolen. And that was probably only the tip of the iceberg.

Huiquan stood at the head of the bed and looked down at his friend. His hair was so neat you would never have guessed he was on the lam. He'd always been like that: as long as he had money, he kept his hair neatly trimmed. A leopard doesn't change its spots. Next after a haircut would be a woman, not food. He said he had done everything but commit murder. What did "everything" include?

Would they shoot him if they caught him? If so, what was the use of hiding him? Why not point him in the right direction and give him a shove to get him going? Huiquan shook Fang awake. Huiquan's back felt sweaty, but maybe things weren't as bad as he thought.

Fang ate slowly, keeping his eyes glued to the food.

"Want to come along with me this afternoon?" Huiquan asked.

"Where to?"

"Don't act dumb with me. You can go alone if you'd rather."

"Is that what you want me to do?"

"It's what your mom wants you to do."

"I'll think about it."

Fang used his fingernail to pick with irritation at a sliver of beef stuck in his teeth. Huiquan handed him a match.

"I've jumped right into the net."

"Who says?"

"Know why I came looking for you?"

"Tired of being hunted down?"

"No, for money. You've done all right for yourself, haven't you? If you'd rather not give me the cash, you can help out by buying me a ticket to Kunming. I'm no thief, and I'm no robber. In Inner Mongolia I foraged grass for a whole month. Can you believe that? Don't look at me like that . . . When I get to

Yunnan, I'll try to sneak across the border, but if that doesn't work, I'll find some work there. I've decided I'm not ready to die yet!''

"You're not far from it, you know."

"Only if you sell me out, Basher!"

They stared at each other.

Having eaten his fill, Fang lay down again. He was still weak, as his droopy eyelids showed. Huiquan went into the other room and scrounged noisily through some drawers. He'd never felt so cowardly before. He was about to do the second really stupid thing in his life. His voice sounded strange.

"Think you can make it south?"

"I can try."

"You've thought this all out?"

"Can we continue this tonight? I need more sleep . . .''

"Want me to lock the door?"

"Go ahead."

"Don't make any noise. And be careful . . .''

It sounded like someone else talking, not him. These were not things he said. What was he thinking? What was he doing? Utterly befuddled, he rode his three-wheeler over to Eastbridge, his thoughts on Spike Fang, who was sleeping against the wall, breathing evenly, when he left. He didn't even glance at him.

Business was so slow he chose not to put up his awning. Instead, he sat on his folding chair with his feet up on one of the tires. He thought about Liu Baotie, who had been admitted to the adult program at the Institute of Law and Politics and given half time off from his job. But for some reason he never went, and Auntie Luo said he was on sick leave this week. He was probably under the gun from his superiors. What would happen to him if news leaked out that Spike had shown up on his beat? A reprimand maybe? He couldn't think of anyone who would be happy to see Liu Baotie in trouble. His girlfriend would have a fit. Auntie Luo would get into trouble, too. But he would suffer the brunt of it. He might be doing a disservice to lots of people, but mainly he was doing a disservice to himself. He had passed up one opportunity after another—morning, noon, and night. What was he trying to do? Did he get a kick out of flirting with danger in the name of bailing out a friend?

Growing increasingly befogged, he sensed that everything bad had caught up with him all at once, and he was totally enervated. Trying to will himself into a lighter mood, he stood in front of his stall to take in the sights. But all he saw was a montage of colors. The setting sun shone lazily, stroking him with its gentle rays. Dark spots danced before his eyes.

Night had fallen by the time he returned home. He unlocked the door and switched on the light. Everything seemed in order. The drawer he had intentionally left open on his way out was now closed. The window in the inner room had been shut from the outside. The quilt was neatly folded on the bed. Only two kinds of people folded bedding that neatly: soldiers and convicts. The chicken bones had been thrown into the waste basket, the vacuum bottle had been put back where it belonged, and the bedpan lay under the bed.

Huiquan opened the drawer. One of his bankbooks was missing, an account containing eight hundred yuan. The other one hadn't been touched. He'd put most of his stash elsewhere, just in case. Now he was embarrassed that he'd done that and didn't know what bothered him the most, the fact that he'd taken the precaution or the reality that Spike had taken the money. Had he given Spike a hint of some sort? Had Spike been worried that his friend would give him away, or had the hint accomplished its purpose—that is, if he really had given him one? He had opened the drawer just enough so the bankbooks were visible. Was that because he had wanted to avoid any responsibility? He didn't think so. When he spotted a sheet of old newspaper on the desk, he realized how grateful his friend must have been. In uneven but readable handwriting a note had been penciled in beneath the headline:

I took 800 and a couple of books for the trip. If you've got time tell my mom I came home. I won't be coming back. Sorry, but I'm scared. You're a good friend. I won't forget you.

Who could forget a big idiot like me? Huiquan wondered as he sat there holding the sheet of newspaper and letting his mind wander. Had anyone spotted Spike as he slipped out through the back? Had they given him any trouble at the bank? Why hadn't Huiquan done it for him—and bought him a ticket and seen him off at the train station, for that matter? Because he was scared. He knew that for a fact.

His bankbook was stolen, and that's all he knew. Huiquan reassured himself as he stood in the middle of the room. He was sure he had given no hint and that his sole subconscious desire had been to keep from getting involved. He had failed, and now Spike was in an even worse fix. But it was too late to do anything about that now.

He carried the bedpan outside and dumped its contents into the gutter at the base of the wall. Spike's rank stench assailed his nostrils. The one gratifying aspect of all this was Spike's embarrassment over imposing on him. He had straightened up the room. Even with his life in danger the dumb bastard had actually straightened up the room. His friend had always prided himself on his neatness.

13

Over the next few days Huiquan didn't set up his stall. His life had come full circle. This time he'd really painted himself into a corner. Barely out a year, and now he was heading right back, like a man dead from the neck up. He couldn't have said how it happened if he'd been asked. Maybe fate had decreed that the straight and narrow was not intended for him and those like him. He had started out in life on the road to nowhere, bordered by traps waiting to claim him and doom him for all eternity. A somber voice repeated in his ear, "You're finished!" He most certainly was. There were too many things that could never be undone. Would he be pleased if his friend were caught and taken back? He didn't know. Like him Spike had fallen into one of those traps, only deeper. Neither could save the other. Society had written them off. They were the dregs of humanity, human garbage, the dust of life. Whether they muddled along or ran helter-skelter all over the landscape like stray dogs, it made no difference, for their chances of ever settling down someplace like normal people were nonexistent. Life had no role for them to play. They were closed off from other people, and they had only themselves to blame. They were reaping what they had sowed. There was no one to blame and no need to look back regretfully. Regret was a waste of time and energy. Besides, where would he draw the line?

Huiquan's morning jogs came to an end. All he wanted to do was lie in bed. His room was like a crypt, his pillow reeked of stale sweat, and as he chain-smoked in bed, he fell under the reproachful gaze of his mother, whose photograph hung on the wall in front of him.

"I raised a worthless son."

She'd said that once. He had rushed to her hospital bedside from camp, but she wouldn't talk to him. Instead, she turned to Political Instructor Xue on the other side of her bed and registered her complaint with him. Later on, when her condition turned critical, Political Instructor Xue took him to see her one more time. By then she could no longer speak, so she just held his hand weakly and stared glassy-eyed at some point behind him. White-gowned people hovered around the bed as he backed up against the wall and watched her breathe her last. Political Instructor Xue stood beside him, holding a superfluous bag of oranges in his hand. At the head of the stairs Huiquan squatted down and refused to leave, and when Political Instructor Xue tugged on him to get him going, the bag fell, and the oranges bounced down the steps like little balls. That was when he started weeping.

He could never repay the debt he owed his mother. And now he had no more tears to shed.

Auntie Luo, noticing that he hadn't brought in his milk for a couple of days, dropped in at noon, worried that he might be ill. He was still in bed, and from the shocked expression on her face he assumed he must have looked like death warmed over.

"What's wrong, Huiquan?"

"Nothing."

"Come on, what's bothering you?"

"Nothing."

"You're still upset with me, aren't you? I shouldn't have—"

"What are you talking about?"

He jumped out of bed as though everything were just fine. She picked up the broom, but he snatched it out of her hands. He wasn't upset. A couple of weeks before, she had tried to introduce him to a girl in West Lane, but he refused when he heard the name. The girl had just been released from a labor-reform camp at Chaoyang Gate, where she'd fucked half the guys there. He knew who she was. But his abrupt refusal made Auntie Luo look foolish, and that reflected badly on him. The girl had a job and supposedly had been voted a model worker the year before. So what? That didn't make up for that other business.

"I'd rather you minded your own business."

He seemed both angry and humiliated. She knew she'd made a blunder and felt terrible because of it. But it wasn't her fault, and he knew that. He did not enjoy trying to calculate his worth in the eyes of others.

Worth-*less* was more like it.

He withdrew all his savings from the bank, just under two thousand yuan. In merchandise he had another four or five hundred. That was the extent of what he had. After buying a gold ring at a jewelry store in the Front Gate District, he stuffed the little bit that was left over into his shirt pocket. It was now clear to him that he would have to choose the time and place for the final act in this drama.

He went to the club on Mill Road. Not many customers were there in the daytime. Manager Han wasn't around; at least he didn't seem to be. A sign on the door said that closing time had been moved up to eleven-thirty. He ordered a double brandy and sat down in a corner booth next to the grimy, laminated wallpaper. The song playing on the jukebox was as dreary as autumn. He smiled at a familiar waitress, who hesitated and then nodded curtly. He ordered a salad.

"Pretty slow this afternoon."

"The novelty has worn off."

"Has Cui Yongli been by?"

"Cui Yongli? Who's—"

"Bearded guy."

With his hands he described a beard on his face. She turned to the service window. "Hey, has that bearded guy Cui been in lately? I've been off the past few days."

"I think he was here the night before last . . . Yeah, I'm sure he was. He came in with Zhao Yaqiu. Who wants to know?"

"That's okay, it's not important." Huiquan waved her off, blushing slightly as though someone had discovered his deepest, darkest secret. He sat and drank till nightfall and then got up and walked out. Business hadn't picked up much, even by then, and he wondered where the big spenders had gone off to. Maybe some new establishment had captured their fancy.

He rode over to the Capitol Gate Hotel, where lights blazed in the lobby. Mainly foreigners there, and very subdued. The red carpet, soft and springy as fluffed cotton, swallowed up the noise. No one tried to stop him. For twenty yuan he bought a ticket to the nightclub, where the majority of people bobbing and twirling across the dance floor were Chinese. A few foreigners sat listlessly at tables, looking as though they were about to nod off at any minute. The rather starchy band was led by a tall, lanky, wasplike Chinese man. There was no singer. One instrumental followed the other, with the trumpet section most noticeably off-key. Were they paid by the song? Whatever the case, they were working up quite a sweat.

After sitting around until eight o'clock, he stood up and gingerly approached a uniformed attendant, whose brass buttons sparkled like shiny medals.

"Zhao Yaqiu? She's here on Friday nights . . . Want to leave a message?"

"No, just asking."

Disappointed, he left the hotel. He patted his pocket. There was something shabby about the ring box, and he didn't have the heart to take it out and look at it.

What had he been thinking?

Would she laugh at him?

The sun rose bright and clear Sunday morning. His first stop was the market, where he bought some food and a toy. When the highway bus pulled up to the overpass, he hesitated for a moment before boarding.

The passing scenery—on both sides of the road—was very familiar. Rice shoots dotted the bone-dry fields; the green buds of winter millet looked like an elegant tapestry. Tractors bumped along the dirt ridges, spewing black exhaust into the spacious skies. Off in the distance a few stick figures worked the fields. He spotted the earthen wall of a canal rising above the fields like a dike or a long train with no locomotive and no caboose—a masterwork created one winter by his labor brigade. There, that was the spot where Political Instructor Xue hurt his back. He was a man who liked to throw himself into his work: either to give the men something to shoot for or to increase his prestige in their eyes; either because he was born to work hard or because he needed to vent his frustrations. Whatever the reason, after digging a hole in the dirt, the top six-inch layer of which was frozen, he stuck a bamboo pole in and pried with all his might. All of a sudden he crumpled to the ground, screaming painfully. Huiquan admired the old guy, so he carried him piggyback to the clinic. After that Political Instructor Xue sort of took him under his wing, and over New Year's, when the other inmates' families sent special food, he slipped him a couple of packs of smokes.

"Try to make 'em last."

He had probably spotted Huiquan picking butts up off the ground, although he never let on that he knew. If it had been anywhere but a labor-reform camp, he'd have followed the old guy to the ends of the earth. If the old guy had said, "I want you to reclaim an acre of wasteland a day," that's what he'd have done. In battle, if he'd said, "Charge the enemy!" he'd have done so without hesitation. He knew he could work himself to the bone, and the old guy would manage to keep up with him. He was, however, in a labor-reform camp, and nothing could change that unfortunate fact, so what was accomplished by dreaming? Besides, he felt sorry for Political Instructor Xue. Once when they were playing basketball, he saw how tattered the old guy's undershirt was, and when he was called for a foul, the pathetic hangdog look on his face made his appearance even worse.

He mustn't let him down. He had to tell him everything if he was to be worthy of his concern and goodwill. Would the news sadden him? Would he chew him out? Would it make any difference? The die had been cast. Now all he wanted to do was sit down with the old guy and have a drink.

But Political Instructor Xue wasn't there. He was off in the Northeast on official business. Huiquan stood outside the reception-room window feeling a bit light-headed. The string bag in his hand seemed terribly heavy. The cute stuffed panda inside had become oddly hideous.

"When will he be back?"

"A couple of weeks. Are you here to visit someone or to bring something for one of the inmates?"

"I came to see Political Instructor Xue. I got out of here earlier this year."

"Sixth Brigade?"

"Yeah . . . He lives somewhere in Liang Township, doesn't he? If you'll give me the address, I'll drop by and see his wife. It's all the same."

The man in the reception room got the address from the Sixth Brigade office, wrote it down, and handed it to him. "Old Xue's got himself a regular fan club!" He sighed for some unknown reason.

Huiquan took the dirt path back to the main road. After carefully planning his little speech, there was no one to try it out on. He was weary to the bone. There went his chance to sit in the political instructor's home, fill a teacup with something considerably stronger than tea, and let the words tumble out. Two weeks—he couldn't wait that long. What a time to go off on official business. If he hadn't known better, he'd have thought the old guy was avoiding him. An invisible hand was holding him apart from other people, manipulating him cruelly. He was too screwed up mentally to work things out as he walked under the autumn sun. Taking a shortcut through a wheat field, he spotted a familiar hollow, picked out the lowest spot, and sat down. During one of those summers—he could no longer recall which year—he'd been assigned to an irrigation team, and here in the grass is where he had lain down to perform that shameful deed, peacefully yet vigorously. The sky had been so blue it drove away his shame. It was every bit as blue today, but now it formed a panorama of painful derision that came crashing down on him. Stripped of his social role, man is reduced to the status of a mole. That's what he had become: an ignoble mole in a darkened burrow.

Too impatient to wait for the bus, Huiquan flagged down a three-wheeled minitractor and hitched a ride behind the scowling driver, who had reluctantly accepted a couple of cans of food from Huiquan's string bag. Liang Township was actually a medium-size town in the neighboring county, which he reached after an hour's bumpy ride. He located Political Instructor Xue's home among a section of single-story buildings at the far edge of town, a dingy two-room flat with mildewed walls that he shared with his wife and three-year-old grandson. Their children were all grown and living on their own, and his wife was such an old hag Huiquan was surprised to learn she was barely fifty. A retired clerk from the town's grain store, she had not been treated well by the passing years.

Huiquan's name didn't ring a bell with her, but that didn't bother him, since it wasn't likely the political instructor discussed camp affairs with her. Huiquan handed the stuffed panda to the little boy, who played with it quietly on the floor. Mrs. Xue offered him a chair, in which he squirmed uncomfortably for a while as his taciturn hostess sat glaring at her grandson while she answered Huiquan's questions perfunctorily. The few framed photographs on the wall appeared to be of peasants. The furniture looked homemade: the sofa's armrests were uneven, the wood stain too purplish, and the springs flat.

"This place is pretty old."

"Old Xue is good for nothing."

"Instructor Xue's a good man."

"You'll never find anyone dumber."

"He takes his job seriously."

"What good has it done him?"

Huiquan, feeling more embarrassed by the minute, rested his hand on his pocket, where the five hundred yuan lay waiting. He didn't know whether he should take it out or not, since he'd wanted to hand it to the political instructor in person. Of course, he wouldn't have accepted it, but that didn't mean he couldn't leave it on his way out. After all, it was Political Instructor Xue who had held on to his mother's bankbooks for him.

He laid the money on the table.

"This is some money I owe Instructor Xue. You can count it if you'd like. Please tell him I'll never forget him . . ."

". . . Never heard him mention it."

He watched her count the bills as he rose to leave. She invited him to stay for lunch, but he said he'd already eaten. She saw him off with a benign comment or two, and that was it. Did she detest him? People like him had used up the greater part of Political Instructor Xue's life and had snatched what could have been a bright future from his wife's hands.

As he stood in the middle of one of the township streets with dust swirling all around him, he didn't know where to go next. It was too early to head back to the city, and what he really felt like doing was hopping on any old bus and letting it take him to the end of the line so he'd never have to return. Now he knew what Spike must have felt.

Had Spike made it to Kunming? Had he been caught? Maybe he had already revealed his Beijing hideout to the authorities.

Huiquan walked into a small café, ordered a bowl of wontons, and sat down to eat them slowly. If Spike hadn't been caught, or if he had but hadn't revealed Huiquan's involvement, was this the right thing to do? What would other people do?

That was his way, grilling himself instead of sitting back

and enjoying life. Then he would make it worse by going off half-cocked and doing something stupid.

Wouldn't it be great if he could sprout wings and fly far away? Or better yet, find some remote, uninhabited place where he could take care of all his needs?

After aimlessly roaming the streets for a while, Huiquan returned to the city, went straight to bed, and fell asleep almost at once. A toad, with only its head exposed above the scummy surface of a pond, glared at him without blinking its marble-sized eyes. He was afraid it might leap at him, with its disgusting, warty skin and all. Did it move just then, or was that the water? He broke out in a sweat as his legs were drawn into the scummy water. He couldn't pull them out; he couldn't do it, and he looked around, panicky, for some kind of weapon with which to strike back.

He was hopelessly trapped when he heard a knock at the door. He lay there confused until he heard a voice, and then he opened his eyes and sat up. It was Auntie Luo, and the urgency of her shouts had him wide awake in no time. He jumped out of bed and opened the door.

"Huiquan, Xiaofen's sick! You have to take her to the hospital. Uncle Luo has been trying to flag down a cab, but no luck."

Tears welled up in her eyes. Huiquan was already throwing on his clothes; unfortunately his foot got tangled in the pant leg and wouldn't go through.

"Hurry! She was asleep, and all of a sudden she had such terrible stomach cramps she bit through the bed sheet."

"Food poisoning?"

"I don't think so. She felt funny tonight and decided not to go back to the dorm. Maybe something to do with the pregnancy."

She was clutching me in bed and was soaked with sweat . . . Huiquan, her husband's not here, so you've got to help us!"

He finally managed to get his foot through his pant leg. He was a bundle of nerves as he pushed his three-wheeler up to the front of the southern wing and ran inside. Luo Xiaofen was as white as a sheet, and her pale eyelids and lips were twitching. She barely knew where she was, and when Auntie Luo's hand brushed against her, she complained softly, "Don't touch me!" That was followed by a shudder, as though she'd been scalded. They obviously couldn't dress her, so they wrapped her in her bedding, straw mat and all, and lifted her up, with Huiquan at the head and the old couple at the feet. Xiaofen immediately curled into the fetal position, and they had to wrestle her onto the bed of the three-wheeler. This was accomplished without shouts or groans, which probably meant she had passed out. Uncle Luo was storming around the compound.

"What's happening? How could this be . . ."

Huiquan climbed onto the three-wheeler, negotiated it out into the lane, and heard the wind whistle in his ears as he began to pick up speed.

"Hold on to her, Auntie Luo, and sit still!"

As they leaned into a sharp left turn at the tiled arch over Spirit Run Street, Huiquan was standing on the pedals, his buttocks not touching the seat, as though he were trying to launch himself into the air. Poor Uncle Luo was having trouble keeping up on his bike. By now Huiquan's case of nerves had disappeared, and he was feeling pretty good, cooled by the crisp autumn air and enjoying free sailing on the deserted streets, the way lit by a stretch of lampposts. He was a taut, powerful machine, and Xiaofen was in good hands. She was his age, much too young to give up the ghost now. She was safe as long as he was around. She'd be fine, and eternally grateful. She would give him some of those looks that had made him feel so wanted as a child. Xiaofen, does it hurt a lot?

"Sit still, Auntie . . ."

They crossed the overpass at Chaoyang Gate and headed toward Dongsi. Life still dangled a few things in front of people to make them feel good, to make them happy. Just not very many. There are lots of things people do that aren't done for the benefit of friends or loved ones, which is why so many stupid things are done and why so many mistakes are made. And not even all the things done for friends and family wind up making *them* happy. A case in point: if saving Xiaofen meant he would have to pedal until he collapsed, he'd do it, but what had he done for Spike?

Again his mood darkened. His shirt was drenched, and beads of sweat wriggled down the ridges of his spine and puddled at his waistband. His legs were turning numb; his veins were distended. He leaned over the handlebars, gasping for breath.

"Huiquan, you must be exhausted—"

"Keep her covered, don't let her catch a chill."

The old woman sniffled and wiped her eyes the entire trip. But the sight of Li Huiquan had a calming effect on her and her husband. Then, when the maternity hospital was only a bus stop away, Auntie Luo finally fell apart.

"Xiaofen! Answer Mommy! Oh, no, she's leaving us—"

"What are you screaming for? That doesn't help anybody!"

Uncle Luo wobbled along behind them like a drunk. They were acting the way people always act when their loved ones are in danger of dying. But what if she had had no loved ones? An unconscious Luo Xiaofen meant nothing to anyone else. The sweet dreams of people in the apartments lining the street were not disturbed by her unhappy passage among them. Inasmuch as her life meant nothing to them, her death was utterly insignificant. No one anywhere, except for her loved ones, gave a damn what became of her. And if her condition worsened, her mother would probably join her wherever she went. Huiquan pondered what the possibilities would be when his turn rolled around: not a ripple. No tears, maybe no sadness.

Their footsteps on the terrazzo floor shattered the quiet of the hospital corridor. Huiquan was carrying Luo Xiaofen in his arms, bedding and all, his face bathed in sweat. Auntie Luo was right behind him, holding a corner of the quilt that had fallen away.

Xiaofen had stiffened. Her face drooped onto her chest, and one arm was sticking straight out, bouncing up and down as though she were waving to someone—that was a disturbing thought. When he saw one of her feet peeking out from under the quilt, he noticed she was wearing little-girl nylon socks.

This was the girl with whom he had walked hand in hand to school, the smug princess who had disdained him in high school, the young newlywed who had rewarded him with a nod and a smile. He should not be doing this. If something had befallen him, she'd have remarked casually to her husband, "That young hooligan who lives in the compound almost died." That is, if she mentioned it at all.

Who would believe that he actually felt sorry for her?

A flock of white gowns fluttered into the emergency room. There was a flurry of activity behind the white curtain and the comforting smell of medicine. Auntie Luo answered the doctor's questions while Uncle Luo stood off to the side, wiping his sweaty face and reddened eyes. When Huiquan realized he was being eyed by the nurses, he made himself scarce. Now that he'd completed his task, he wasn't needed any longer.

In a small room some distance from the emergency room some haggard men caught his attention because they were smoking. He joined them and lit up. It took only a few puffs for him to sense that he didn't belong there. The others, all expectant daddies, belonged to a different species.

Daddy. A curious word. He had no daddy. He had nothing. He knew neither where he was born nor who had brought him into the world. All his misfortunes were linked to this mystery. Were his real mother and father still alive? He hoped not. His stepfather and stepmother were both dead, and it wouldn't be fair if the others were still living.

A newborn baby is truly blessed.

Luo Xiaofen was wheeled into an elevator at the end of the corridor. Her pert little nose had the waxen paleness of death, which was quite fetching, actually. The surgery was on the fifth floor. Uncle Luo, so nervous he could barely hold the pen, signed the forms and then sat in a waiting room chair to moan and groan.

"She's in shock, an extrauterine pregnancy. A Fallopian tube ruptured. Hemorrhaging." Auntie Luo looked at Huiquan as if she wanted to say something to him, but instead she told her husband to fetch their son-in-law. He rose with difficulty.

"Okay, I'll go . . ." But after a couple of feeble steps he looked imploring at Huiquan. "My legs are so weak I can barely walk. Huiquan, I hate to ask, but . . . here's the key to my bike."

"Is there enough air in the tires?"

It was a curt response. He wanted to help, but something just didn't feel right. Xiaofen's genteel university assistant had got her pregnant, had placed her at death's door, and now where was he? In bed, asleep. Huiquan was repulsed by the thought of having to see the fellow who looked as if he would have been crushed under a lousy easy chair that time he'd delivered the furniture for them. Xiaofen had fallen for the pansy because he was a university assistant. Huiquan wasn't, and where was he now? Even with the same title, he wouldn't measure up to the other guy.

Other people had it all over him, Huiquan thought as he rode past Scenic Mountain Avenue East, Earthly Peace Gate, the Drum Tower, Desheng Gate, and Little West Heaven. He saw hardly another human being. An occasional truck rumbled past, filling the air with engine noise that lingered for a while. The few people on the street hugged the shadows suspiciously.

The apartment was on the second floor.

The assistant was frantic at first, but he soon calmed down.

"Is she in any danger?" he asked with all the passion of a doctor asking, "Where does it hurt?"

"She's in shock."

"Really? Then let's go . . ."

The assistant straddled the passenger rack. It was hard to believe he could be so composed at a moment like this.

"She'll still be able to have children, won't she? Fallopian tube . . . that doesn't sound good at all . . ."

Blood was sloshing around in her abdomen, and she wasn't out of danger yet, and his only concern was for future children. Asshole!

"Slow down, will you? This is a steep overpass, and we don't want to fall . . . She's in surgery, so what's the hurry?"

A real asshole!

His wheels barely touched the ground as he crossed the overpass, ignoring his passenger, who had his arms wrapped around his waist like some little slut. It was four in the morning by the time they reached the hospital. After handing Uncle Luo the bike key, Huiquan moved out of the way. Superfluous again. An excitable Auntie Luo was filling in her son-in-law, aided by an occasional remark from Uncle Luo. The assistant had his back to Huiquan, who merely saw him nod from time to time.

Huiquan sat on the outside steps, his legs aching and his head feeling as if it were filled with cotton. The flickering stars showed that daylight wasn't far off. A taxi was parked in the compound, the napping driver cradling his head on the steering wheel. Under the streetlamps the dead leaves at the base of the wall looked like scraps of confetti or cloth. Dawn at the hospital meant a skyful of cool, medicinal odors swirling in the breezes. A bicycle glided past the metal gate, its mud guard maintaining a patient, rhythmic clang. An infant's wail drifted over on the wind, but when Huiquan pricked up his ears to listen closely, it stopped.

He was reminded of the toad in his dream. Why in the world had he let it scare him so? What real terror had it symbolized? As a boy he'd been afraid of death. As an adult the only things that scared him were not knowing what to do next and loneliness.

Had Xiaofen's condition improved while he was gone?

He imagined a woman's glossy white belly being opened up and blood spurting all over the place. If she were his loved one and she were dying, he would run headlong into one of the hospital's concrete pillars and end it all. He didn't doubt that for a moment. Cut and dried. But if Xiaofen stopped breathing, the assistant would squeeze out a couple of crocodile tears and nothing more.

He flipped away his cigarette butt and tried to stand up, but his legs wouldn't hold him.

14

Huiquan slept around the clock, not waking until dusk. The bowl of egg noodles on the table jogged his memory: Auntie Luo had awakened him so that he might eat something, but he had drifted back to sleep. He slid out of bed and ate the noodles, warming them up first, and then went outside.

Uncle Luo, full of pep, was working on his fishing pole.

"Well?"

"Everything's fine, Huiquan, thanks to you! Tomorrow I'm going to catch you a nice carp to go with your wine."

Huiquan handed him the empty bowl, and stood there for a few moments. The pug-dog from the western wing was rinsing off some vegetables under the faucet, looking suspiciously cheered by her neighbors' misfortunes. Her old man was squatting in the doorway wiping down his bicycle. Once again a loving couple.

The streetlights hadn't come on yet. Some kids out in the street were kicking a ball around, the poor deflated thing hugging the surface like a household pet rolling back and forth. They never let it stop, kicking it each time it began to slow down—*ke-thunk!*

When he was their age, marbles had been his game, not with those pretty agates, but with opaque, not-quite-round two-for-a-penny glass balls. He always lost. In fact, losing was his goal, since all winning ever got him was a drubbing. He was one of those kids who went through life being bullied, and without making so much as a whimper.

He never knew what happened to the bullies from his childhood, but they were probably doing well, since as kids they had had it all over him, and most likely still did. No one made the mistake of bullying him now, but his life was as miserable as ever. Being bullied or not had no effect on the quality of his life; at least it didn't seem to.

Blink! The streetlights came on, casting ghostly shadows all around. The kids' faces took on a metallic cast.

The following day Huiquan went to pay his November taxes. Might as well pay December's taxes while I'm at it, he mused. The clerk wrote a receipt and handed it to him with a wary look.

"Saves me a trip."

He smiled, free and easy.

From there he rode to All Virtues Restaurant, where he ordered half a Peking duck; it wasn't until he began eating that he realized he had no appetite. Be that as it may, he sat there, carefully spreading the duck sauce on thin crepes, wrapping them into tight cones around shredded leeks, and eating them halfheartedly, as if they were fruit wraps.

He killed a couple of hours that way and then rode aimlessly around Loop Two. At the Xibian Gate intersection he realized he was at the spot where Hobo had been killed—not that there were any traces of the accident—and he wondered which of the concrete lampposts had taken Hobo's life. Whichever one it was, it had to have been the hardest, the most rigid, and the scariest thing his friend had ever encountered.

Leaving Xibian, he swung round to North Sea Park, where the surface of the lake was calm and autumnal—whitish and cold looking—since the boating season had ended. Lakeside trees showed a mixture of yellow and green, as though life were ebbing away. As he rode past the art museum, he noticed a paper cutout on the marquee, announcing an exhibit of folk art from Northern Shaanxi. It showed a pair of oxen with locked horns, both with double-fold eyelids.

At Goose Cloud Restaurant he ordered dinner and then barely touched the sea cucumbers, although he did manage to polish off a plateful of scallion mutton.

Restaurants always reminded him of his past. They were places where, like a prize idiot, he was always being treated to a meal for one thing or another, only to drink himself into a stupor as whoever the host happened to be praised him to the skies. Everybody's hero.

These days he was spending his own money, which was clean even if its owner wasn't. Where were all his benefactors now, all those loyal fans? By letting Spike take his money, he had compromised himself irreversibly. The cops could be at East Lane right now, just waiting to nab him, for all he knew.

He mustn't let things go that far.

Back home again, he chain-smoked in bed as he stared at the ceiling. A voice inside was urging him, "Turn yourself in!"

Suddenly everything went black. Spike had been there and was now gone—hard to believe, even if it had only been a dream. He had done some dumb things in his life, but this took the cake. Still, dwelling on it did no good.

He spent all of Wednesday at his stall at Eastbridge, and when he sold a dozen woollen knit shirts for fifteen yuan apiece, the other vendors knew something was wrong. They kept staring at him with looks of either loathing or suspicion. The wholesale price was twenty-four, which meant they should sell for at least thirty-eight. Only someone who had an adversarial view of money would pull a stunt like that. Either that or someone who needed money for a cinerary urn, or simply someone who had suddenly turned math illiterate.

He slapped a canvas cap on a kid's head and asked for only one yuan. The mother took it off and examined it inside and out. That really pissed him off.

"Nothing wrong with it, is there?"

She was still examining it as she crossed the street. She would have felt more at ease if he had demanded five yuan. And if he had given it to her for nothing, she'd have assumed there was a bomb or some poison hidden in it somewhere.

As he watched the stream of apprehensive customers, Hui-quan could no longer tell who was toying with whom. Like his merchandise, the people were absolutely devoid of value.

As he began taking down his display rack when it was time to close up and go home, his hands shook. The sight of all those rusty screws and the graying canvas awning was unsettling. He took one last look at his rectangular space, with its painted white boundaries; the 025 was nearly obliterated. How many people had trampled on it during all those days? Sooner or later it would disappear altogether, and there would be no one to give a second thought to this spot, this meaningless piece of ground fated to be his for a little while. In an open field a piece of land this size would be of no significance. So why had he grown so attached to it? Whatever the answer, the time to leave it had come.

As he passed Oceans Bookstore on Chaoyang Boulevard, he

spotted a familiar figure in the crowd just before an eastbound trolley blocked his view. A taxi and a refrigerator van followed in its wake.

"Brushes!"

The man's head snapped around. It was him, all right, but by the time there was a break in traffic, his friend was nowhere in sight. Inching along on his bike, Huiquan spotted Yifu some forty or fifty yards down a narrow lane beside an apothecary, running like a bat out of hell. He had been heading away from the Workers' Cinema, and from the panicky look in his eyes it was obvious that not only was he still scalping tickets, but he hadn't quit gambling, either. Brushes was a born loser; you could tell that by the sight of him running away—flustered and faltering, the very picture of defeat. He would keep on losing until he had nothing more to lose. In all likelihood he had lied to just about everyone. Was he really a worker at the Jeep factory? Was the chubby girl his sweetheart or just another victim of his lies? It wasn't farfetched to assume that nothing Brushes had ever said was the truth.

Huiquan sensed that he was the biggest victim of all. The man had been his friend, but lopping off one of his fingers would no longer clear the books. This time he'd have to kill him to square things, and he'd have to do it before the cops nabbed him.

Number 18, East Lane, Spirit Run Street. He had passed through this gate thousands of times, but never on such tenterhooks as now. Would he run like a scared jackrabbit, as Brushes had done? He hoped not. No, he would calmly offer up his wrists and smile complacently. That was the only way to do honor to his reputation as the Basher.

Nothing amiss in the compound. Auntie Luo smiled warmly and told him Xiaofen was much better. Uncle Luo's fishing expedition had, as usual, ended in failure. Two baby carp were splashing around in the washbasin. The sound of a cleaver on a chopping board emerged from the west wing, a comforting sound, no longer reminiscent of the terrifying noise of a woman being chased around the compound, trying to keep ahead of that same cleaver.

Everyone seemed to be doing just fine.

Maybe things weren't as bad as he'd thought. We all have our deep, dark secrets. All that domestic harmony was unnatural, and maybe the cuckolded husband had reached a secret agreement with the "other man." That should have been easy for a wimpy asshole like him. Meanwhile, Auntie Luo couldn't praise her son-in-law enough, even if the dog-turd assistant might already be stepping out with someone else's daughter. It's possible to keep anyone in the dark as long as you pay attention to appearances.

Huiquan had calmed down enough to read the newspaper before bed. A reader had sent a letter to the editor, complaining about a pair of high heels that became a pair of flats only a few days after she bought them. She claimed she had written only to call attention to the issue of quality control, but her real reason was probably to shame the manufacturer into replacing the defective shoes. A plane crash in Italy. The death toll was 128, with five survivors. Bad things happen to people everywhere. Good things, too. A self-employed bicycle repairman was plying his trade free of charge, when all the dumb son of a bitch had to do was lower his prices.

He slept like a baby that night. No dreams.

The next day he went to Sha Family Inn. The door was opened not by Cui but by a short, balding man with fishy eyes. He could have been anywhere between twenty and forty.

"He's not here."

"Where can I find him?"

"He went home."

"Where's that?"

"Don't know."

"Is he coming back?"

"Don't know."

The little man blocked his way and kept him from getting in. The tall girl was moving some cardbord boxes. She didn't see him.

He left, confident he'd find his man soon enough, just so long as he didn't get impatient. Since he didn't know what he'd do when he found him, there was no sense of urgency in his search. No rolling pin this time. No need for it. He just wanted to talk. The next day was Friday, the day Zhao Yaqiu was supposed to sing at the Capitol Gate. It had been a long time since he had last heard her voice.

The mud has dirtied my shoes
My shoes are sinking boats

She sang only in his heart, and only those two lines. They were stamped in his memory, and whenever they rose to the surface, he was really thinking about that layer of fine hairs. His full lips often felt tingly, for each time his imagination lost its edge, his lips were brushed by silky, cool, fresh leaves.

The area around Bright Horse Bridge was nearly deserted. A solitary high rise with ground-floor shops stood on reclaimed farmland. Work had ceased on the surrounding sites, which were no more than foundation pits, dirt piles, prefabricated slabs, and rickety work sheds. It looked like a disaster zone.

Cui Yongli had claimed Zhao Yaqiu's virginity. It was only a hunch, but at the thought Huiquan's muscles grew taut, and he

clenched his hands into mighty fists in his pockets. Do it! But
another voice said, Why? You're a bigger man than that.

I don't have a damned thing, and I'm not being big enough,
he replied in his thoughts.

"Bearded guy? . . . Fourth floor . . ." The wary old woman
shut the door and then reopened it and said, "Center stairwell."

Finally he had found someone who knew Cui Yongli. It was
a well-constructed apartment building, but the hallways were a
mess, with dust everywhere. A palm-fiber doormat lay before the
door on the fourth floor. He wiped his feet and rang the bell. The
sound of a xylophone inside stopped abruptly, and there was
silence.

He rang again.

Slippers shuffled across the floor. The lock turned. The door
opened a crack, revealing Cui Yongli's bearded face. The man
was surprised, and not very pleased, by the look on his face,
maybe even a little fearful. He was wearing plaid pajamas—
pajamas in the middle of the day!

"What are you doing here?"

"I came to talk to you."

"Is something wrong?"

"Why should anything be wrong? I just thought we might
have a drink."

". . . Give me a minute."

The door shut. Huiquan lit a cigarette. Carpet, wallpaper,
chandelier, large fridge. Cui was no stranger to the good life, even
if he was a liar and a cheat.

He emerged wearing a windbreaker and a different expression.

"My wife doesn't like visitors," he said, patting Huiquan
on the shoulder. "That damned carpet means more to her than

life itself, the stupid bitch . . . How'd you find out where I live?''

"Asked around. You don't want to know.''

"Where do you want to go?''

"It's up to you.''

"You don't look so good.''

"Is that so?''

Huiquan rubbed his chin, feeling a little deflated. They had walked about halfway to the second bus stop beyond Cui's building when the bearded man steered them into a highway diner. Huiquan tossed some money down on the table. Cui looked at him and then picked up the menu and ordered.

When the bottle arrived Huiquan poured a drink and took a big swig.

"What hot items did you bring back from Guangzhou?''

"Not a thing. I meant it when I said I needed to take some time off.''

"I saw some boxes over at Sha Family Inn.''

"They belong to my cousin. I sublet the place to him. He wanted to take over, so I let him. I really do need a rest. Too damned tired—''

"What about the recording session?''

"Didn't pan out.''

Huiquan stared at him. "I thought it had all been arranged.''

"That's the way things go sometimes. People change their minds. Today everything's cool, but tomorrow it's 'Huh, did I say that'? Little Zhao was upset at first, but she got over it. We took in the sights on the coast, and I arranged some gigs for her. She had a great time. Me, too . . . You have to take things as they come.''

"She . . . How's she doing?''

"Wising up a little.''

"It was her first time away from home, wasn't it?"

"Apparently so. She was like a kid in a toy shop. But that's how people are. First day in school, first business deal, first love, first . . . The first time's always the toughest. It gets easier after that."

"Did you guys . . ."

How should he ask? Cui lowered his head and pretended to be absorbed in studying his food.

"Did she mention me?"

"Hm, let me think . . ." Cui patted his forehead. "Oh, right, there was a waiter at Always Welcome Restaurant who resembled you. She said you look Cantonese, but that's it."

"I said some things to her. She didn't mention them?"

"Nope. Why would she? What did you say to her?"

"Nothing. Just a bunch of crap about learning something. But what right does somebody like me have to do that?"

"Nope, she never mentioned it."

They clammed up as each refilled his own glass. No toasts this time. It was a tense moment. Huiquan ground his teeth and looked up. His eyes were bloodshot.

"Did you do it to her?"

"What's up with you, Basher?"

"I asked you if you did it to her."

"You're drunk."

"What are you scared of?"

"Me? Scared?"

Cui laughed at that, laughed real loud. Specks of food stuck to his beard. Huiquan clutched his glass tightly. Don't do anything stupid. Don't! he commanded himself.

"Basher, you're like a kid who wears his emotions on his sleeve. I'm not going to say anything more about it. It's not worth it. Instead of asking all these questions, why don't you do

something? Friends should be frank with each other, so I'm telling you it's your own fault if somebody beat you to it. Use your
head!''

Cui wiped his beard with his handkerchief.

"I feel sorry for people like you. If you fell for her, why
didn't you go after her and tell her how you felt? If she wasn't
interested, you could have used a little sweet talk, and if that
didn't work, you could have banged her first and asked questions
later. It can't be much fun just thinking about it. But choose
wisely, or you could be right back where you started from." Cui's
laugh had a nervous edge. Huiquan worried him, and he knew it.

"Fuck your old granny—"

"Go ahead and swear if it makes you feel better."

"I admire you."

"Now *that* worries me. I know how big a deal loyalty is to
you, that and speaking your mind. I take off my hat to you."

"No need to flatter me, I'm not going to do anything."

Cui was genuinely startled by this comment, and it
showed. But he quickly composed himself and made light of his
comments. The wine tasted a little funny to Huiquan; it was
probably not the genuine article. At first he'd assumed he
wouldn't be able to endure more than a few minutes of Cui's
company, and he was surprised to see how fragile his loathing
was. He still believed a dinner plate would look good flattened up
against Cui's face, but he was no longer interested in putting one
there. Cui was a stronger person than he. Once again his self-
esteem was dealt a crippling blow. He took another look at Cui
and was forced to admit the man had an intelligent face, and his
neatly trimmed beard made him handsome in his own way.

He blurted out his terrible secret, maybe to salvage some
self-respect, and he knew he had accomplished his objective
when he saw Cui's face turn pale.

"You let him stay with you?"

"I even gave him eight hundred."

"He's gone?"

"He's gone."

"What are you going to do now?"

"Don't know. Got any ideas?"

Cui Yongli laid down his chopsticks and stroked his beard thoughtfully. Huiquan could barely keep from laughing.

"I can't figure you out, Basher."

"You're not going to help me out?"

"Look, I don't know you, and you don't know me. I haven't heard a word you said. End of discussion."

"What does that mean?"

"Nothing, it means nothing. It means it's time for you to solve your own problems. You can either cover it up or toss your bedroll over your back and head for the nearest police station."

"You mean turn myself in?"

"I didn't say that. I didn't say anything."

"Don't think I don't understand you."

Huiquan refilled Cui's glass and then his own and drank the dregs straight from the bottle.

"Want to join me? Bottoms up!"

"No more for me. You . . . you must be joking."

"I never joke."

"Basher, you don't think things out before you do them. You can't do . . . I used to think you were pretty steady."

"Don't give me a fucking lecture! I don't know who the hell you think you are, but thank your lucky stars I'm not interested in fucking you over."

Cui shook his head helplessly and said nothing. The two men got to their feet and just stared at each other. Cui, feeling increasingly awkward, was the first to look away.

Dust was swirling on the street as they walked outside and went their separate ways. Suddenly reminded of something, Cui turned and called after Huiquan in a conciliatory tone, "Come see me if you need anything. Friends have to look after one another . . ."

Li Huiquan kept walking westward without so much as a backward glance; his hands, thrust in his pockets, were clenched so tightly he could hardly bear it. He mustn't stop. He knew that if he did, he might turn and beat the shit out of Whiskers. He'd done enough stupid things for one lifetime already. Friends? What the hell were friends? He didn't know the meaning of the word. Cui Yongli probably wished he'd never met him. Of course, he would keep living the good life, but not without knowing what it felt like to keep looking over his shoulder. That thought made Huiquan feel a little better; he'd won a sort of moral victory.

Although he felt pretty sober, Huiquan had put away enough to make riding his bicycle a perilous proposition, so he decided to walk to the nearest bus stop. The 48 stopped at Loop Three, which was still a long way off. Walking was the only way to get there, so off he went, hugging the side of the road. The fields on that November day had an expected bleak, unkempt look; distant high rises reached up into the polluted sky, their tower cranes standing above them like lonesome trees. He had nearly reached the end of the line.

Back home Auntie Luo informed him that someone had come looking for him. His legs nearly gave out when he heard that, but he fought to compose himself. She told him that the Self-Employed Workers Association had nominated him as a model worker. It had not been the police. That was a relief, since it meant there was still no hitch in Spike's quest to leave China. He was about to make his way into Burma, a nation whose citizens got away with murder. He would take to the place like a fish to water.

The water here, on the other hand, had dried up, leaving Huiquan like a beached fish. Waking up in the middle of the night feeling parched, he put on a kettle of water and then sat on the edge of the bed and waited for it to cool off. He was gasping for breath as he looked in the mirror across the room; it was a dried-up, defeated fish that stared back at him.

She said he looked Cantonese.

She had already rolled in the gutter with Cui Yongli, and that no longer bothered him. And what if it did? He was consumed by desire, the desire to be destructive. That layer of fine down was like the blackened bottom of a pot, which he wanted to scrape off roughly with a sharp rock or a broken tile.

On Friday night he showed up at the Capitol Gate Hotel at seven sharp. A spotty turnout in the nightclub made it possible for him to find a table near the bandstand. A waiter wheeled up a serving cart and placed a Coca-Cola, a plate of pastries, and a fruit plate with two bananas and a large mandarin orange on the tablecloth. Every table got precisely the same thing.

By the time he had peeled his orange, laid it back on the plate, and peeled the bananas, the band members were filing in through a side door, their instruments bumping and scraping against the folding chairs as they passed. Once they were in place, a middle-aged woman with a hand mike took the stage and opened the show with a light monologue. Then she nodded to the conductor, who struck up the music as she moved to the side of the stage.

The sound of shuffling feet accompanied the dimming of lights on the dance floor. Though the woman had a pleasant, emotion-filled voice, Huiquan kept his eyes on the side door the whole time she was singing.

He spotted her. Smiling broadly, she was chatting in the doorway, dressed in a light-colored suit and wearing her short hair loose, with a single lock curled over her forehead. Her pert nose and tiny mouth looked as innocent as ever, but she had loaded up on blue eye shadow, which made her eyes look too deep and too large for her face. The area around her mouth was pale and free of shadows. She wore the expression of a girl who knew what she wanted and how to get it. Huiquan experienced the strange sensation that he didn't know her.

Where had that line of fine hairs gone?

A group of Japanese tourists filed into the dance hall: young men, all dressed about the same—probably students. The first singer finished her set and left the stage, handing the mike to Zhao Yaqiu, who confidently strode up and stood in the spotlight.

As soon as she began to sing, the normally reserved Japanese burst into applause and broke for the dance floor. It was one of their songs. Since he didn't understand Japanese, Huiquan just gaped at her like a man watching the sun as it rose or set.

She smiled at the audience, and he wondered what life looked like through the eyes of someone so young. What did all these strangers look like through her eyes? Was she happy? What was her first thought each morning?

He went out into the lobby for a smoke. Tonight he looked as good as anyone else in the crowd, with a new haircut, a suit he'd ordered back in July, a brand-new Great Wall gabardine overcoat, and shined shoes. Everything was just perfect. So why did he feel like a square peg in a round hole? He knew he was different from the other patrons and that the differences could never be erased no matter what he did or how hard he tried. They were better than he. He was a solitary, thoroughly stupid person.

Clap, clap, clap! Another burst of applause as the next

singer took the stage. Huiquan threaded his way across the dance floor, heading toward that mysterious side door. The new singer was a young fellow who jumped and writhed all over the stage, sounding like a donkey in heat—*hee-haw*. The audience went crazy.

The side door opened onto a dark corridor cluttered with instrument cases and folding chairs. No one stopped him, and one old fellow actually went into the dressing room area to tell Zhao Yaqiu she had a visitor.

She emerged eating a piece of chocolate, and the moment she saw him, she rushed over and shook his hand. He saw her brow crease into a frown as she turned and shouted into the dressing room, "See how loyal my fans are—they even come looking for me here."

Heads popped out through the doorway, male and female, all heavily made up, and then retreated back inside after giving him the once-over. Muffled giggles emerged.

"Did you bring flowers?" She turned up the volume.

"I . . . um . . ."

Her crisp laughter joined that of the people in the dressing room, the sound echoing off the walls of the narrow corridor. It wouldn't take him five minutes to wipe the smiles off those faces once and for all. Oh, what the hell, let them laugh; let her laugh. Maybe he'd been nothing more than a joke all along. The beautiful people needed someone to laugh at, after all. Why not him? Maybe they had never seen such a ridiculous creature before. His presence enriched their experience. At least now they'd know how a class-A idiot looked and acted. People love to humiliate those they consider beneath them. That was a lesson he had learned long ago. But he never expected to be mocked here. Apparently he brought shame to people just by living among them.

"I'll wait for you at the hotel entrance."

"Please, Little Li, don't get the wrong idea."

"I said I'll wait for you at the hotel entrance."

"I haven't finished singing for the night."

He turned and stalked out the door without another word. The dance floor was packed with couples slow-dancing to the gentle, cheery music, creating a swelling atmosphere of pleasure. He threaded his way across the neon-lit dance floor without seeing a thing, not stopping until he was in the wind-swept autumn night. Taxicabs with blazing headlights came and went while their idle brethren packed the hotel driveway. The relative absence of stars in the sky made the moon appear larger and yellower than usual. He leaned against a marble column by the entrance and smoked as he listened to the gibberish dripping from the mouths of foreigners as they alit from their taxis.

He waited an hour. By then she had removed her makeup, which gave her a softer look. The collar of her thin wool duster was turned up. He felt his resolve dissipate, little by little, in the wind.

"What is it you want, Little Li?"

"I wanted to see you."

"They always laugh and giggle when I have a male visitor. They get a big kick out of it. Don't take it to heart."

"No problem . . . You're a lot tanner after your trip to Guangzhou. Did you have a good time?"

"Not bad. Things went pretty smoothly, thanks to Cui's connections. Almost everything was new to me."

She had been standing with her eyes downcast, but her courage kicked in, and she looked him straight in the eye. Her face became a blur to him. She was an altogether different person now. He was clutching the ring box in his pocket so tightly his palm was sweaty. He didn't have the nerve to take it out, afraid he might make a fool of himself.

"How is our friend Cui?"

"Pretty slippery, but he's okay."

"He . . . he's married."

"I know."

It just slipped out, to her chagrin. She looked at Huiquan, who seemed not to have noticed.

"You shouldn't hang around with people like that."

"Oh? There's nothing wrong . . ." She bit her lip and looked at him out of the corner of her eye. "What did Cui tell you?"

"Nothing."

"Is there something special you wanted to talk to me about?"

Her attitude quickly hardened. She puckered up and whistled lightly to show contempt. He knew it was all a show, and so did she, to her embarrassment. Who should be ashamed, her or him? He took out the ring box, screwed up his courage, and handed it to her.

"My goodness, a gold ring! I can't take this!"

"I like the way you sing."

"Is it real gold?"

"You keep getting better."

"I can't accept a ring. If it were a necklace, I might think about it."

"Why?"

"Because I don't want any formal relationship. We're just friends. I hardly know you."

"I didn't mean it that way."

"That's what they all say, but in the end they won't let go. I know you're different from the others, but I really can't accept it. I've got all the jewelry I need. Now if you gave me a stuffed animal, I'd be happy to take it.''

"Really, I didn't mean it that way."

She was always putting on an act, smiling or frowning—it was like a mask she never took off.

"Do you like me?"

He said nothing.

"If you do, you should respect my wishes and not try to force the ring on me. Give it to some lucky girl someday. We'll still be friends. Anyone who likes my singing is my friend.''

Her patience was running out, and she turned to glance at the hotel's automatic door. That was when Huiquan spotted a man in a dark suit on the other side of the glass door: her new bodyguard. He recognized him as the drummer in the band, the strange-looking guy who controlled the light show with a foot switch.

"For the last time, I didn't mean it that way."

"It's getting windy. I should be getting something to eat."

"I won't be coming back."

"Why not?"

"Because just the thought of it makes me sick to my stomach!"

"You—"

"Take care of yourself."

Huiquan took the ring box from her and flung it down on the steps. It bounced in the air and came down in two pieces, its shiny contents flying away and landing under a nearby Toyota as if it had been sucked away. Zhao Yaqiu gasped. The man in the dark suit came rushing outside.

When Huiquan reached the bottom step, he looked back one last time. With the light behind them, the two people standing side by side appeared as one large, dark object. Her profile

blurred; her features disappeared altogether. She had been de-
stroyed. The innocent little girl who had resided in his heart for
so long was gone. Not only did he no longer understand her, but
he no longer understood himself. With fear and trepidation he
had put her on a pedestal, only to discover that his idol was
nothing but a clever whore. He hadn't touched a hair on her
body, revering the image of fine down above her lip. Had she
smiled sweetly while she was wallowing in promiscuity? He had
engaged in no seamy sexual dealings with her, not even in his
dreams!

Out in the street in front of the Capitol Gate Hotel he
released a torrent of filth at the top of his lungs. The sound was
unbelievably weak. Some of the windows in the beehivelike
hotel were bright; others were dark. Arc lamps above distant
work sites looked like will-o'-the-wisps. A bright hole shone in
the sky above the airport at the far end of the highway, a splotch
of white amid the blue. The city at the other end of the highway
was asleep. Darkened villages dotted the surrounding countryside. The red landing lights of an airplane on its final approach
flickered; the roar of its engines was nearly deafening. Eventually
the plane was on the runway, returning the night to darkness and
quiet.

Huiquan flagged down a taxi, which screeched to a nervous
halt. He jumped in.

"Spirit Run Street!"

At the entrance to East Lane the apelike cabbie demanded
thirty yuan. He glared at the man as he fished out a wad of bills
and flung it through the window. "Wipe your ass with the
change!"

In the taxi he had reached a decision. He had nothing to be
ashamed of, having lived a clean life. Tomorrow he would man
the stall, and the next day, and the day after that, over and over

until the day he could no longer do it, until the day he died, or was run over by a car, or was arrested. He had nothing to fear. Spike Fang, the cop, Auntie Luo, Zhao Yaqiu, Brushes, . . . male and female, old and young, more than he could count—they were all alien to him. Other people lived for themselves, so he would live for himself. Everyone lived for himself, period! If Spike showed up again in the middle of the night, he'd throttle him on the spot. If anyone else laughed at him as those painted boys and girls had, he'd knock their teeth out! If another girl smiled at him as Zhao Yaqiu had, she had better not expect him to hem and haw or waver before threatening or forcing her to do what he wanted. He feared no one.

"Fuck 'em all!"

He had another sudden impulse to scream at the top of his lungs in the narrow confines of East Lane. This time the sound was extraordinarily loud. Loud enough to make the whole lane rock and to throw him off balance. Something wet and salty slid down the lines in his face and slithered into the corners of his mouth. He crouched down beside the gate of number 18. He was surrounded by silence.

The moon hadn't moved, but now it was white.

Epilogue

Since the Neighborhood Committee had nominated Li Huiquan as a model worker, the Street Committee sent a form for him to fill out and return. Auntie Luo brought it over. She found him in his room, sprawled across the bed, dead drunk.

There was no food on the table, just a nearly empty bottle of strong liquor. The floor was littered with a half-eaten carrot and cigarette butts. He lay, fully dressed, on top of the covers in the freezing room. His feet were at the head of the bed, shoes and all.

"Huiquan, what's wrong?"

". . . Uh . . . who's that?"

"How can you do that to yourself?"

". . . I'm okay. Have a seat . . ."

He sat up, but his head reeled, and he had to struggle to keep from toppling over again. When she told him about the form, he just nodded uncomprehendingly and took it from her, staring at it without really knowing what he was looking at.

It was a dark, wintry day. Raindrops that had fallen in the afternoon turned to snowflakes toward evening. But the ground was too warm to keep the snow from melting before it could stick. The black roof tiles glistened as though covered with a layer of oil.

It was early evening by the time Huiquan was fully awake. His head felt light and airy, which was only fitting, since it was virtually empty. He found a ball-point pen and wrote his name on the form. He was out of practice. "Li Huiquan" came out looking like somebody else's name. *Ethnic origin:* Han Chinese, of course. But could he really be sure? *Native home:* What had his biological parents called home? High cheekbones and thick lips like his couldn't be a legacy of Beijing natives. *Age:* twenty-five. No. Another year was coming to an end, which meant it had been twenty-six years since he was lifted out of the underground-cable ditch and into the world of man. *Adult family members. Previous awards and disciplinary actions. Notable achievements. Neighborhood Committee comments. Street Committee comments.*

My adult family members? He snapped the pen in two and walked into the late-autumn, early-winter night, finding himself engulfed by swirling snow. The streets were wet, as though rain swept, but a thin, uneven line of white had accumulated at the base of the walls. Pedestrians scurried along, spraying water as they trampled through countless puddles. Cars found the going tough in the swirling snow, even with their high beams on.

At a stall west of the theater he bought a skewer of lamb, which he nibbled on as he walked aimlessly. He had nothing to do and nowhere to go. His mind was a blank.

For a while he headed east; then he turned north and went into the karaoke bar on Mill Road, which was flooded with music. He ordered a drink, tossed it down, and ordered another. He was sitting in his favorite booth, from which he could reach out and touch the grimy, laminated wallpaper. His eyes were glassy, his mind a blank. The young faces around him were as dull as marionettes; the music went its merry way, to be understood by no one. The waitresses eyed him suspiciously.

He drank till closing time and then, instead of walking home, he staggered in the direction of a place called the Water Treadle. The nearly deserted streets were lined with occasional patches of snow that encased dark footprints. He sat on the steps of the free market at Unification Lake to rest for a while. After scooping up a handful of clean snow from the base of a wall to suck on, he scooped up some more and rubbed it all over his face.

Back on his feet again, he turned down a lane west of the marketplace, where single-story homes lined the left side and brick high rises were going up on the right. A safety net hanging above the lane made him feel as though he were walking through a dark, sinister tunnel, sandwiched between rows of buildings all the way to the end, wherever that might be. He knew that Hu Family Tower was up ahead somewhere, and beyond that was Eastbridge. Once he passed Eastbridge, he wouldn't be far from home. So that was where he was headed.

This was the road home.

Someone tapped him on the shoulder. He stumbled.

"Had a bit too much to drink, pal?"

Another one appeared on the other side, real close.

"Lend us a little so we can get something to drink, too."

He tried to say something but was manhandled into a recess, where his head banged against the wall. His tongue was thick, and he felt like throwing up. Hands moved quickly over his body, popping several buttons from his overcoat.

He was grinning, sneering even. The hands stopped, and a fist thudded painfully against his temple. He quickly hunkered down, only to be kicked in the knee. A hand thrust its way into his coat pocket. With his overcoat spread open like that, he was like an animal being skinned.

"It's useless to resist! The place is deserted, so no one can hear you if you scream."

"Do as we say or we'll cut your fucking guts out!"

Should he do as they said? It all sounded so familiar. These young punks were either high school students or dropouts awaiting job assignments. He could tell by the rough treatment that they were as tough as he had been at their age; but they lacked his style. Sneaking up on him like that!

"Take his watch!"

"The guy's got lots of meat on his bones . . ."

Here it comes! Now Huiquan had them where he wanted them. Pretending to stumble, he scooped up a broken brick with one hand and covered his head with the other as fists and feet rained down on him. Then, suddenly straightening up, he swung at the head of the punk nearest him. *Thunk!* He was slightly wide of the mark, and the brick shattered in his hand. The guy's shoulder slumped, the rest of his body following. As he was driving his shoe into a firm, young thigh, the other guy buried his fist in his belly. It wasn't much of a punch, so how come it doubled him up with pain?

The hurried sound of footsteps resounded in his tunnel like a herd of stampeding horses. He felt sick to his stomach. After steadying himself by leaning against the wall for a few moments, he started moving slowly westward. There was snow on the ground beyond the area covered by the safety net. He frowned. His mind was still a blank. It contained nothing, not even sorrow. His first drubbing. All those fights, and this was the first one he'd ever lost. It was a new and unusual experience, and it left him feeling relaxed, even strangely giddy.

The little bastards!

He walked down the sidewalk of Hu Family Tower Boulevard. The whiteness was spreading, and the wind chilled him. Several buttons were missing, and his coat pockets had been cleaned out. But when he checked, he was surprised to discover that they hadn't got around to his pants pockets: his handkerchief, cigarettes, cash, matches, and—inexplicably—a bottlecap were all still there.

He felt like puking, and his legs were unusually rubbery.

He leaned up against a lamppost to light a cigarette. The match went out, so he lit a second one. After a puff or two he found he could barely stand. The street had begun moving like a conveyor belt.

He keeled over like a toppled tree, his head banging the snow-covered ground. He felt a sharp pain in his belly. When he reached down to see what was wrong, he touched something wet, sticky, and warm. He spotted his cigarette on the ground a little ways off and reached out to get it. The sight of his hand, bright red, terrified him. He shoved the cigarette into his mouth, but it wouldn't draw. No telling where his matches were. The cigarette had turned red, as had little spots in the snow, the red stuff having dripped from his fingers like a leaky faucet.

Back went his hand to his belly. His mind was still a blank.

A solitary truck rumbled down the boulevard, the roar of its engine lingering long after it was out of sight. It took a while, but he finally realized that the red stuff on his belly, his hand, and his cigarette was blood—his blood.

Hu Family Tower was just up ahead. Beyond that, Eastbridge. And beyond that, Spirit Run Street. He wasn't far from home. His three-wheeler was parked in the yard. He'd forgotten to cover it with the plastic tarp, and if it sat out in the rain too long, it would begin to rust. It was his last friend in the world.

Two people walking hand in hand on the steppe. He and a little girl heading toward the bright red sun. Now she was gone, and he was alone. The sun had set.

Political Instructor Xue was looking down at him.

"Get up!"

"Master Xue, I'm so sorry."

"I said, 'Get up!' "

She smiled at him, the fine hairs above her upper lip looking like a faint shadow, the shadow of her lip.

"I love you!"

"I love you, too!"

"Pull me up!"

"Give me your hand . . ."

It's not her! It's not, it's not!

He lay on the snowy ground, racked by pain. The streetlights lit up a multitude of tiny snowflakes floating down to cover him. The image of his gaunt father, stone faced and mute as he sat up in his sickbed, floated into the void of his mind. He was sitting on the edge of his mother's sickbed as she weakly stretched out her hand to him, her eyes gazing off into the distance behind him. He stood by dumbly, wanting to crawl into a hole and die.

"I raised a useless son."

The blood scalded his hand. He was lying in the underground-cable ditch, and its sides had begun to cave in. When he tried to stand, he heard the fouled snow mock him, and he was afraid.

"Help me!"

Across the street a cyclist dressed for the cold dismounted like a cautious hunter and searched the area with his eyes.

"Help me!"

The hunter stayed put, looking first at the tower, then at a nearby home, then up into the sky, ready and eager to capture that illusory, feeble sound. The frustrated hunter climbed back onto his bike and headed south, one of his tires rubbing against the fender to produce a cautiously gentle, rhythmic melody.

"Somebody help me!"

He was pleading with every person who entered his mind, but his voice was too weak to be heard. Finally he laughed loudly, like a drunk caught up in a fabulous world of his own creation. His body reeked strongly of alcohol and blood, fouling the fresh, chilled snow.

"Good luck to all you dumb fucks!"

Two husky, handsome youngsters fled in panic, running as fast as their legs would carry them. He followed them with his eyes, wondering which of them had done this terrible thing to him, or had done him this favor.

A trail of dark footprints in the bright snow led off into the distance.

Slowly his body gave up its superfluous fluids; his mind released its superfluous thoughts. As he closed his eyes, his fears and loneliness were swept away. Like a wounded animal, he relived the pain and joys of his life in the final moments before the hunter arrived to claim his kill. He thought, too, of the boundless sorrow stretching out in front of him all the way to infinity.

Snowflakes continued to kiss his thick lips, as though to compensate him for what he had been through. The middle of the night. From the bowels of the city came the heavy thud of footsteps.

Calmly he listened to them draw near.